As a Texan and r_____ has strong
opinions on 'rea_____es, please),
and wearing white after Labor Day _____') Lindsay writes
books with mystery and romance fea_____
sassy heroines who drive them crazy_____
plains with two big dogs and her ow_____
lets and raising two STEM warrior_____

F__
c__

leisure $\&$

Raves for *The Royal Runaway*:

'Thea is a whip-smart princess for the modern era . . . The story's greatest strength is its twisting spy tale, as it takes one unexpected turn after another' *Entertainment Weekly*

'Captivating! Full of twists and turns, *The Royal Runaway* will keep you guessing and cheering for a Royal happily-ever-after!' Geneva Lee

'Happily ever after gets a refreshing update. This imaginative, absorbing, and empowering story is a must-read' *Kirkus Reviews*

'Whip-smart, engaging, and relatable, *The Royal Runaway* is an all around delightful must-read romance. I couldn't put it down!' Nina Bocci, *USA Today* bestselling author

'*The Royal Runaway* is paced as swift as a speeding bullet, showcasing evocative action and an edgy romance. Absolutely killer!' *Romance Junkies* *****

'*The Royal Runaway* is the perfect royal romp, like *The Princess Diaries* meets James Bond, which I never knew the world needed until now. It does, trust me. Royal lovers like me will adore it, and rom com fans will love Lindsay Emory's fresh, fun voice' Teri Wilson

'Filled with intrigue, romance and a kingdom that feels real enough to visit, *The Royal Runaway* is sure to delight. It's a thoroughly modern fairy tale with characters whose motives will keep you guessing until the final pages. Prepare to be charmed by Thea, a duty-bound princess with an independent streak' Victoria Schade

By Lindsay Emory

The Royal Runaway

The ROYAL BODYGUARD

LINDSAY EMORY

HEADLINE
ETERNAL

First published in Great Britain in 2019
by HEADLINE ETERNAL
An imprint of HEADLINE PUBLISHING GROUP

1

Cataloguing in Publication Data is available from the British Library

ISBN 978 1 4722 5820 5

Typeset in 10.69/14.75 pt Fournier MT Std by Jouve (UK), Milton Keynes

Printed and bound in Great Britain by Clays Ltd, Elcograf S.p.A.

HEADLINE PUBLISHING GROUP
An Hachette UK Company
Carmelite House
50 Victoria Embankment
London EC4Y 0DZ

www.headlineeternal.com
www.headline.co.uk
www.hachette.co.uk

To Meghan and Harry. After the hope, love and
beauty of your wedding, I had to re-write this book.
So thanks for that.

one

WHEN MY HUSBAND DIED, A STRANGE CALM SETtled over me.

I saw the past, present and future unfurl, clear as the images of smoke and fire on the television screen in front of me.

My life had always been captured in such detail. My birth was announced with heraldry and pomp. My parents' marriage disintegrated piece by piece in the columns of newsprint and between commercial breaks.

And now . . . my husband's death. Excruciatingly slow. Replay. Replay. Replay.

I had spent the last few hours watching the race on television from a small cottage just yards away from the press and fans and sponsors. Other wives sat in the stands, but Stavros preferred me out of the public eye. One couldn't blame him—our relationship and elopement had sparked an intense media glare. A Formula One driver winning the hand of Caroline, a royal princess of Drieden? It was a scandal for the ages.

I loved Stavros as soon as I met him, and he moved as quickly as the cars he drove. I let myself go along, recklessly perhaps, giving up my title and my position as third in line to the Driedish crown in exchange for the delicious thrill of being with him.

We married in Monte Carlo, in a small chapel overlooking the sea, right before the Monaco Grand Prix.

Twelve hours later, after he lost the race and he was sulky and accusing me of bringing a bad energy to it, I started to wonder if he was right . . .

Was I a bad-luck charm?

And yet I felt sorry for him. Because he'd lost his race, because our relationship had caused such stress for him. I felt guilty. If I hadn't been born a princess, hadn't invited the public to gawk at us, at him, then he would have been able to focus—on the car, the track, the competition.

So I stayed. After all, I cared about him, even if the first blush of passion soon faded. When he won, we smiled. Laughed. Made love. When he lost, he drank. Pouted. Stormed out and left for hours. And I started hiding in cottages.

He said it was easier to concentrate on the race if the world wasn't reminded of who I was. Or who I used to be.

Stavros was losing the race when he crashed and flipped and his car exploded into a huge inferno on the thirty-second lap of the Slovenian Grand Prix. My dashing, intense husband, the great Stavros DiBernardo, was gone forever, in one last, furious blaze. Dying like he lived.

Leaving me to face the flashbulbs alone.

I had never thought of myself as psychic, but I saw the future then in headlines and captions.

Poor Caroline. Grieving Caroline. The widow. The disinherited. The disgraced. The despondent former princess.

The drama would never be enough. The stakes would never be too high. The intrusion never too deep.

After my parents' divorce, I saw first hand the two paths available to a royal post-scandal.

I could be like my father, Prince Albert of Drieden. Retreat to a country home. Spend my days fishing and planning gardens. (Because the only thing more boring than gardening is planning a garden.)

Or I could be like my mother. The one who sucked up media attention like an almost-melted ice cream on a summer day.

It was my terrible luck that neither option was acceptable to me.

I was only twenty-nine. Too young to play dead in the backwoods of Drieden and too young for the magazines to ignore me if I didn't.

I needed time. Time to think, time to plan, time to regroup. And the clock was spinning fast.

Pieces of my plan snapped together, as if my subconscious had worked on this problem for years.

Everything fell into two categories: things I could take with me and things I would leave behind.

I had time for two short emails—one to London; one to an Italian village.

There was a knock at the door.

"Come in!" I called out, in a hoarse voice that sounded strange to me. The last twenty minutes had been a blur and I wasn't sure if I had been crying or screaming.

It was Stavros's manager. Luis Caballero walked into the room, his trim figure nearly vibrating with adrenaline. He stopped dead when he saw me.

"What happened to your hair?" he gasped, shock making him switch to his native Spanish. His eyes grew round with horror as he stared at the long blond ponytail lying on the carpet at my feet.

Even though my grandmother, Queen Aurelia, had stripped me of my titles when I married Stavros, my princess blood ran true. I lifted my chin and said, "I'll need a widow's veil for the funeral. Thick enough that no one can see my face." Luis inclined his head, a gesture of respect or a gesture to grant me privacy. "And a bottle of hair dye," I told him. "Jet black."

two

"DON'T JUMP."

Elena's voice was grouchy, but Elena's voice was always grouchy around me.

I made a point of stretching my neck out to look over the balcony edge, down to the softly lapping water of Lake Como below. "I won't," I promised her. "Just because it's only four stories down. I'd likely survive it."

Elena grunted. "And then I'd have to clean up the mess."

"And here I was, thinking you'd started caring about me."

Another dismissive sound, although I wasn't quite sure yet how to translate it. My Italian was fluent, but the slight difference of meaning between "pah!" and "bah!" still escaped me.

I slid my hands along the stone balustrade and lifted my face to the sun, soon to set in the west. It was the first glimpse of sunshine we'd seen in weeks, as the shores of Lake Como had been hammered by one dreary winter day after another.

I closed my eyes and smiled, treasuring the thin layer of warmth to be found underneath the chill from the water.

For a moment, I was reminded of Drieden.

Home.

A tiny nation on the North Sea, Drieden suffered long, stormy winters that were dark and gray. My people knew how to treasure slivers of sunshine.

Elena muttered something I didn't catch. I swore she did it on purpose, some sort of trick-the-Driedener game she played. "I'm sorry, what did you say?" I said politely.

"For a woman who doesn't like to be seen, you're showing yourself off to the world."

I opened one eye and squinted at the view of the lake. This was about the farthest I could get from "showing myself off." On the penthouse-level terrace of my house on the outskirts of Varenna, there was no one around who could see me, except maybe the people on the few boats that had braved a February day. And even then, I had taken care to wear my large Sophia Loren sunglasses and a chic wide-brimmed felt hat. Just because I was in hiding didn't mean that I couldn't bring it in the fashion department.

But I wasn't going to get defensive with Elena. Or explain it all to her.

I had hired her almost a year ago to help me manage this property. Villa Cavalletta teetered on terraced land above the lake on the outer edge of the village. I had bought it as an investment, just before my marriage. Years ago, the villa had been split into three apartments. The basement and ground level I offered to Elena, as part of her salary. She would then manage the two apartments above, renting them to the near-constant stream of tourists and vagabonds that flocked to Lake Como every year.

I had never planned on being one of those vagabonds myself.

But now I lived like a hermit in the penthouse apartment. It was rather grand for a single woman who had no family, no friends and as little interaction with her property manager as possible. But it was rather humble for a former royal princess, so I supposed the whole thing balanced out on some universal scale of justice.

"Can I help you with something?" I asked Elena. "Or did you come up here just to criticize me? Again," I added pointedly.

Elena refused to be intimidated by me. For the first few months, I tried keeping a proper employer–employee distance in our relationship. But Elena had a way of irritating me so much I couldn't help but feel warmly toward her. I know it's sick, but I had grown up in a royal family full of—let's call them difficult—personalities. If someone acted superior toward me and chastised me for the way I chose to dress, I was reminded of dear Big Gran back in the Palace in Drieden City.

Home.

My issues would make a therapist's head spin.

"I'm going to my sister's for the next two nights. I just wanted to let you know." She crossed her arms and nodded her head, all business.

"What about Signore Rossi?" I asked, referring to her elderly father, who lived in the ground-floor apartment.

"Two nights." She held up two fingers. "*Due.*" She said the word in Italian, slowly, as if I hadn't understood her. "He's fine. I have left him food and water and a partially charged cellphone. Hopefully, he won't use the battery up, texting his girlfriends."

I couldn't help but laugh. Disgraced princess, widow and recluse I might be, but I could still appreciate that Elena's sharp wit hid a soft heart.

"I'll check on him while you're gone," I said.

"*Grazie, Lina.*"

After six months of hiding in Italy, I was still not used to hearing my Italian alias on someone's lips. *My name is Lina DiLorenzo*, I'd told Elena that first day, when I had arrived at Villa Cavalletta with nothing but a hat box and two Louis Vuitton suitcases.

Perhaps that was why it always took me an extra second to regroup after she used my name. "No one's made a reservation?" I asked, referring to the middle apartment we still rented out to tourists.

Elena shook her head. "You can stay up here and watch the water, for all I care."

I smiled slightly at that. "And the newspapers?"

She grimaced. "Pah! I forgot!"

"It's okay," I assured her. "I can go."

Her answering frown reminded me that she wasn't as grouchy as she pretended. And I wasn't as scared of the outside world as I pretended.

Mostly.

I GREETED THE GENTLEMAN BEHIND THE NEWSSTAND AT the train station in brief no-nonsense Italian. He handed over my papers, the same ones Elena usually collected every week. This newsstand was the only one in Varenna that carried a wide range of European publications, thanks to the tourists who regularly passed through the station on their way to and from their various holiday destinations.

I did not know the man's name, and he did not know mine. Besides Elena and Signore Rossi, no one knew my alias in Varenna, which was just as I liked it.

After another short errand, I hefted my bags back through the streets and up the steep steps in the hillside to my home.

I put my shopping on the pale marble table that served as a desk in my salon and cracked open a window that looked out over the water. Even though it was winter, I needed fresh air. Craved it, in fact. I had spent my entire life, it seemed, in houses and castles and manors where windows were sealed tight.

Here in Varenna I wanted to breathe freely.

Through the open window, I heard music coming from the streets below. For five, six days, it had been the same. A guitar and a sad, yet strong, baritone. It seemed like most of the songs were in English, although a few were in a language I couldn't identify. Gaelic, perhaps? The lyrics were mostly about women who had left. Maybe that's why I liked them so much.

But I couldn't listen to a busker's song all day long. Lina DiLorenzo had to finish a chore.

Not that reading was a chore. In fact, reading took up most of my days here in my northern Italian hidey-hole. But reading the newspapers from my home country made me feel like acid was eating a hole in my stomach lining.

At first I had resolved to leave everything behind. When I escaped from the reception held after Stavros's funeral, I knew it would be hours before anyone looked for me. And when they did, they would be looking for the blond Driedish princess they thought they knew, inconsolable with a grief they could not imagine.

They didn't know that the highlighted hair had been left in Slovenia. The title of Princess had been dropped on her wedding day. And my Driedish heritage had been forgotten as soon as Lina DiLorenzo stepped off the train in Varenna.

Or so I had thought.

Until a Driedish paper left behind in the rented apartment brought a part of my past back to me. The language of my childhood, the stories about familiar places and names were a balm I hadn't known I'd needed. But it wasn't a soothing balm. Oh, no. It was more of a burning liniment, a necessary discomfort for a sore back or aching muscles.

I still told Elena to start buying the papers, though. If anyone asked, they were for my guests.

Computers were out of the question. Too many sites kept track of who came and went. Consistent clicks on articles about the Driedish royals from an Italian backwater town could raise flags. But the newspapers provided me intelligence on what my distinguished family was up to now and were my aversion therapy when homesickness reared its inconvenient head.

I settled into an emerald-green velvet chair and started flipping through the Driedish news. My grandmother was Her Royal Highness Queen Aurelia, and there was a lot about the preparations taking place for her fortieth-anniversary celebration next summer. I skimmed through and, as always, I kept an eye out for my name.

After Stavros's death, the papers had been crammed with stories about me. Most of it was speculation—about my future plans, whether I was returning to Drieden (no) or begging for my grandmother's forgiveness (certainly not.) Finally, my sister, Princess Theodora, made a statement to the press: "The Royal Family of Drieden thanks the entire country for their prayers and well wishes on the death of Stavros DiBernardo. On behalf of our beloved Caroline, we ask for privacy and the time to heal."

It was typical, perfect Princess Theodora. Saying just the right thing, in just the right way, and no one noticed that she said absolutely nothing at all about anything important.

Still, I was in her debt. The press coverage about me, my dead husband and my whereabouts trickled down significantly after my sister's statement. Everyone assumed I was in deep mourning on a mountaintop or on a cloistered island and, apparently, if I hadn't had a scandalous affair with a race car driver, I would have been very boring indeed.

Which suited me fine.

And speaking of my perfect older sister, here she was in the newspaper. Again. Months ago, they had heralded her new "Princess Theodora Trust," which seemed to be some sort of charitable money-laundering operation for my grandmother, if I knew my grandmother at all. Now my older sister was constantly appearing at philanthropic events and good causes dressed in chic suits and holding up big checks.

Driedeners loved her.

PRINCESS THEODORA BREAKS GROUND ON HISTORICAL MONUMENT.

Yawn. That was right up Thea's alley, though. She always paid more attention to Driedish history than the rest of us did. My sister Sophie barely knew how to spell her own name. My brother, Henry, liked the bits about wars and battles but tuned out the rest.

Me? I learned what I needed to learn to navigate life in the palace. Make everyone happy. Negotiate and collaborate. Be perfect.

After finishing the Driedish papers, I breathed a sigh of relief. There were no imminent threats to my way of life. At least, for today.

One more newspaper had to be reviewed. I had saved it for last.

I found what I was looking for on the second page of *The Times*. The latest in a series of reports revealing a massive corruption scandal in race car driving under the byline of Clémence Diederich.

All right, fine. Clémence Diederich was me. It was my pseudonym.

I know, I could drag this secret out and play coy with it, but really, I am quite proud of the work I do.

My journalism career—for want of a better word—began years ago. I had made friends with an American reporter through some charity work. One thing led to another and I started quietly explaining (off the record, of course) some of the finer points of Driedish divorce law to him. Then, I wrote a small piece about the opening of a cultural exhibit in New York, and maybe a few more that I wish I hadn't, under the name Cordelia Lancaster.

To cut a long story short, once I was free of my royal shackles and just a commoner married to a race car driver, and I saw first hand what was going on behind the scenes in Stavros's profession, I contacted my friend about a tell-all.

Now, my series had been published in *The Times* over the past four months. This was the last article.

And then what?

It was the question I kept ignoring.

There wasn't much investigatory journalism I could do while hiding in the attic of a remote Italian villa.

And I couldn't go out in public yet. And what sorts of stories could a disinherited royal princess report on, anyway? I didn't want to talk tea parties and etiquette or film-festival fashion.

I wanted to write about interesting things. Important things.

From bitter experience, I knew that no one really wanted me to be interesting. Or important.

They would want either bland and banal or shocking and fabulous.

It was my bad luck to be somewhere in the middle.

I gathered up the papers, intending then to check the reservation website for the villa to ensure that no guests had made a last-minute booking. Since it was February, tourism was at a low, but one never knew if a couple of frugal Americans had taken advantage of a low fare and decided to visit Lake Como in the coldest month of the year.

But before I could get the website up, I heard the baritone again on the streets below and it made me stop in my tracks.

How long had it been since I had felt anything like this stirring in my chest? Since my husband's death? Since his kisses first took my breath away? Since our wedding day?

I had been numb for so long. The day that Stavros died, I screamed, trembled, felt my heart break.

We hadn't had the perfect marriage, but then, I wasn't a perfect wife. Our notoriety, my fame, my impulsive *yes*, had led directly to his death.

For a fleeting moment when Stavros proposed I thought I was loved for myself, for the woman I was. But then I learned the truth. I was not a perfect wife, or daughter, or sister. Not fit for a crown, not fit for anything, really. So I shut down and locked the door to the past.

I was living the life I had now out of necessity. I was nothing but an anonymous Italian woman in a small tourist village. No one looked twice at the dark-haired Lina, who kept herself to herself and didn't cause any trouble. I lived behind high walls and stayed invisible. Like a ghost.

It had to be like this. Distance and anonymity meant safety. For everyone. For me.

Songs like that, though. Flowing through my window like a cool, peaty stream, made me want to feel again, like I used to.

I marched across the kitchen and slammed the window down.

There would be no more feeling. No chances taken.

Until it was safe.

three

SIGNORE ROSSI HATED THE WAY I MADE COFFEE, BUT I gave him a cup anyway. "Bah. Australian coffee," he said as he made a face.

I should explain that. When I met Elena and her father, they commented on my accent. Instead of giving them a reasonable explanation, such as I was Italian but grew up in Drieden, I told them that I was Italian but had grown up in Australia.

It should probably be a point of pride that I don't lie adroitly.

So Signore Rossi and Elena blamed all my idiosyncrasies on my Australian childhood. I had no family nearby, because they all still lived in Australia. My Italian was a bit formal—because Australians were like that. Now, my coffee-brewing technique was Australian.

I hoped a real Australian never rented the guest apartment. They would be very confused about the misconceptions that awaited them.

As we did every time I visited, Signore Rossi and I settled around the television. Signore Rossi was almost completely blind, but he stared at the screen as it played the news all day and, in the evenings, he enjoyed soap operas and talent competitions.

The international news station was on, so I watched and he listened to reports about a drought in India and a hurricane in Mexico. There was a woman turning one hundred and twelve in Osaka (it was all the fish the Japanese ate, Signore Rossi observed, and the cigarettes) and a boy who had been miraculously rescued after spending fifteen days in a boat off the coast of Florida. "He's lucky it's warm there," Signore Rossi said. I pulled a cashmere scarf tighter around my shoulders and agreed wholeheartedly.

After a commercial break featuring Italian coffee pods endorsed by the soccer superstar Mastropieto, the news anchor returned and read the next report, about the World Economic Forum in Davos, Switzerland. "Among this year's influential attendees are President Salovic, noted economist Madeleine Berger, biotech billionaire Karl Sylvain von Falkenburg and, for the first time, advocating the education of girls in the engineering and science fields, Her Royal Highness Princess Theodora of Drieden."

I froze as a photo of my family shot up on the screen. Why they couldn't have used a beautiful formal portrait of my sister, I don't know. But there she was, at one of the Driedish national holidays, with the rest of us, on the steps of the city hall. She stood on my grandmother the Queen's left, my father on the right.

And there I was, shoulder to shoulder with Thea.

It had been taken two or three years ago, I guessed. My hair had been blonder, and my blue eyes, the same as my sister's and my father's, were not hidden behind dramatic oversized sunglasses. I remembered those giant amethyst earrings, a gorgeous deep purple that had looked so well with that fresh green dress but had nearly made my ears bleed from the weight.

Signore Rossi. I jerked, remembering where I was. That I was not reliving that day with my family, waving at the crowds, but I was here, hiding, in a cold Italian apartment with a blind man.

He was blind . . . wasn't he?

It was a crazy suspicion but still I searched his face, his blank eyes staring at the screen. If he saw anything, or was able to recognize my face through his hazy vision, he showed no sign of it.

The television reporter was still talking about Thea. What was she saying?

"The princess achieved worldwide notoriety last year when her royal wedding was canceled at the last moment. But in the last few months, she has stepped out and resumed her work as an activist in the arts, science and education. Her appearance in Davos signals a new commitment to bring those causes to the world stage."

They moved on to another story. I looked down at my frigid hands in my lap. They were shaking slightly. Too close a call? Or something else? Maybe seeing my family—myself—on television was too intimate. I should probably stick to newspapers. Static black-and-white newsprint seemed safer, somehow.

Signore Rossi had said something. "I'm sorry, I missed that," I said to him.

He lifted a chin at the television. "That royal wedding. The one that was called off. Did you hear about that?"

I closed my eyes. If Signore Rossi only knew. I had been the one to go into Thea's dressing room to tell her that her fiancé, Christian Fraser-Campbell, had gone missing. That he had left her at the altar in front of the millions across the globe waiting to watch a romantic spectacle. It had killed me, to watch her confusion, her humiliation, and know there was nothing I could do about it.

"I did hear about it," I said carefully.

"I wonder who had to pay for it all. A royal wedding can't be cheap."

"What is money, to those people?" I asked rhetorically. Truth was, I doubted Thea had any idea what her wedding had cost. It wasn't like royal princesses were shown the bills for occasions such as that. Hundreds of government and palace staffers had orchestrated the event—and then methodically taken it all down, piece by depressing piece.

Signore Rossi grunted. "Still, you have to sympathize with those young people."

"Which young people?"

"That princess and her groom. Clearly, they were caught up in a passionate love affair and it burned out. Poof. It's probably better that they found out they weren't suited before the wedding. So many first loves think they'll last for ever."

Strange. I had never heard an outsider give their opinion of my sister and Christian's failed relationship. I had still been in the palace bubble in the aftermath, and no one had been allowed to speak his name. And after my elopement, no one brought up Thea and Christian to me; they only gushed about how romantic my elopement with Stavros was.

Of course, I knew people would have ideas about Thea, about me, about Big Gran and my parents and the institution of the monarchy in general. But after a lifetime of being a princess one learned to just . . . filter them all out.

But here was a man—an elderly Italian man in a remote village— who had the most curious and incorrect preconception about my sister's love life.

I had to correct him.

"I don't think it was a first-love situation," I said.

"No? Aren't big, grand weddings for first loves?"

"Not for people like that, I don't think."

Signore Rossi's eyes crinkled at the edges. "I wouldn't have taken you for a cynic, Lina. We Italians are passionate, and Australians also seem to be fairly gregarious folk."

"I'm not a cynic," I said, surprised at the defensiveness in my voice.

"That's right. You told me you eloped with your husband. No cynic would do that with their first love."

"He wasn't—" I broke off. Recovered. "I don't believe I had a first love."

Signore Rossi chuckled. "Of course you had a first love. Everyone has a first love."

"Love? I don't know about that," I replied drolly. "Maybe the first man I lost my head over."

"There you are. First love." Signore Rossi spread his arms dramatically. "Losing your head, it's the same experience."

I stood, instinctively heading for the window. Of course, this apartment was on the ground floor so the view of the lake wasn't the same. But I saw sky and clouds and open space. I took a deep breath. "Yes, maybe it is," I replied, mostly to placate the old man, not because I agreed with him.

"Well, tell me about him," Signore Rossi urged. "Was he young and awkward? Or someone your parents did not approve of?"

A flash of a face in my memory made my stomach tighten. Embarrassment—I identified the emotion. Extreme and total embarrassment.

"No. Yes." I shook my head and remembered that Signore Rossi couldn't see me. "I mean, no, he was not young and awkward. And my parents never knew about my . . . feelings," I ended inadequately.

"A short affair, then."

"It never even got to that point, I'm afraid." I raised my arms. "He rejected me when I approached him."

Signore Rossi's gray brows shot up in surprise. "No! He was not a real man, then?"

I closed my eyes tightly and remembered that day. A tall, broad-shouldered man with eyes that watched my every move, luring me into a false feeling of intimacy. "He was a real man," I said. "That was the problem. I was just a girl. Young, foolish, with no experience with the opposite sex. And he was full of himself and a complete egomaniac." For months I thought we had flirted, sparring verbally.

I had considered myself so witty, so adorable, such a cosmopolitan match for his dry, sexy comebacks.

"How old were you?"

"Nineteen."

Signore Rossi made another sound of disbelief. "Nineteen? Were you raised in a religious family?"

"It was Australia," I explained.

"Ah. Australia," Signore Rossi nodded. "Yes, I see."

The door had been unlocked, and now memories were coming back, almost tangible. I could smell the hay in the barn. Feel the sweat under my jodhpurs, the clinch of my riding boots. The way my pulse danced when I was alone with him. The anticipation of matching him, move for move. "I was so carefully guarded . . . in Australia. And he was older. He . . . worked for my father's company."

"Hm . . . Many fathers wouldn't mind their daughters marrying a man with employment in their own business. A steady job means he's a good worker."

I smiled. "Perhaps. But like I said, it never got that far. I had carried a torch for him for months and, when I finally approached him, my feelings were not reciprocated."

Not reciprocated. What polite language. It completely glossed over the truth of the event. How Hugh Konnor had looked shocked, then repulsed. How he stepped away from me. Held his hands out, even, as if to shield himself from the teenage princess about to jump his bones.

How he left me in the barn.

How he was reassigned to my mother's detail the very next day, presumably after storming to the security offices and demanding a transfer.

"I was humiliated," I finished, surprised that those words came out of my mouth. I had never admitted as much to anyone. A young Princess Caroline of Drieden had never dreamed that she would be rejected by a commoner. But speaking to Signore Rossi was almost as good as a confessional booth. He would never tell anyone, and if he did . . . I dismissed that thought. Ten years had passed since that excruciating encounter in the palace stables. Ten years since Hugh Konnor had been within restraining-order distance from me. Even the past few years, when he'd been assigned to my older sister, he always conveniently had the day off when I was back at the palace.

Not that I noticed. Or asked.

As if he could read my mind, Signore Rossi asked, "Do you still think of him?"

"No." That sounded abrupt, so I tried to soften it. "It's been years. I had a husband," I said, as if an impulsive set of marriage vows wiped clean one's memory of all prior infatuations.

"And you no longer live in Australia," Signore Rossi said, with a little wave at the building around us.

"No," I agreed, with a small laugh. "Australia is very far away."

A comfortable silence settled between us. All the things I had said to Signore Rossi were true. It had been a decade since Hugh Konnor rejected my heart. My body. I had eloped, was now a widow. There was no reason to hold any feelings for the man now.

"But still . . ." Signore Rossi mused, staring off into the middle distance, at shadows only he could see. "First loves can haunt us for many years."

I opened my mouth to disagree. To say emphatically that my first love was ancient history.

But the spinning nerves in my belly begged to disagree.

four

I SAW THE GHOST TWO DAYS LATER.

Or, what might have been a ghost. There was no other explanation for seeing a dead man, was there?

Ten months ago, the previous April, my sister's fiancé, Christian Fraser-Campbell, had left her at the altar, which promptly traumatized the whole nation of Drieden. Here they'd been, happily anticipating a royal wedding, with all the romance and drama, and then . . . all the tea towels had been for naught.

Months later it was reported that Christian had taken his own life. I tried calling Thea, using the only number I knew (and the only one that wouldn't go through thirty secretaries), but there was no answer and I didn't try again. Perhaps she didn't want to hear from me. Perhaps it was my cowardice, or my misplaced guilt that this was the one thing I couldn't help her with.

Either way, given that I was in the middle of my own marital drama, I was not entirely sure of all the details surrounding Christian's death. The newspapers were certain, however, that he was dead. Which made seeing his ghost in Varenna that much more shocking.

I remembered vaguely that he'd had a sibling. Perhaps this was another relation of some sort. Another Scottish duke or earl on holiday.

In February. In Italy.

Or perhaps I was missing home. Missing family. It happened more often than I cared to admit, and today there had been a story in the Driedish newspaper that only my siblings would appreciate. The groundbreaking of the historical monument that Thea had presided over had dug up bones. Archeologists were shouting that the monument's location was near the spot where one of our ancestors, the one who had founded the House of Laurent, had died in a battle.

This was why reading the Driedish newspaper was not healthy for me. I wanted to gossip about the discovery with Thea, Henry—even Sophie. No one laughed at the antics of our family tree like my twin brother Henry. No one took them as seriously as Princess Thea, heir to the throne.

So that explained it, really. I read an article about Driedish history, which made me think about Thea, remembering the last time I saw her on her wedding day, and of course this would make me recall her long-lost fiancé. Obviously, this would make me see his face in a nearby café during my morning walk to the market.

I did a double-take when I saw the man. So similar to Christian, yet leaner, perhaps. More unkempt. An air of nervousness that the urbane Christian Fraser-Campbell had never given off.

So I continued my day. A quick stop at the ATM. A new automatic coffee pot for the rental apartment, as the last review had said the current one was "glitchy." Rain started to fall, cold and offensive. As a Northern European myself, I found the very idea of Italian rain to be extraordinary. To my mind, Italy was supposed to be languid heat and endless hazy days. It should not have winter of any sort.

But I kept thinking of Ghost Christian. It wasn't him, I knew that for a fact. All the news outlets had reported his death by suicide.

I decided to go the long way back home. Call it restlessness, call it boredom, but four months of doing nothing but hiding like some overly dramatic diva of Italian cinema was wearing thin.

Thin enough that I walked through the freezing rain to settle the question once and for all.

I passed by the café again; it was rather sad-looking in winter. The awning was bedraggled and a tent of clear plastic formed a kind of a vestibule around the door. I gazed in the window where I had seen the Ghost's reflection and saw nothing but mine.

Whoever the man was, or whatever resemblance he bore to my sister's dead fiancé, would be a mystery I would never solve.

I turned back to the street that led home and *smack*. Someone ran into me. A man, a bit taller than me, his face turned down as he clutched his coat around him in the rain.

"Pardon," he said.

In English.

And with a Scottish accent I definitely recognized.

I grabbed at the man because he stumbled as he coughed. But then his face lifted and I knew with one hundred per cent certainty that this was a ghost. Or a long-lost twin. One of those highly unlikely possibilities now was one hundred per cent.

The name Christian got stuck in my throat. Ghost or long-lost twin of Christian Fraser-Campbell—his name wouldn't be Christian . . . would it?

So he was the first to speak. "Caroline?" He croaked. "You aren't—"

He broke off in another fit of coughing.

It would be rude to ask, "Who are you?" so instead I stuttered. "You're not . . . I mean, how . . . who . . ." He rubbed his eyes and looked back at me. "Christian? How are you?" I finished lamely, as if we were old classmates who had just run into each other at the cinema.

"Fine, fine," he said, but his voice was rough and raw and I saw now there was purplish bruising under his eyes.

I knew this man. He knew my name. Somehow, improbable as it was, my sister's ex-fiancé was not dead, as the whole world believed, but very much alive.

With me. Here. Now.

He started coughing again and I realized he really was ill and had no place standing in the winter rain rushing in off the lake.

The next thing I realized was huge.

Princess Caroline of Drieden and Christian Fraser-Campbell were standing in the street. In public. And we were the potential news story of the decade.

"You must come back with me," I heard myself saying. "You're too sick for this weather."

Of course, I was tremendously concerned about the health and wellbeing of this man who had been just hours away from being my brother.

But it would be a lie if I said I was unconcerned about anyone seeing us together.

AFTER I HALF HAULED CHRISTIAN THROUGH THE TOWN then up to my apartment, he passed out in my spare bedroom.

For nearly an hour, I couldn't relax. So many questions were flying through my mind, not least of which was—what if whatever Christian had was contagious?

To be fair, I didn't know where this supposedly dead person had been. If this was a case of some sort of zombie virus, I didn't want to be cavalier about it.

I went over the possibilities. One—Christian Fraser-Campbell had an identical twin brother that no one knew about. One who answered to the same name. Coincidentally.

Two—Christian Fraser-Campbell had committed suicide but

had been reanimated by either a zombie virus, a mad scientist or some miraculous act of God.

Three—Christian had faked his death. Because that was something it was well known almost-royal princes did *all* the time. /sarcasm font/

Still, of the three explanations, when the one about a faked suicide seemed most likely . . . I got a funny feeling in my stomach. This was a Big Deal. I could see the headlines now. Classy ones, of course, not those tabloid conspiracy-theories ones. An exposé on the stress of public life, perhaps, or the need for more mental health care among Europe's aristocratic class.

And not to brag, but . . . I had tons of expertise in those two topics. A yelpy groan broke the silence. I ran into the spare bedroom and saw that Christian had reanimated himself. He was still pale and sweaty, but his eyes were clear and bright.

I picked up the glass of water and aspirin I had left earlier and offered them to him. "Do you think you can manage these?" I asked.

He nodded, gave me a small, grateful smile and took the pills and water.

"Do you think—" I broke off, not sure how to phrase my question. "This is probably just the flu, right? I mean, you haven't been in an equatorial jungle or around any secret government labs?"

I got a frown and a little shake of the head, which I chose to interpret as a negative response to my question. "Can I get you anything else? A cup of tea? Some toast?"

Christian made a face. "I think I just need some sleep. That is, if you don't mind me being here?"

"Of course I don't," I assured him. "You must get better." I smiled. "There will be all the time in the world to catch up."

A wretched cough erupted from him and I stayed until he could recover his composure, in case he wanted to take me up on that offer of tea.

But he said something I never expected.

"Clémence Diederich."

Now it was I who needed some water. "What?" Maybe it wasn't what it sounded like.

"Or is it Cordelia Lancaster?" Christian grimaced. "I haven't seen her in a bit, though."

It felt like the bottom of my stomach had just disappeared. "I don't—"

He cut me off. "I know, Caroline. I know your secrets."

I should not have been so terrified of a thin, pale ghost of a man.

"How?" I managed to ask.

He waved a hand. "Unimportant." Christian's wide, serious eyes met mine. "But I need your help. Clémence's, that is."

If I had known everything, I wouldn't have offered my assistance so readily. But as I said, I was bored, and concerned about this man who had almost been my brother-in-law and who seemed to be on the brink of death.

"Yes, what is it?"

"I want Clémence Diederich to tell my story. The true story."

five

AS WAS TO BE EXPECTED FROM A PRINCESS, MY COOK-
ing skills were barely adequate. Still, it was one of the
unexpected benefits of being a commoner for the last nine
months that I now knew how to boil water, toast bread and sauté
eggs.

As Christian slept off his hopefully-not-fatal flu, I tried to keep
busy preparing a simple meal and a short list of questions.

I know. I'm sure it seems very selfish of me. A man was on his sick
bed and I was trying very hard not to use his illness in my self-
interest. But as I scribbled my questions on a notepad, I decided it was
evidence of my boredom.

It was all well and good to opt out of public life, to adopt a new
name and an anonymous presence but, clearly, I needed a little more
excitement.

And the Christian Fraser-Campbell story was going to be just the
hit I needed. As soon as he woke up and could string coherent sen-
tences together.

Here I had been, simply biding my time out of the public eye, counting the days until I could fashion some sort of new life for myself, and now, the perfect story had dropped into my lap.

Who better to interview Christian, to explain the trauma he had gone through, put it in a larger perspective for the world?

There was no one better than me. Or Clémence Diederich. Since she was me.

I itched to open up my computer and send a quick query to my editor at *The Times*. It would be informal; I couldn't give anything away. *Hi, it's me. Been tossing around a few ideas for my next piece. Heard a crazy story about an infamous person who may have faked their death* (or become a zombie. Or maybe he's Jesus.).

Right. I might need some more information from Zombie Christian before I send that email.

But the thought of reanimating Clémence Diederich and Christian Fraser-Campbell at the same time . . .

It could also end in further disaster.

Personal disaster or career reinvigoration. Decisions, decisions.

An alert sounded from my laptop and I jumped, guiltily. No, I hadn't emailed my editor. Yet. I was going to ask Christian for permission first before I spilled all of his personal details over the international media. Obviously.

I pulled the laptop over to me and checked my email. A very unprincess-like oath fell from my lips. It was the website where I listed the villa apartment for rent.

I cursed my Driedish practicality all those months ago when I listed it. I had thought it was wasteful, having the whole villa for only my occasional use. Yes, it was my escape house, but why not make some extra money and let Elena earn her rather substantial house-keeper salary?

Oh, why did Elena have to leave? My finger hovered over the email buttons. I could reject the reservation. The money wasn't

important to me, but the thought of Elena's judgy face made me hit
the "accept" button.

TO: Cavalleta@villacavalleta.iy
FROM: Stone@firewall.dr

Re: Varenna Rental inquiry

Apologies for the late reservation. I am running through
Varenna this evening and wondered if you had availability.

Two nights, one guest. Please respond as quickly as you
can, so that I may find other accommodation, if need.

Grazie.

Two nights. One tourist who had obviously used a translating app
to write an email in Italian. Easy enough. I could do this.

What did I have to do again?

Elena would never let me live it down if I screwed this up. Worse,
she might quit in a fit of Italian pique and then I would have to find
another tenant, another manager, another face for the outside world.

Not that it would be terribly hard. All sorts of celebrities and notable
persons were able to buy help—if they threw enough money and legal
contracts around. But honestly, the thought of trying to find someone
else exhausted me and I liked Signore Rossi and his irascible daughter.
They were the only people in the world who cared if I woke up each
morning.

I typed out a quick response to the last-minute renter: "Yes, there is
availability. Please see the attached policies and payment instructions."

I would have to double-check the rental apartment. Make sure
there were linens and amenities. I wished I had paid more attention to
what Elena usually did, but I had spent the last few months recovering and working, burying myself in the Formula One piece.

But just as I made my mental list of things I'd need to prepare and got up to go out via the back stairs, I saw Christian in the doorway.

His shirt hung open and his brown hair was dark from the shower he'd obviously taken.

"You're feeling better, I see?" I said hopefully.

"Very much so," he said with a grimace. "I hate so much that I've imposed upon you."

He'd always had such perfect manners. It was no wonder my sister had thought him prince material.

"Please, Christian. It's no imposition at all." I went to the toast I'd made earlier. It was cold and slightly charred, but that made it dry, and wasn't dry toast supposed to be just the thing?

I held the plate out. "Are you feeling up to some food?"

He nodded and sat down at the table in the kitchen where I put his plate. Perhaps I really had conquered the whole domestic-goddess thing because he actually ate the toast, blackened edges and all.

And as he was apparently feeling better, I felt I could start a conversation without being too cold-hearted. "This comes as a bit of a shock, so I have to ask."

"Which part is a shock?"

"Seeing you," I admitted. "Alive. Here in Varenna, especially." When he didn't explain his still beating heart, I wondered if perhaps he didn't know. "You heard, of course, that the entire world believes you're . . ." I paused because suddenly this felt a bit rude. It was all those years of royal etiquette training. Say this, not that. Address this topic, not those.

No one had ever explicitly given me permission to call someone "dead" to their face. It seemed a bit indelicate.

Still. I reminded myself that I was no longer a royal. No longer bound by formal protocol. I was an international journalist who had exposed a safety scandal after watching my husband die on television.

I could certainly tell a man to his face that he was dead. Or not, as the case might be. *Just spit it out, Caroline.*

"I was led to believe that you were no longer living," I said, slowly picking out the words.

Christian did not seem surprised. But then, he seemed to have almost no reaction at all. He frowned slightly, pushed back his plate of toast crumbs and regarded me solemnly.

"I see. And who gave you this information?" His eyebrow rose. "Your sister? Theodora?" He said her name carefully, like he hadn't said it in a while.

Just like a zombie would.

I shook that silliness out of my head once and for all. Obviously, whatever had happened to Christian was far more catastrophic than zombiehood. He was a changed man—I could tell just by looking at him. Yes, he was leaner, his hair different, and there was a tattoo on his chest that hadn't been there on that last holiday we'd all taken to Mykonos. But also, this Christian was less suave, less charming, than the man who had laughed loudly at the house parties with a royal princess on his arm.

A chill ran down my spine. This Christian was a different person and he'd signaled that he knew . . . things . . . about me. He knew about my pen names, so what else did he know?

I needed to handle this delicately. The way he'd said Theodora's name, the way he'd reacted to my "news" of his death, there was something I had to unravel, tissue by tissue, like a surgeon. Or catastrophe would strike.

"Thea and I don't speak," I said, not quite answering his question.

"Ah."

I waited. No need to respond to that.

"You don't speak often? Or not at all?"

There was a gleam in his eye when he asked these questions, which seemingly sounded an alarm in the distant part of my brain.

But then I realized. My brain had not just emitted a beeping sound. It was my security system.

I murmured an apology to Christian and went to the front door, where I had several discreet monitors placed. I saw nothing, but the system showed that someone had just let themselves into the building.

Either Elena had come back or my new tourist tenant had already arrived. Ugh. I should have specified a check-in time. "Christian, I have to run downstairs for just a moment!" I called out as I traversed the hall to the back entrance.

Of course there's a back entrance to a penthouse apartment in a villa overlooking Lake Como. I may have had my royal titles stripped, but I wasn't living in some sort of hovel.

When the villa was split into the three apartments, they kept the servant's stairs that connected them and I had installed code boxes to get into all three. What use was a hidey-hole if I didn't know all the ins and outs?

I skipped down to the second level and punched in the code, wincing at the loud beeps it made and already regretting saying yes to letting out the apartment. What if the beds weren't made? What if I had to restock the toilet? This could be supremely awkward.

The back door to the apartment, like the other two, led to a utility area. This one had once been a small kitchen and the sink and storage still remained. I quietly opened the door to a broom closet and was relieved to find that yes, my intuition was correct and this was where Elena kept the spare soap, towels and washcloths. Excellent. I tucked several of each into my arms and decided to act like I was just running in and out.

"Hello?" I called out in English, then added in Italian, "*Scusami?*" The apartment was dark, I noted as I carefully crept out into the main rooms. Perhaps I had been mistaken—or my security system had. Perhaps the new tenant had dropped off their bags and then left to find dinner or meet a friend.

When no one replied, I exhaled with relief. Perfect. I would just go put these extra supplies in the washroom, check that there were sheets on the bed and sneak out. Elena would be so proud of me.

Then I was hit by a truck.

six

RIGHT BEFORE I WAS HIT, I SAW A FLASH OUT OF THE corner of my eye. A blurry movement. Gray rubbed on black and then I was slammed into a wall.

I was face to face with a monster.

Dark, angry, the size of a bear. Golden eyes gleaming in the night. His heavy forearm was pressed against my collarbone and throat. He could crush me, but then . . . he froze. He wasn't expecting me. Good. This was my chance.

I opened my mouth to scream. I should have used that energy to run instead. Because before I got a breath in, his forearm rolled just so slightly into the soft flesh of my neck, cutting off any ability to scream. His other hand, he clamped over my mouth.

Terror scraped along the inside of my skin, crawling like biting ants, but something strange and fierce in my brain told me not to fight.

The huge bear loomed over me, body pressing ever so slightly into mine, his mouth lowered to my ear.

"Don't move," he growled as his palm relaxed only slightly against my mouth.

"Where exactly do you think I'm going to go?" I hissed, pushing back ineffectually at the solid mass of muscle that was currently pinning me into place.

He pulled back. "Do be quiet, Your Highness."

I froze. Shock, surprise, fear tumbled together as it hit me.

The man had spoken to me in Driedish.

A perfect, *native* Driedish accent.

Your Highness.

He knew who I was.

And I knew those eyes, even in the dark.

"Hugh?" I said, my voice barely more than an exhalation against the heat of his still-hovering hand.

The bear nodded, a precise movement. No energy spared, because all one million kilowatts were totally focused on me.

All of that muscle tensed against me, to keep me in place.

All of the ferocity, leashed only for me.

All of his attention.

On.

Me.

It was all a goddamned lie.

I pushed back, my hands free of the soaps and towels that had flown everywhere when Hugh Konnor sprang out of the fucking shadows and scared the shit out of me. "What the hell are you thinking?" Scratch that. "What the hell are you doing here?"

Let the record show that while I had pushed him with quite a bit of my available strength, the man barely budged. But he did move his palms to the wall beside me, so perhaps I should have been grateful.

I was not.

"Let me go!" I slapped at his arms, but he caught my hands easily and wrapped them around my back. If anyone saw this, they would assume we were in the middle of a passionate embrace. In the dark, against a wall. Tangled together.

But this was Hugh—no, I mentally adjusted the way I saw him. This was *Konnor*. A royal bodyguard. A man from my past had found me.

Not only that, but it was *that* man.

The man I had told Signore Rossi about, the man who had definitely *not* been my first love.

He was also the man who was most definitely about to get his ass kicked out of my apartment as soon as I could figure out how to put on an extra hundred pounds of muscle and win an arm-wrestling contest with an ex-soldier who had at least fifteen years of military and national-security experience.

"Let me go," I hissed again. "You have no right to barge in here and take me prisoner!"

Konnor's grip relaxed, but he didn't let me go. "There's a man in your apartment."

I paused for a moment, processing the strange way he said that. A declaration, not a question. But . . . "Seriously?" My voice rose. "Don't tell me you've come all this way to throw a man out of my boudoir. I'm seriously flattered. Last time we met you couldn't have cared less who I had in my bed. My grandmother must not be giving you enough work to do back at the palace."

His golden eyes glinted in the dark. "Do you know that there's a fugitive in your apartment?"

"Which one?"

His dark brows crunched together.

"I own this apartment we're standing in. Are you a fugitive?" Oh. My mouth dropped as I drew a quick breath. "Is that why you're hiding in the dark?" So many possibilities flew through my imagination. "Are you kidnapping me?"

"Christ," Konnor swore. He let my hands go but he still loomed in front of me, as solid and unyielding as the plaster wall at my back. "I didn't even know you were here," he spat. "So stop playing games and tell me if Christian Fraser-Campbell is upstairs in that apartment."

This was about Christian? That pale, sickly shadow of a man? I opened my mouth to confirm that yes, Christian was recovering from a bad bout of flu in my spare room, but something made me stop.

That something was my intense irritation at this current situation.

"Did you rent this apartment?" I demanded. His head tilted slightly. I'd take that as a yes. "And you did it with the purpose of interrogating me about who I invite into my home?"

"Look. I don't have time—"

"I'm a private citizen now, Konnor. I don't have to do anything you—"

He swore again, slapped the wall and took three steps back. "We can do this the hard way or the easy way."

"Or no way," I offered, quite reasonably, I thought.

"You let me in and introduce me to your guest," he said with a grimace. "Or I bust down the door with a team of my colleagues and we take him by force."

A flush of heat and I saw red. "How dare you!" I sputtered. "You can't do that!"

He leaned in and smiled without joy. "Like you said, you're a private citizen now. I assure you I can."

And while Konnor was thoroughly pissing me off, I realized that what was most maddening was . . . he was right. I was not a princess. I had been cut off from the family. I couldn't threaten him with retribution from the Queen because she wouldn't answer my phone calls anymore.

I was simply a woman. Powerless in the face of sheer brute force. Or was I?

"On whose authority do you enter these premises?" I demanded.

He shrugged, an infuriating posture. "I rented it out. Paid for two nights."

My fists clenched. "And that gives you the legal authority to enter my private apartment?"

"I'm an officer of the law—"

"In Drieden," I interrupted, trying desperately to find a loophole that would put me back in control.

"There's international reciprocity, especially in the case of imminent danger, like when . . ." He cocked his head. "I heard something. Did you hear that?"

"What?"

He started walking toward the back entrance.

"What did you hear?" I demanded, following him.

"That cry for help." His steps quickened as he entered the utility area and reached for the door that led to the stairway.

"I didn't hear—" I broke off because I realized my idiocy. He was already half a flight ahead of me, taking those stairs three or four at a time, and I knew he'd find the door lodged open because I had left it like that just in case Christian called out for me.

Stupid. Stupid. Stupid.

I heard a crash, a shout, a Driedish curse.

I ran into my apartment and saw the back end of Konnor running out the front door. The security system monitors were all ablaze and lit up.

Christian.

I knew he was gone even before I looked for him. The apartment felt deserted. But still I checked the spare room. His shoes were nowhere to be found.

I barely had time to think through my next steps. It was really instinct telling me what to do.

Christian had left his small leather bag.

Take it.

My computer.

Shove it in the bag.

A coat. My keys. My wallet.

I'll buy what I need later.

Any second, Konnor and/or his buddies from the Royal Secret Service were going to come back in here and demand that I give them whatever they were looking for.

They expected me to be a good little princess, docile and obedient and completely okay with them ruining the story of the year.

Like hell I was.

Go.

seven

HAD FALLEN INTO BED AROUND THREE IN THE MORN-
ing, after I had gotten lost in the back roads outside of Santa Chiara,
which was understandable. It had been nearly five years since I had
visited my mother's Tuscan villa, and in those days I was still chauffeured behind tinted glass.

The warmth of the late-morning sunshine through the window
was comforting, even as the memory of the night before crept back
to me.

My home in Varenna, the little enclave of semi-normalcy and
independence I had carved out was, likely, gone.

Finding Christian Fraser-Campbell wandering about the town
was an unlikely coincidence. A palace security officer in my rental
apartment was not.

Somehow or another, my location had been discovered. I would
not be able to return to Varenna, not unless I was ready to have my
door beaten down by the press and other obnoxious persons like
Hugh Konnor.

But even in the blessed silence of my mother's house in the middle
of the Italian countryside, I was living on borrowed time. Someone,

sooner or later, would visit this villa. And with the kind of luck I had, it would most likely be Felice.

I was lucky, though. Not every woman had a mother who had collected extravagant real estate while she was married to the Crown Prince of Drieden. Her "hidey-holes," she called them. When I was twenty-one and decided to study art history in Rome, Felice had taken me aside and given me the access codes to this particular hidey-hole. "In case you need to escape the city with someone tall, dark and Roman," she had purred.

I won't be coy. Mother's villa had come in handy, a time or two. And for that reason—and others—a few years later, I invested in my own first hideaway in Varenna. But maybe this Tuscan villa had always been my back-up, I realized. Maybe I'd known, even then, that a well-prepared woman planned multiple escape routes. As Mother had taught me.

The not-too-musty linens reminded me that someone must keep an eye on my mother's house and that, even here, I could not count on privacy for long. I would keep the lights off for a few days while I plotted my next steps—whatever those were going to be.

I was ranking the possibilities as I slid out of bed and washed. I could go into hiding again. The mountains? America? If I mixed a bit of both, I could run off to Patagonia, as Mother had done. Nothing but hundreds of miles of open air and the occasional South American polo player/cologne model. The idea had merit.

But so did the story of the disappearance of Christian Fraser-Campbell. I patted his leather bag, which I had picked up the night before. When I was safely out of Varenna, I had pulled over and looked through it briefly, searching for any possible clues about where Christian was going next—and what he was running from. I had found only one piece of evidence—a pad of paper from a hotel in Rome. I'd go there next, and maybe someone would have contact information for him—or anyone who knew him. It could jeopardize my privacy to start asking questions in public, instead of anonymously in an email or over the phone, but the pay-off would be worth it. A mystery solved. A huge, shocking revelation. It would cement the journalism career of Clémence Diederich.

If I decided to do the piece, I reminded myself. I wanted to talk to Christian again. Get some answers. And some assurances.

It was habit that made me go to the kitchen, even as I knew there would be nothing fresh to eat. But this was one of Felice's hidey-holes, and what good was an impromptu assignation spot without some coffee or basic pantry staples?

Still thinking about the best way to travel incognito and how to cautiously approach Christian's friends and associates, I didn't notice the man at the kitchen table until it was too late.

I screamed.

Backed up against the wall.

He didn't move, but he did look mildly irritated.

"What are you doing here?" I demanded. "How did you get in?"

Fucking Hugh Konnor, of Her Majesty's Royal Guard. In the bright morning light, I saw him much more clearly than I had in the apartment. His usually close-cropped dark hair had grown, along with an auburn beard and mustache. It had been years since I'd seen him like this, in close quarters, without a crowd of people around.

His arms rested on the table, the sleeves of his thermal woolen shirt pulled up to reveal muscular forearms. A thick black tattoo skated along the outside of his right arm. My attention wanted to linger there. To decipher the code. But it didn't matter what it represented.

I needed Hugh Konnor out of this house. Immediately.

"I'll ask once more. What are you doing here?" I hadn't been a princess in so long, I'd forgotten how to sound princessy, and my voice showed it. It was thin, flimsy. Useless.

"I followed you, Your Highness."

"I'm not a royal princess anymore. Please don't call me that."

His jaw tightened. "Mrs. DiBernardo."

"Oh, please, no." My stomach heaved at the sound of my married name. I put a hand over my mouth. Something flickered in his eyes and his lips pressed tightly together.

"You followed me," I echoed, hoping to get back to the topics I was most concerned about. "I don't know why you would do such a thing. You can leave." He stayed seated at the table. "Any time," I added. Still, the man didn't move.

A flutter of fear caused my stomach to flip. A small black canister on the kitchen table caught my attention. My pepper spray. Something I had bought when I first lived on my own and was jumping at every sound. I had left it in my car the night before . . . hadn't I? Or had I brought it in, left it there when I stumbled through the house in the dead of night? I couldn't remember.

Konnor noticed me looking at it and he pushed it toward me. "You can have it, if it makes you feel better."

I lurched forward and clutched at the pepper spray, bringing it back with me against the wall. Konnor had been right. The small cylinder in my hand comforted me, but only a little.

Hugh Konnor's presence wasn't disconcerting, exactly. No more than that of any other member of Her Majesty's Royal Guard would be. *Lie.*

Okay, yes. Hugh Konnor was exactly the worst person to find me. To follow me. No other guard despised me as much. And the feeling was mutual. No other officer made me this nervous, this . . . panicked.

I wanted him gone, immediately.

Which is what I said. "Please leave, Mr. Konnor." I held up the can of pepper spray. It was somewhat of an automatic gesture, more defensive than a threat.

"I'm afraid I cannot." To his credit, he looked sincerely regretful. But also—strangely—pissed off.

"You can. There's nothing stopping you." I waved in the direction of the door. "Please remove yourself from this property." *And if you could, oh, I don't know, manage to not tell anyone that you saw me, that would be great.*

I didn't add the request for his silence. Of all the palace security staff, Hugh Konnor was the most by-the-book officer I had ever known. As soon as he left, he would have a form filled out in triplicate detailing what had happened the day before. "Shit," I said. "You've already reported this, haven't you?" My chest started to hurt. "You're waiting for back-up or something, aren't you?"

I had to get out of here. My car was in the drive. My bag was in the bedroom. Would he stop me if I ran back to get it? Would he tackle me? Force me to stay?

"You can't stop me from going," I said, in a voice that didn't sound like my normal self. I was shaking. A little hysterical. I hated being emotional in front of Hugh Konnor. "I'm a private citizen. I have rights," I added, even though I knew how little that had meant to him when he was in my apartment in Varenna.

He stood slowly, holding his hands out in front of him as if he were calming a snapping dog.

"What are you doing?" I leaned back into the wall, wishing it would swallow me up. Anything to get me out of here.

"Your Highness—"

"No."

"Your . . ." He broke off, then recovered. "Caroline."

My name. The first time I'd heard my own name in months. And it was out of the mouth of *this* man?

"I haven't called anyone." His voice was still low, as if he meant to soothe. "But I can't let you go, either. Not until—"

I leapt at the opportunity. "Until what?"

"Until you tell me what you were doing in Varenna with Christian Fraser-Campbell."

Oh, right. Okay. I could do that, just to get him to leave. I opened my mouth to explain, to tell the simple truth about how I'd coincidentally run into Christian on a village street, but just then a bell rang at the front door of the villa.

Konnor snapped to attention, all alert and straight. "Were you expecting someone?" he asked in a low voice.

I shook my head, biting my lip in silence. He nodded and held a finger out to me. "Stay right there. I'll take care of it."

When he left the kitchen I allowed myself to slump with relief, and it was as if the moment of relaxation triggered my brain to start problem-solving again. Putting the pieces together.

Konnor seemed surprised by someone ringing the bell, which gave credence to his statement that he hadn't alerted the Secret Service—or anyone—as to my whereabouts.

And, I reasoned with myself, why would he? My grandmother had stripped me of my royal titles and removed me from the line of succession. There was no reason for Her Majesty's Royal Guard to keep tabs on me anymore.

But I had still disappeared from the public eye. Knowing my grandmother—and the rest of my family—the way I did, I was sure they were dying to at the very least monitor my movements.

Maybe. If they still cared.

Maybe that's why Konnor hadn't called anyone. No one cared. And if so, that meant he hadn't been looking for me in Varenna. He had certainly seemed surprised enough when he had his arm against my throat.

But how had he found me, if he hadn't been trying to search for me . . . Why had he followed me to my mother's Tuscan hidey-hole?

My stomach twisted—from nerves, from the exertion of survival, from the execution of secrets. Footsteps sounded down the hall—just one set. I had lost my chance to run.

When Hugh Konnor appeared in the doorframe again, his eyes

were serious, sharp and staring right at me. I had the uncanny feeling that a shark was circling me.

"Who was it?" I rasped. I had to know.

"The groundskeeper. He saw the cars in the drive."

"What did you say?"

Konnor shrugged a wide shoulder. "I showed him my palace badge. It seemed to be enough."

My head spun. Wasn't this what controlling men did? Wave off the neighbor who was checking to see what the banging and crashes were about? God, I was so sick of this patriarchy shit. And how did a normal woman fight back when she wasn't a princess and couldn't order the stubborn ass of a man around?

Natural instincts flipped on. I lifted the small can of mace and sprayed.

Nothing came out.

Konnor fixed me with a bland stare.

I screamed the F-word. In Driedish.

"I thought you didn't want people to know where you were!" he shouted irritably.

"Don't come any closer," I warned him, but it sounded pathetic and weak. What was I going to do? Claw at him? Spit? My mixed-martial-arts training was non-existent. Shocking, I know.

"I'm not here to hurt you, Caroline. I'm here to protect you from making questionable decisions."

"Protect me?" I scoffed. "From making questionable decisions? Since when is that your job?"

Konnor's brows furrowed. "Since I was hired by the palace and I took an oath."

I blinked. "You think you're protecting me as my *bodyguard* right now?" I laughed. Oh, okay. "Then I release you. Go. Shoo. Go forth and guard someone else's body, please. This body is perfectly, totally, one hundred per cent fine without you."

"Caroline." There was no fumbling with "Your Highness" or "ma'am" or whatnot. No, he said my name with all his bodyguard authority, like he had that last day in the royal stables, when I was nineteen. The last day he'd been my bodyguard. "Do you know who you had in your apartment yesterday?"

I took a second to process his ferocity. There was something that was being miscommunicated. "Yes, I think I'd recognize the man who was going to marry my sister."

He shook his head and smiled bitterly. "No. That was the man who was going to murder your sister."

eight

HE WAS RIFLING THROUGH MY MOTHER'S CUPBOARDS, cursing in Driedish, instead of answering my question.

What the hell was he talking about? Christian was trying to kill my sister? I mean, yes, he left Thea at the altar, but it was a bit overdramatic to equate that with murder.

Finally, he pulled two bottles of wine out and mumbled, "This will have to do."

"Are we having a party?" I asked.

He ignored me and plunged a pocket knife into the cork of one of the bottles. It was the most savage wine opening I had ever witnessed. I shivered and took a step back.

"It's not even nine o'clock in the morning," I said as he started drinking straight from the bottle.

When he finished guzzling, he wiped his mouth and gave me a look of disbelief. "You just tried to mace me. Now you preach proper comportment?"

It was an excellent point. I thought I had walked away from all the requirements and rules of my former royal life, but these things were deeply ingrained. Old habits revealed themselves in all sorts of inconsistent ways.

Like the way I was acting with Hugh Konnor right now. Staying here, talking to him, expecting that he might treat me like an equal and answer my questions like a reasonable person. What was that old saying? Something about being insane and expecting different results after people showed you who they were?

Hugh Konnor had shown me who he was nearly ten years ago. He did not respect me enough to speak to me like an adult. It was useless trying to reason with him, especially when he was a member of the royal security staff, who were the very people I wanted to avoid like an incurable STI.

"Are you going to tell me what you meant about Christian and Thea?" I asked again. "Because, if not, I'm leaving."

Konnor's eyes narrowed on me. "Why would you leave? You just got here."

He had a point. I thought quickly. "I don't like you. I want to be alone."

"Where are you going?"

I pushed away from the wall and headed back the way I had entered this morning, intending to go to the bedroom I had slept in, collect my (Christian's) bag and exit my mother's villa like a civilized woman of the world.

Hugh Konnor couldn't stop me. Except, of course, he could.

I made it as far as the bedroom. I had the bag in my hand. I turned. He was at the bedroom door, a hand on each side of the frame. "I'll ask again. Where are you going?"

Standing like this, arms outstretched, he loomed huge. Threatening. His sleeves had pulled back more and the black ink on his forearms seemed sharply outlined.

And the look on his face . . . stern. His golden-brown eyes were deadly serious.

My heart started to pound. It was the struggle of my life. Obey. Or rebel. Listen to the authority of those trying to "protect" me, or . . . Not.

Who are you? I asked myself the same question the day I decided to walk away from Stavros's funeral. The answer had come back immediately, like it did just now.

"It's one hundred per cent not your business," I told him, with my chin up, trying to invoke as much authority as possible. "Please stand aside."

He stared at me for a moment and a shadow crossed his face. Then he changed his posture. He dropped his arms and stepped away from the bedroom door.

Wow. That really worked. Since I'd lost my title, I'd become even more fearsome. I was unstoppable. No one could argue with me now. I clutched the leather bag to my chest and half ran, half walked past Hugh and down the hall, through the living area and out of the front door while my Jedi mind trick was still working on the stubborn bodyguard behind me.

The Tuscan sun that had seemed so gently reaffirming this morning now glared into my eyes. I felt exposed, as if spotlights had flipped on to track my escape from prison. Of course, I resented the fact that I hadn't had a chance to think up the best ways to hunt down Christian but maybe Hugh was doing me a favor. I was taking a leap of faith. I'd go to Rome, see where the trail led, without being burdened with this stone monolith with a misplaced sense of duty.

Two cars were in the gravel drive. So Hugh had followed me by car. He could do the same right now, I supposed, but I threw the thought away. I didn't have time for strategy. I would figure it out as soon as my foot was on a gas pedal.

I threw my bag in the front seat, followed it and reached into the dash, where I had left the keys the night before.

They weren't there.

I ducked down, searched the floor, between the seats, and tried to ignore the hollow panic that was growing inside my gut.

I knew where the keys were even before I turned and looked.

Hugh Konnor stood in the drive. He opened his palm and my keys dangled from a finger. But he wasn't taunting me with them. The look on his face was sympathetic. Bordering on pity. "Come inside. Please."

The kind word was not what I wanted. None of this was.

"I can't let you leave," he repeated. What was this—the third time he'd said it? If I knew anything about Hugh Konnor, I knew that he was a man of his word. He always meant what he said. I should have believed him the first time.

Hugh Konnor was not letting me go.

I swore loudly and got out of the car. In a sort of rebellion, I left my bag in the front seat. If he wanted to treat me like a princess that he could order around, then he could fetch it for me.

MY MOTHER MUST PAY HER GROUNDSKEEPER HAND-somely, because as soon as he realized that there were visitors at her villa, he arrived with baskets of provisions: fresh eggs, cured meats, a still-warm loaf of bread and a carton of winter vegetables.

Hugh set about making breakfast. I sat at the table in the kitchen and watched him. If a man was holding me captive, I wanted to see everything he was doing. If he reached for a cellphone, a knife, a bottle of wine, I wanted to know.

This is Hugh Konnor, the voice inside my head reminded me. *You know him.*

I did. And I didn't. Ten years ago, I thought I knew him. Then I learned I didn't. Our relationship had been short and confusing and, in the end, humiliating.

And now this. He was still confusing me, Mr. Tall, Dark and Cooking Breakfast. My stomach rumbled at the smell of toasting bread.

My next steps were plain, then. Eat a much-needed breakfast, discover what it was that Hugh Konnor needed from me, convince him to let me leave without alerting anyone who cared about my location. And then I'd be on my way, tracking down Christian and/or finding a secret spot to live again. Which reminded me, I needed to send a message to Elena and Signore Rossi, whenever I could access the wifi and I didn't have the Bear Man looming over me.

I didn't offer to help—with the coffee or setting the table. Another small, bratty rebellion. He prepared the food and brought me a plate and a cup of coffee—black, as I liked it. *Because we have no cream*, I reminded myself. *Not because he gives a shit about your coffee preferences*.

He sat at the table with me and, for the shortest of moments, I was disconcerted. Konnor was a bodyguard, and a member of the palace staff did not sit with the royal family. Ever.

I shook my head at myself. Officially, I wasn't a royal at all. I had not been since my elopement and since my beloved, punitive grandmother had stripped me of my royal titles. But somehow, that reality had been different when I lived with Stavros, then during the last few months in Varenna. I had been living a fantasy life—someone else lived with a handsome, moody race car driver—not Princess Caroline of Drieden. Then it had been Lina DiLorenzo living a quiet, reclusive life in Varenna, not the woman who had once been fourth in line to the throne of one of the oldest monarchies in Europe.

Now, sitting at a table with someone—a flesh-and-blood, brooding someone—from my past, the loss of my identity—or perhaps my identity regardless, was once again a startling reality.

I was no longer a Driedish princess. And Hugh Konnor could sit anywhere he wanted. He could do anything he wanted to . . . including keeping me hostage.

What would the repercussions be, really? If I called and reported this behavior, would anyone care, back at the palace? And why was he doing this, anyway? He was clearly only making up these tales about Christian. Probably just wanted to control me, like the rest of the palace staff—

"You're not eating."

Hugh's voice startled me from my thoughts. "Oh." I blinked and refocused on my plate. He was right, of course. I hadn't even picked up a fork.

"It's not like you not to eat." Hugh's gruff observance reminded me of our history. And my usually healthy appetite. My cheeks warmed as I realized it looked like I was either a food snob or trying for some sort of hunger strike, neither of which was like me, truth be told.

"I'm sorry," I stuttered. "I'm a bit distracted, since I'm being held against my will."

Hugh's brows drew together, as if he was confused. I decided I had to clarify. "You know. When someone doesn't let you have the keys to your car, it's generally considered kidnapping."

His brows rose, an expression of understanding now. "Oh, I see. So for the first twenty-seven years of your life you were actually being kidnapped? All that time with the chauffeurs and the limousines? Right under our noses?"

"I . . ." My mouth snapped open then shut. "You're deliberately twisting what I'm saying."

"No. I'm accurately interpreting what you said, Your Highness."

My gut tightened at that honorific. "I'm not—" I restarted. "I mean, don't call me that."

"Old habits, Your Highness."

"Just call me Caroline," I said through clenched teeth.

His head dropped, but I could see his jaw tightening, like he was trying to keep himself from heaving up his breakfast.

"That's right," I drawled. "I forgot how much you can't stand me. So much so that you won't even use my name."

He raised his eyes and they met mine. "It wasn't right then and it's not right now."

The reminder of what I had done ten years ago wasn't necessary. To be honest, the past was a thick, heavy thing sitting on the table between us. Maybe that was why I didn't lift my fork or drain my coffee cup, as I normally would. We had other things to deal with, Hugh Konnor and I.

I decided to be the adult in the room. "Do you want to talk about it?"

He picked up his coffee and drank heavily. Apparently, I was the only one whose appetite was affected by our shared history, which seemed about right. Then he said, "Yes. We need to talk."

Suddenly, my mature aspirations were a very, very bad idea indeed. Ugh. Why did adulting have to be so hard?

"Fine," I said, wincing at the incoming awkwardness.

"Christian Fraser-Campbell. What do you know about him?"

My eyes flew open. "Really? You want to talk about my sister's ex-fiancé and not the reason why you hate me?"

Now he was the one looking distinctly uncomfortable. "I don't—"

I cut him off. "You do hate me. Otherwise, you would have taken my virginity when I asked you to."

nine

KONNOR LIFTED ONE VERY SERIOUS BROW AT ME. "Really." So much was contained in that one, flat word. *Really? This is what you have obsessed over for the past ten years? Your schoolgirl crush? You're still not over me—this prime piece of sexy manhood?*

Now would be a good time for the floor to swallow me up. Seriously.

Not to worry, he moved on as if what I had said wasn't a big deal at all. Which made me feel as small as a snail. "Tell me, have you looked at a newspaper or turned on a television in the last year?"

"Yes," I snapped.

"Then you are aware that your sister's fiancé was reported to be dead by suicide last summer?"

"Yes," I said, avoiding his eyes. The shame of not calling my sister Thea when the shocking news hit was matched only by the shame that, at the time, I was hiding in darkened rental houses because my marriage was a failure and my husband wanted to forget he had ever married me.

Two months later, when Stavros died, I needed space. Anonymity.

Time to focus on righting the injustice that had caused his death. I put my needs before my elder sister's and didn't reach out then, either.

"But he's not really dead," I said defensively. As if that made me a better sister.

Konnor blinked, crossed his arms in front of him and, once again, I tried to ignore the lean, corded muscle and the black tattoos along each bone. A line of numbers on one arm, scrolling words on the other. Then something hit me in his patient silence.

"You knew he wasn't dead," I said with a little gasp. Then the rest of it struck me. "Did everyone in the palace know? Did Thea?" And if my sister Thea, second in line to the throne, knew her fiancé had faked his suicide after he had abandoned her on their wedding day . . .

"What the hell has been going on at the palace?" I asked. This was a kind of insanity that my grandmother had never allowed when I was there. She ruled the palace, the family, the entire monarchy with an iron fist. That was, I suppose, the job of a queen, but still. If one person stepped out of line, acted against her expectations, like say, eloping with a Formula One race car driver, that brought the velvet guillotine down.

The palace covering up that Christian hadn't killed himself was out of character, to say the least.

Konnor seemed as if he was carefully weighing his words before he spoke again. "Christian Fraser-Campbell is a threat to Drieden. Last summer it was discovered that he was involved in a plot to bring down the monarchy."

I blinked several times. It was a lot to take in. Of course, I knew my family was also the capital-R Royal family of Drieden. But in all the usual family squabbles, sibling rivalries and testy divorces, sometimes it was easy to forget that Big Gran was also the Big Monarch. And that our family portrait gallery represented the people who filled the nation's history books.

So to hear that the man who was going to marry my sister was a threat to our country? Our whole way of life? My brain had to adjust to that idea.

"And so my grandmother came up with this suicide story?" I guessed, still trying to process all of the craziness.

Konnor shook his head. "Christian released the fake photographs of his body as a way to get your . . . your sister's security off his trail."

"Thea knows all about this?" And now I felt like the worst sister in the world again. That Thea had had to deal with the abandonment of her almost-husband but also his betrayal to her country? No one was more patriotic than Princess Theodora. She was the one who always had all the history facts and figures memorized.

Me? I'm the sibling who just tried to keep the peace. And look where that got me.

Konnor hesitated before he answered me. "Yes. Your sister has been very involved in the search for Christian. For obvious reasons."

"Yes, of course," I murmured.

"No. You don't understand. Christian drugged me and locked me away. Then he did the same to your sister. He conspired with her bodyguard to sell state secrets to the people who would have your grandmother and your entire family exiled to Bolivia."

Shock silenced me. Utterly. This was far more than some bad feelings about an uneaten wedding cake.

"And this is what brought me to Italy. We've been searching for Christian since late last summer. I had a lead and caught up with him in Milan, followed him to Varenna." He paused. "To your house."

I closed my eyes and shook my head. Of all the random, awful coincidences. "Christian and I literally ran into each other on the street," I explained. "He was sick, it was raining." I shrugged. "He needed a place to stay."

"But you said you had heard he had died." Konnor's eyes narrowed at me. "Wasn't it slightly suspicious that you saw him, walking, talking . . . alive?"

Now I reached for the coffee, suddenly needing the strength of caffeine to help me answer these questions. "Suspicious? No. Strange? Curious? Perhaps." I took a sip and smiled weakly. "There have been fake news stories about me my entire life. Only a fraction of them have been corrected. There are probably still people in the world who believe that I was abducted by aliens after Stavros's funeral. Or that I'm living in an ashram in Arizona."

"You thought Christian's death was *fake news*?" The disbelief in Konnor's voice was understandable, but so was my explanation.

"Only when I saw that he was still breathing," I said. "It's entirely reasonable," I added, a little defensively.

"Reasonable. Similarly, that he showed up in the same small Italian village you were living in. On the same street."

His sarcastic suggestion hung in the air, lingering like a bad odor. "Are you suggesting something?" I asked.

Konnor merely cocked his head and looked at me, letting silence be his answer. "You think I *invited* him over?" My voice rose. "You think this was planned? Why in the world would I meet my sister's presumed dead fiancé in secret?"

"You've been living in secret for four months."

The accusation came sharp and quick as an arrow. "What does that have to do with anything?" I demanded.

"People living in secret are generally trying to hide someone."

He was one hundred per cent correct. But the someone I wanted to hide was not Christian Fraser-Campbell. So I said, "You have no idea what you're talking about." I pushed away from the table and stood up, feeling a little sad about my uneaten breakfast. I was going to regret not eating, but there was no way I was sharing a meal with Hugh Konnor right now, not with his insane accusations.

Konnor stood, too, his chair squeaking over the rough wood floors. "I know that Christian Fraser-Campbell was involved in a conspiracy to destroy the Driedish monarchy. That to do so he committed murder and assault and kidnapping. That he is one of the most wanted men in Europe, but he's stayed beyond our reach for six months. Until he was found strolling up to your doorstep." Konnor's lip curled. "Men like him aren't this good unless they have powerful people helping them. And no one's more powerful than a royal princess."

"I'm not a royal princess—"

"Especially one who was so adept at keeping herself hidden for nearly as long."

I turned away to face the window, feeling uncomfortable with Konnor's interrogation, under his intense gaze. "This all sounds pretty crazy," I finally said, as I tried to process everything Konnor had described. Plots, murder, kidnapping? It was truly hard to imagine that the man who had slept the day away weak and wasted in my spare bedroom had anything to do with Konnor's tales.

My back was toward him, but I knew what I'd see if I turned around. Hugh Konnor had that perfect bodyguard face—serious, keen, *aware*. He took in everything around him. Maybe that's why I couldn't help but be attracted to him when I was a young, innocent teenager. He seemed so engrossed in every detail about me. As if he was memorizing my skin, my breath, my pulse. When he'd been my guard, he had anticipated my every move. Always in step, always right there.

It had been too much for nineteen-year-old Caroline's hormones to handle.

But twenty-nine-year-old Caroline could control herself. She could control the situation. *Control him.*

The thought made me shiver.

But still. Maybe I was onto something. He said habits were hard to break, that he still saw me as a royal princess.

Fine. I'd be his princess. Until I could escape him.

I straightened my posture. Cast a disdainful look over my shoulder. Just the way princesses should. *Why are you still here?*

Konnor's face was exactly as I expected. He didn't blink when I gave him princess attitude. He never had.

"Tell me about your plan. Where were you going this morning?"

My heart skipped. That was too familiar. Too intimate. "No."

"Why not?"

"Because it's a secret plan," I informed him haughtily, deigning to turn back to him. I eyed the bread on the table. If I picked up a slice, would it ruin my whole untouchable-princess demeanor?

"Ah." He gave a half-nod. "I see."

A proper princess would let that go because she wouldn't care about what he saw or didn't see. But me? I just couldn't resist poking at sleeping bears.

"What do you see?"

"You don't care anymore. About the House of Laurent. Your family," he added pointedly.

"I . . ." I stopped. What was the right answer? Should a princess care or not care?

My sister Thea would know the answer to this. She always knew exactly the right amount of royal disdain to slather on. My sister Sophie would, as well. Either one of them could easily manipulate any man they wished. They'd probably inherited that gene from our mother.

Me? I had only received Felice's forthright pragmatism, none of her sexual wiles. That was why I ended up in apartments by myself and struggled with convincing mule-headed men to leave me alone.

But I had to keep trying . . . something. My freedom was on the line, here. "Of course I care," I said. "But my family, like my plans, my living arrangements, even my relationships, are none of your damn business."

Konnor took a slow, deliberate step toward me. "Six months ago, Christian Fraser-Campbell restrained me, drugged me, and left me for dead. I have been searching for him ever since." Another measured step. "Believe me when I say that anything—any information that you have—is very much my fucking business."

If he'd moved any closer, maybe I would have panicked. After all, here was this powerful, intense man crowding me. But right then, I didn't feel frightened. Possibly because, knowingly or unknowingly, Konnor had shown me what I needed to do to manipulate him.

"I'll tell you what I know on one condition," I said.

His eyes narrowed. "What?"

"That you'll leave me alone afterward."

He lifted his head and studied me for a moment. "Yes. After you tell me every detail, I will leave you alone."

Like I said, I didn't inherit my mother's devious ways, or else I would have seen Konnor's words for what they were.

Manipulation.

ten

TOLD HIM ALMOST EVERYTHING. ALL OF THE PERTINENT information, at least. I left out the parts about Clémence Diederich, Cordelia Lancaster, and what Christian may or may not have known about me. Hugh Konnor wasn't my bodyguard anymore; he didn't need to know my deepest darkest secrets. Not until I could learn what Christian's true intentions were. After my explanation, I sat back down at the table. My breakfast was cold, but I would not be so proud as to go without eating. Starving princesses aren't very attractive.

But if I had expected that Konnor would brush his hands, say "Thank you very much," and get in his car and drive off (and I had, in fact, hoped for exactly such a turn of events), then I was disappointed.

Instead, he started pacing. "He was sick? What were his symptoms?" Konnor asked about Christian.

"I told you. He was sweaty and pale."

"He could have faked that."

"And a fever? How does one fake a fever?"

That earned me a look like I was an idiot. "There are drugs that speed up the heart rate, make a person sweat."

"That seems excessive. Why would he pretend to have an illness? He could have approached me and simply talked to me."

Konnor dismissed that with a wave of his hand. "He wouldn't know what you knew. He needed subterfuge."

I rolled my eyes. "But *why?*"

That made Konnor's feet stop moving. "*Why?* He needed something from you, perhaps. Or perhaps to kidnap you."

"Really?" I rolled my eyes as I tried to ignore the fact that Konnor was dangerously close to the truth, perhaps. That Christian wanted something from me. "No one else has been able to find me—not the tabloids, not the secret service. But you're claiming that Christian Fraser-Campbell has the intelligence capability to show up at my house, the venality to try to topple the Driedish monarchy, the skills to hide himself for six months, and—"

He cut me off. "And the backing to support his acts, yes."

"I'm not buying it," I said, to Konnor's scowling face. "I liked him well enough for my sister's husband, but he's really only an impoverished minor noble. And British, at that. To attach all this drama to it is excessive." It was too complicated, so far beyond all the reasonable explanations for Christian's disappearance that I had imagined back in Varenna.

"Next you'll be telling me he's a zombie or something," I scoffed.

Konnor mumbled something like, "Tell that to your sister."

I wanted to snap back and order him to stop bringing up my sister, but I probably needed to be more diplomatic. More tactical. So I picked up our breakfast plates and carried them to the kitchen sink.

After I rinsed the plates, I moved back to the table, where Konnor seemed to be deep in thought. Nice and quiet, perfect for a calm, reasonable suggestion from me.

"Now that I've told you everything, it's time for you to hold up your end of the bargain," I said lightly.

"What is that?" Konnor frowned at me.

"You said that after I told you about my contact with Christian, you'd leave me alone."

"Sure," he said easily. "I'll drive you to the train station." He checked his watch. "Should be a train to Milan that would be good for you."

I nodded and tried to keep hidden any hint of disappointment. Milan? Train station? I really needed to get on the train to Rome. And I had hoped that Konnor would be the one leaving. But it was just as well. I would just come up with a new plan on the fly. Or maybe I would simply travel to Milan, turn around and catch a train to Rome next. Doubling back. That was something they did in spy movies, right?

Konnor got up from the table and, with quick, efficient moves, cleared the kitchen. I left a note for the groundskeeper, thanking him for his attentive assistance. Next time I spoke with my mother, I'd be sure to let her know how well her staff had performed.

Because he still had my keys and because my bag was still in my car, Konnor got into the driver's seat and took the wheel. Again, I would have preferred to drive myself, but I bit my tongue and put my seatbelt on in the front passenger seat. Princesses get chauffeured, I reminded myself. And I was getting what I wanted this way. A one-way ticket, far, far away from demanding, over-attentive security professionals.

In less than a half hour we were in the nearest city with a train station, Santa Chiara. Konnor had been following a map on his phone which directed us through the narrow streets and to the station.

But as soon as he pulled into the car park, I saw them. I reached over and clutched his upper arm. "You bastard," I hissed.

The Driedish police stood out the way that tall, burly blond men in ill-fitting navy suits would in an Italian train station. They were practically klieg lights of Northern European DNA.

"You promised!" I accused Konnor as my fists rolled up into balls. I had never struck anyone but, God help me, I wanted to pummel

Hugh Konnor for double-crossing me. I wanted to make his stone face flinch for once.

And damn him, he stayed his impassive self. "I promised I would leave you alone after you told me everything."

"I did!" I insisted. "I told you everything."

"Did you?" He cocked his head, reached into his pocket and pulled out a slip of paper.

My handwriting. My questions, which I had scribbled down to ask Christian.

I had no good way to explain that. Not without telling Konnor that I sometimes wrote newspaper stories on the side under a different name or two. And no one at the palace ever needed to hear about *that*.

"You can't do this." I thought quickly. "I'm not an heir of the Queen's anymore. I'm a private citizen, I can't be whisked away without my consent."

"You're still entitled to protection, especially when your life has been threatened. And it has." He met my eyes then, and I could tell he believed what he was saying. He was absolutely convinced that Christian Fraser-Campbell was a danger to me.

Why?

"I won't go with them. I'll run away. And I'll still be in danger."

"They'll follow you."

I knew he was right. Once the rest of those palace security officers saw me, my privacy was over. Even if they didn't manhandle me back to Drieden and Big Gran, they would not stop once they laid eyes on me. I couldn't be that smart—or that lucky—again. Not without some time to come up with a plan—and time was one thing I had just run out of.

So I only had one bargaining chip left.

"Yes, you're right. I didn't tell you everything," I said as quickly as possible, before he could wind around to the parking spot where that big black Mercedes van was, presumably, waiting for me.

Konnor's foot hit the brake. "What is it?"

"Drive me out of here and I'll tell you."

He nodded too quickly. Turned too readily. Did he think I was stupid?

Well, yes, I probably was. But I was a very quick learner.

I reached over and took his cellphone and hit the power button so he couldn't send a location signal. His foot hit the gas pedal.

I guessed he was a quick learner too.

KONNOR HAD GONE TO THE KIOSKS AND BOUGHT A ticket to every bus that was leaving in the next hour, and now he handed those tickets over to me. I still had his phone, and I knew that he hadn't tried to contact anyone during our drive to Florence, but I wasn't taking any chances. Now I was paranoid that there were other ways that Konnor had signaled them. Or maybe he'd put a GPS tracker on my car. *My* car! The idea made me indignant. He'd used my car and my gas to turn me in! If I saw any of those palace security staffers in the bus station, I was hopping on the first bus that was leaving. Then I would . . . well, I'd figure something out. It wasn't the most foolproof plan, but it was my best shot at getting out of here.

We were standing in a smelly, dark corner of the bus station. It was a new experience for me. I'm sure we looked shady to anyone who looked over at us. The big, hulking bearded guy handing slips of paper to the nervous woman in large Prada sunglasses and dyed hair. "I probably look like your cheap date hiding in the corner," I muttered.

Konnor looked irritated. "That's not very flattering."

Strangely, I was touched. "Thank you." Especially when I hadn't had a chance to brush my teeth that morning.

"I mean, I would never . . . do that."

My stomach went sour. "Oh, right," I said between gritted, grinding teeth, feeling like a fool for the fifty thousandth time around Hugh Konnor. One of these days, I'd remember how unappealing he found me. Or . . . "that."

"Your . . ." He stopped himself from saying the "Highness" part. "Caroline," he said instead, in a heavy, even way. "You said you had more information to give me."

Quickly, I glanced over his shoulder. I scanned for anyone who looked like a Driedish police officer. Then I glanced at the departures sign. A bus to Rome was leaving in ten minutes. Perfect.

"There was one thing that had changed about Christian since I'd last seen him. It might not mean anything. I mean, it's not like I was the one seeing him naked."

Konnor blinked in rapid succession. "He was naked?"

"He took a shower, in my apartment. I told you that. And when he came out, I noticed a tattoo on his right side, under his heart. One that he hadn't had when he was with my sister." I paused. "Unless he did. But I don't think so. I would have noticed it."

Konnor's jaw clicked. "You pulled this stunt to tell me he got a tattoo. That may or may not have been there ten months ago."

"It should be easy enough to check. There are photos of all of us when we went on holiday to Greece. And then my sister would also know, since she was engaged to him and all."

"What does this tattoo look like?" Konnor asked reluctantly.

I pulled a pen out of my bag and grabbed his hand. It was wide, rough and warm and, for a moment, I had the crazy impulse to thread my fingers through his. To confess all my sins, knowing they would be safe in those hands.

But they wouldn't. Konnor had shown me he was ready to turn me over to the wolves, sins and all.

Still, I upheld my end of the bargain. In blue ink I drew the symbol on Konnor's palm that Christian now displayed on his chest. A horizontal diamond with sunshine rays radiating from the bottom half.

"That's it?" Konnor's voice was rough.

I nodded. "It's not a lot, but . . ." I raised my eyes to meet his. "I can't let you take me back. Not yet."

And with that vow, I grabbed my bag and left Hugh Konnor in a darkened corner of the Florence bus station and ran toward my Plan B. Or maybe it was Plan C? Whatever it was, once again, I heeded the voice in my head.

Go.

eleven

THE APARTMENT ON THE VIA GIONOVIA WASN'T AS isolated as Mother's Tuscan villa, nor was it as anonymous as my Varenna house, but hopefully it would serve, for a few nights at least.

As exhausting as the trip from Florence had been, I would not let myself collapse in a heap and sleep, like I had when I escaped to Mother's last hidey-hole. First, I had to make sure all measures were taken to . . . secure the perimeter.

No, I did not know what the hell I was doing. I was an exiled princess, not a security expert, but I forced myself to go through the apartment and ensure all the doors were locked. All the windows were shut tight. All the security systems were set appropriately. Or not set. Or at least not silently triggered, bringing down a small army in the middle of the night.

This lavish apartment had been where I'd lived for over a year when I studied in Rome. Back then, I still had guards, but they'd taken a smaller apartment on the floor below. It was a risk for me to come back here, but a measured one. After all, it had been seven years since I'd left Rome and, besides my mother, there was little chance that any other member of the family had spent a significant amount of time here.

As I walked through the apartment's halls, I stared up at the paintings that hung around me. Since I'd been an art history student when I'd lived in Rome, I'd taken time to go through this collection, here.

The Rome apartment was part of my mother's portfolio, but it was not one of the properties that she'd acquired during her marriage to my father, Prince Albert of Drieden. No, she'd received the apartment as part of her Sevine inheritance.

Let me explain. Although I was born royal through my father's line, my mother's family was, if not royal, almost equally distinguished, and extremely wealthy. The Sevines of Drieden had been merchants involved in shipping goods throughout Europe and the Far East. Reportedly, the king at the time wished to ensure that such wealth stayed in Drieden. Thus, the Sevines received titles in the early seventeenth century, and for four hundred years their fortunes were permanently intertwined with the Royal House of Laurent . . . until my mother, Felice, divorced the heir to the throne.

Thus, the Roman apartment was decorated with lesser European artists and Sevine family acquisitions over the centuries. Some of them felt like old friends, as I had given them names when I lived here. There was "Franco, the Duke of Snooty." And there was the Loose-Lipped Lady of Lalique. My sister Thea would probably know if there were historical figures of note in the paintings. Me, I just saw color, texture and composition.

When I was sure that no one could enter the apartment without my knowledge, I retreated to the relaxing pale apricot bedroom I had used years before. The wide bed beckoned me, with its taupe upholstered headboard and thick satin draperies that hung from the canopy. But before I allowed myself to swan-dive into those luxurious linens, I took a small tablet out of my bag.

If I had been careful with locking the doors and windows of the apartment, I was similarly cautious with connecting to the internet here, using software that would protect my location and search history. When my parents divorced, I had learned too much about the capabilities of third parties to access presumably private information.

I yawned. Just a quick check of my accounts and I'd feel comfortable enough to sleep.

My finances were secure. No one had accessed those, thankfully. The only email account I had used since Stavros's death was the one for the Varenna rental account, but I wanted to make sure there hadn't been another last-minute registration.

Sure enough, there was one new email. I clicked.

TO: Cavalleta@villacavalleta.iy
FROM: 1717vx7171@eulink.eu

Re: Varenna Rental inquiry

Hello dear Caroline,

My apologies for running off like that. After you extended such exquisite hospitality to me, it was really quite inexcusable. I regret that we were unable to discuss my proposition for you.

Perhaps I'll catch up with you soon and we can discuss the matter.

In the meantime, Signore Rossi says he hopes to see you again.

Yours,
Steading

I reread the email four, five times before the shivering started. A million questions zoomed around my head, like cars on a race track.

Who was this from? For a brief moment, I thought it was from Konnor. An apology from him made me briefly warm and emotional but, rereading it, I knew the language wasn't right. Hugh Konnor didn't use words like "exquisite" and "inexcusable," and he'd certainly never apologize for leaving me.

The truth crept up on me like the slow, cold tide of the Northern coast of my homeland. Only one person would have used my full name on this account. Only one person.

One person who once had the title of Duke of Steading. Before he faked his death.

Christian Fraser-Campbell. And he ... I pulled my knees up tight to my chest as I reread the line again: *Signore Rossi says he hopes to see you again.*

Was it a threat? Or more empty pleasantries? Or ...

My fingers itched for a telephone. But who would I call now?

The palace.

That answer came far too quickly. The memory of that line of pale, stern palace security at the train station sent another shiver down my spine. Once I called and made the request that they go check on the Rossis, then I might as well just book a first-class ticket back to Drieden.

Who else?

The Varenna police.

Yes. Of course. I could place a quick, anonymous call. My Italian was nearly perfect; no one would connect the former Princess Caroline of Drieden with a concerned neighbor who simply wanted to ensure that Elena and Signore Rossi were fine.

The telephone in the kitchen had a different line from the rest of the residence, I remembered. Perhaps it would be an extra shield of anonymity, I reasoned as I hurried out of the bedroom and down the hall.

I referred to my tablet for the number of the Varenna *polizia* before lifting the old-fashioned receiver from the wall-mounted telephone and punching the digits in. One ring, two rings, a women's voice answered.

"*Buona sera,*" I said, right before a man's hand reached out from the dark and hung up the receiver.

I screamed.

"Your Highness."

I swung around and punched Hugh Konnor right in the nose.

"*Stop doing that!*"

I flung the phone at his chest for good measure but, since it was attached to the receiver with a cord, it sort of boomeranged back and clunked against the wall.

But it was oh so satisfying when Konnor reached up to his nose with a scowl.

"Get out!" I yelled. Then I changed my mind. "How did you get in?"

"A key," he growled, still rubbing his face.

"Always with the keys. I'm telling my mother." I paused. I knew how that sounded. But still, my mother needed to know she had given way too many keys to her houses to way too many men. Although . . . knowing my mother, it wasn't exactly surprising.

I mean, I was here. And I, too, had used a spare key.

Konnor still sounded miffed when he said, "This property belongs to a former future queen. The manager responds well to a palace identification. Especially when it's for the security of an heir to the throne."

"I'm not—"

"Yes, I'm clear on who you are not," Konnor said grumpily.

"I'm not clear on why you're here. When I've explicitly told you I don't want you around me!" My voice rose substantially, possibly into the screeching area of volume. But me playing coy and femme fatale and bratty princess hadn't convinced him that I was serious, so now he was getting the real Caroline. The one who wasn't afraid to sound like a fishmonger's wife.

"You're Princess Caroline of Drieden! You don't get to choose that!" He actually pointed a finger at me. Like I was a naughty school-girl. Pointing fingers made my blood boil.

"I do!" I threw my arms out. "Or I did, before you came along and ruined everything!"

"Your Highness." He used the title with gritted teeth. Appar-ently, he was now going to be stubborn about that as well. "Your life is in danger and I took an oath to protect you, no matter if you throw a tantrum or not!"

"So you're just following me around now? What happened to your search for Christian, then? Wasn't that your *raison d'être*? What happened to that?"

Konnor's jaw worked. "I'll resume it when you're safe."

"When I'm safe?" I laughed bitterly. "When I'm locked away on some distant royal estate? I'm not good enough for the palace, remem-ber. But I'm sure Big Gran and Father would love to send me away. Like to Perpetua, where they sent Thea—when she'd done nothing wrong, except pick a jackass fiancé."

A curious expression flashed across Konnor's face when I brought up that cold island, but it dissipated when I decided I had more to say. "Besides, it's not me that I'm worried about." I pointed at the dead telephone in frustration. "I was trying to check in on my neighbors in Varenna."

"Why? What happened?" Konnor focused on me like he was a shark and I was bloody chum.

Oh, right. I might have not thought through this bit as carefully as I should have. But that's what happens when bullying palace body-guards busted into my not-so-secret getaway spot.

"It's nothing." I tried to brush him aside, but he was quicker than I'd expected a man of his size to be. His hand shot out and immediately latched around my wrist. Pulled me closer, as he looked me over for, I don't know, obvious signs of violence or infection.

"What. Happened."

I may be stubborn, but the specter of Signore Rossi's kind face got the better of me. "I got an email, about the apartment, there was something in it about my neighbor, Signore Rossi, and . . ." I met his eyes and knew if I didn't tell him the truth, he'd find it eventually, even if that meant he barged into the headquarters of my email service provider, flashed his stupid identification badge and received access to my messages.

"If I show you, do you promise to call Varenna police for me?" I asked, hoping that at least my immediate concerns for Signore Rossi would be addressed.

Needless to say, that question did not erase the ferocity on Konnor's face, which deepened once I showed him the email. Thankfully, he immediately whipped out his cellphone and placed a call to the Varenna police, handing it over to me only when I waved demandingly and started shouting Italian into his ear.

The receptionist promised to have an officer check in with the Rossis and, after hanging up, Konnor pulled the tablet back to his lap and studied the email.

"Steading?" he asked.

"Christian's ducal title," I reminded him.

"He's using it as a message."

"To me?" Well, sure, I guess. It was in an email to me.

But Konnor dismissed that. "No. To your sister's new chief of security."

That was strange. "I thought you were assigned to her."

Konnor was clicking through my emails. "I am," he said. "But so is he."

"Who is he?"

"When you go back to Drieden you'll meet him."

Ha. "Nice try. I'm not going back."

He closed my tablet and looked up at me. "This isn't a joke. For some reason, Christian is coming after you. This matter he wishes to discuss—"

I needed to steer him away from that. "Could be a simple discussion. Perhaps he thinks I'll be able to smooth things over with Thea." It wasn't too strange an idea. Everyone in the family thought of me as a peacekeeper. Someone who could be counted on to mediate both sides in rough times. Even Mother had leaned on me after the divorce, using me to talk to Father, to Sophie's tutors, even to Big Gran's advisors, on her behalf. I had been exceptionally good at all these tasks, since I was the only daughter to be rewarded with the keys and codes to Mother's extensive network of hidey-holes.

Which, unfortunately, had been infiltrated by an annoyingly persistent Hugh Konnor. Bastard.

"He's threatened your neighbor. Hopefully, that's all he's done. But Caroline, you have to believe me, he's capable of much worse. And until you're safe, I can't stop him."

"That sounds like a personal problem, *Hugh*." For some reason, I emphasized his first name, as it was not lost on me that he deigned to call me Caroline whenever he wanted to convince me to do what he wanted. "And honestly, it seems like you don't know how to catch up with Christian anyway. You've been chasing him for six months and didn't get close enough until he surfaced, ostensibly, to meet up with me."

Konnor seemed to shrug that off, like the stubborn man he was, but a tiny flame of an idea had sparked in my brain.

No. I couldn't.

You can.

There was no way.

But there is.

Okay, then. Here went nothing.

"In fact, you know what? I have an idea that will help you achieve your goals—both catching Christian Fraser-Campbell and keeping me safe."

He couldn't help but look curious. Because what I was offering was irresistible to a man like him.

"What is your idea?" he asked reluctantly.

"I'll email Christian back. And set up a meeting."

twelve

B UT NO. IT COULDN'T BE THAT SIMPLE.
Konnor pushed up from his chair in one single bound.

"Don't throw my computer!" I cried.

He looked quizzically at the tablet he still held in his hand and then back at me. "Why would you think I would throw your computer?"

"Because I punched you . . . ? Because, in the past few days, you keep trying to make my life more difficult than it should be? Because you enjoy being a pompous prick and we do this tit-for-tat thing—"

Konnor interrupted me. "Okay, fine, you think I'm a jerk."

I finally felt heard. "Yes, I do."

"I was going to keep it with me, though."

"And there you go, proving my point." Because he got his kicks from controlling me.

"If something else comes in from Christian tonight, I'll need to know about it immediately." He paused and then mumbled, with a touch of shyness, "And I thought you'd want to get some sleep."

"Oh." Maybe Konnor wasn't the heartless asshole that he always was around me. Maybe he actually cared a little bit.

"Because you look like you need the rest. You look like hell."

Strike that change of opinion. Konnor was still totally the same asshole he'd always been. Because nice, kind men don't tell women they look like hell.

"I don't need to sleep," I snapped. It was a huge lie. I'd been fantasizing about that plush canopied bed the entire trip from Florence. "I want to know what you think about my idea."

He lifted his broad shoulders. "It has merit."

Ah. Faint praise, indeed. "Merit?" I echoed. "It's brilliant. Christian says he wants to meet me, I show up, we talk and then I convince him to go back to Drieden to go to couples therapy with my sister . . ." I trailed off, because the most unlikely thing was happening.

Hugh Konnor was *chuckling*. At what I had said.

"Did I say something funny?"

"Well . . ." he hedged. "The idea of Princess Theodora going to therapy with that man is . . ." He shook his head. "She'd sooner shoot him."

Okay, now he was the one who sounded like a lunatic. My sister would one day be Queen of Drieden. She was civilized and proper. There was no violent bone in her body. "Fine. Whatever." I dismissed his distracting mirth with the palm of my hand. "The point is that setting up a meeting with Christian is the quickest way for all of us to get back to our normal lives."

Konnor's smile faded now, and he regarded me with very serious bodyguard eyes.

"You have to agree with me," I said. "Clearly, my plan is the best plan."

"One, I have sworn an oath to protect the members of the royal family with my life. Two, using a princess as bait to catch a volatile, vicious criminal would, almost always, violate that oath, and three." Konnor held up three fingers for emphasis. Then he put them back down again and, with a short nod of his head, signaled that he was through with the conversation. He gestured toward the door. "I'll see you to your room."

On the walk to my bedroom, it killed me not knowing whether his third point was seeing me to my room or something else entirely. The man was so frustrating. He always had been, really. And I wasn't going to ask him to clarify what he had been talking about. Which was also something that I had always done. Or not done.

When we arrived at my bedroom door, I turned to say one more thing to him and pulled up short. I had not realized he was so close. Here in this shadowy hallway, surrounded by centuries of antiques and art, Hugh Konnor seemed more alive by comparison. He was vital, muscular yet agile, and so very, very large.

My breath caught. I hated that it did so. Cursed whatever pheromone or esoteric science it was that made my body react to him like this. Ten years may have passed since I had made my virginal passes at him, but clearly my hormones had not outgrown a burly, cranky bodyguard who always looked at me as if he saw right through me.

"That's the problem, isn't it?" I asked softly. His brows drew together at my sudden non sequitur.

"What problem?"

"You know what I'm trying to do, with this plan to meet Christian."

His eyes reminded me of a topaz pendant my mother had passed down to me. Rich, golden. Alive. And right now, they were nearly hypnotizing me. "I don't want you running off again."

Curse the blasted warm feelings that immediately curled through my torso. "Why?" I had to ask.

He swallowed. "Because you make it very hard for the security staff to do their duty."

I shouldn't have asked why. I don't know what I expected from him. "We're talking about this in the morning," I said, trying to sound like I was the one in charge.

But when I shut the bedroom door behind me I knew. Even as a princess, when it came to Hugh Konnor, I was never in charge of anything, least of all my involuntary emotional reactions.

THE SMELL OF COFFEE PULLED ME FROM MY SLUMBER the next morning. Even though I was still thoroughly irritated by Hugh Konnor not leaving me alone, there were benefits to traveling with someone who always seemed to know where the coffee pot was.

After visiting the same lovely Italian espresso machine that Hugh had put to work this morning, I found him in the living room, where the remnants of his overnight stay on the couch contrasted with the elegant decor. Although the apartment was a luxurious and extremely expensive piece of real estate, it wasn't overly large. From this location, Konnor would have immediately heard me leaving the apartment during the night, should I have been brave—or stubborn—enough to try to escape his clutches again.

"Good morning," I said, as a way of announcing my entrance into the salon.

Konnor was studying a pad of paper he'd dug up from somewhere. He looked up distractedly. "Oh, right. You're up."

He really had a way of making a girl feel treasured and important.

"Yes, I'm up. And I'm ready."

"For what?"

"To pick up the pieces of my life again. So if you'll just let me write Christian a quick email, then we can get started with my plan to convince him to turn himself in."

But he didn't immediately hand over my tablet. And he barely acknowledged my presence, let alone that I'd suggested that we take prompt, concrete action.

"Konnor?" I fought the impulse to go over and wave my hand in front of his eyes. Maybe he'd lost his vision and his hearing over-night. Poor thing. Maybe I wasn't being ignored, he just couldn't hear or see me.

Yes, I made a lot of excuses for people. It was a problem, I know.

He glanced back and forth between two pieces of paper. "No," he suddenly said, in that decisive, authoritative way that bodyguards had. "We won't be contacting Christian just yet."

"Yet?" I echoed that one, key word. "What are you waiting for? Let's do this!"

Now I had his full, alert attention. "Do you know what he wants to speak with you about?"

"No, but I'll ask when I email him back." I tried to sound breezy and confident about it. Oh yes, it was so straightforward. What do I have to lie about? Not pretty little, innocent Caroline.

Hugh stood, and stretched out his neck as he did so. The move-ment did nice things to his arms and shoulders, too, not that I was noticing or anything. "Do you know why he came to Varenna to find you?" Now he rolled his shoulders. Like a man who had been stuck on a couch all night long. Poor thing. "Or, for that matter, how he found you?"

"No . . ." I said carefully. "But again, these are all things I can ask when I have a conversation with the man." I emphasized the word. *Conversation*. Simple. Safe. Benign, really.

Konnor shook his head. "There are too many unknowns. I don't like unknowns."

I tried not to let my frustration show. "You don't like me either, but you're putting up with me because it's your job." He furrowed his brow and opened his mouth as if he was going to protest. "Don't. I get it, okay? The point I'm trying to make is that sometimes we don't like something but we suck it up and get it done." I held out my hand, intending for him to place the tablet into my fingers so that I could do the thing that needed to be done.

But no. Because why would Konnor do anything that I wanted him to do? Instead, he handed over one of the pieces of paper he'd been glaring at when I'd walked in.

It was a drawing of the symbol that was tattooed on Christian's chest. He'd copied the one I'd inked on his palm the day before.

A horizontal diamond with rays extending from the top. I flipped it around. Now the rays were extending from the bottom.

Konnor frowned at the flip. "It goes that way?"

I held it up to my chest, over my right breast, to demonstrate. "On Christian, yes."

"Does it matter?" Konnor asked.

I shrugged. "I don't know. Depends on what it is, I guess."

He eyed the paper, which I was still holding with a very serious frown. Most men don't stare at my right breast with that vague disapproving look. It was discomfiting that Hugh Konnor was doing it, but, I supposed, par for the course with him. Finally, he nodded. "Yes, it matters."

"How do you know?"

"Because I know the man. He's not a tattoo guy," Konnor explained with a decided disdain in his voice. "He likes custom-made suits and, back in Drieden, he had someone iron his boxer shorts."

"People change," I said, thinking of my life and all the fashion stages I had gone through.

"Sure. One day we're buttoned-up dukes with law degrees, the next we're homicidal rebels without a cause." Konnor lifted a wry brow. "People are who they are. We don't change. And someone like Christian Fraser-Campbell doesn't get a tattoo that no one can interpret and that no one can see while he's running from Interpol." He gestured toward the paper I had now lowered from my breast. "So what the hell is that and what does it mean?"

I looked at the symbol for a moment and then back at Konnor's pushed-up sleeves and the tattoos that were visible on his corded forearms. "What do yours mean?"

He twisted his arms and flexed so he could examine his ink. I was sure he wasn't doing it for my benefit, but I can't say I didn't enjoy the view. "This one's Latin," he said, shaking his left arm a little. "And this one's just numbers," he muttered about his other arm.

"And presumably they mean something to you as well," I observed, ignoring the little flutter in my stomach while I gazed at Konnor's tattoos. It was strangely intimate. When he was on the official job back in Drieden, he was always properly dressed. Cuffs buttoned, jacket on. But here in Italy, he was fitted for comfort and stealth. I kept talking to distract myself from checking out the rest of Konnor's muscular body—and wondering what else he hid underneath his nearly skin-tight thermal shirt. "I mean, what are tattoos? They're usually a symbol of something meaningful to a person. A name, a flower . . ."

Konnor wrinkled his nose at the drawing. "That's a horrible flower."

"Or it's a symbol of some kind."

"It could be anything. How could we ever know?"

Out of the corner of my eye, I saw a painting over the fireplace that I'd looked at fifty, a hundred times. The Roman—or was she Greek?—goddess Persephone holding a pomegranate as a peace offering to a wolf, while frightened soldiers stood behind her. The painting was by Giulpione, from the sixteenth century. An example of Renaissance art.

Of course. "As a matter of fact, I know someone who could possibly help us."

thirteen

THE SMALL, NONDESCRIPT PLAQUE OUTSIDE THE BELL read "Monsignor Francesco Baldoni" in an elegant script. I took a deep breath before I pressed the button, avoiding Konnor's eyes. He had been against this, against anything that didn't involve wrapping me in a satin bow and sending me back to Drieden City, to be honest. Since he hadn't been successful when he tried, once again, to convince me to return to my grandmother's palace, he had agreed to accompany me to my old professor's office to inquire if there was any religious or hidden meaning in Christian's tattoo.

We were shown into Father Baldoni's studio by a young Franciscan friar who introduced himself as Giovanni. I stumbled as I used the name that Father Baldoni had known me by—Caroline Laurent—my maiden name. My Driedish name. It didn't feel quite right, but neither would Caroline DiBernardo. Or Lina DiLorenzo.

How many other identities would I have to try on until I found the one that fitted me as I was? It was an uncomfortable question and one I pushed aside as soon as Father Baldoni joined us in his dark, dusty study.

He was a few years older, so perhaps that was why he squinted. Or it could have been my cropped, dyed-black hair, so different from my former long blonde ponytail. "Carolina? Is that you?" he asked in Italian, adding the extraneous vowel at the end of my name, which made it sound so much more feminine. So musical. "Princessa Carolina?"

I greeted him with an embrace—a real one. I had always enjoyed my time here with Father Baldoni, reviewing his huge collection of art and illustrations, listening to him discuss saints and symbols for hours.

"And who is this?" Father Baldoni asked about Konnor.

"A colleague," I replied. "Who doesn't speak Italian."

Father Baldoni scowled. "He's not an art historian, then. All the world's art history is in Italy, all the masters are Italian, one must speak the language."

"Yes, I quite agree," I murmured, with a slight smile at Konnor, who frowned back at me. "But he is helping me with a . . . documentary," I finished, borrowing my older sister's past profession. "We were doing some research and found a symbol that I had never seen before. I was hoping you would be able to identify it."

As I expected, that immediately intrigued Father Baldoni. He was one of the world's pre-eminent experts in religious iconography and cryptology, having spent the last fifty years in the shadow of the Vatican, religiously indexing and cross-referencing the vast collections of the Holy See. If anyone knew what this symbol might be a reference to, it was Monsignor Francesco Baldoni.

He drew wire-rimmed reading glasses from the pocket of his woolen cardigan and gave me a smile. "Of course. Let us see what has given you such trouble."

I had redrawn the symbol carefully onto a new sheet of paper, and I handed it over to him under Konnor's suspicious eagle eyes, as if a seventy-year-old priest would take my outstretched hand and flip me onto the ground with some Franciscan judo move. Seriously. The man had some trust issues.

I switched to Driedish to tell Konnor, "I studied with Father Baldoni for nearly a year. I think he's safe."

Konnor did not look reassured by this but continued his baleful glare at the senior priest. Thankfully, Father Baldoni barely registered Konnor's watchful animosity, as he had become immediately engrossed in my drawing.

It was just like I had seen on Christian's torso: a diamond stretched out on the horizontal, with rays extending from the bottom.

"This is it?" Father Baldoni asked. "It is complete?" He gestured to the top. "There is nothing extending from these sides?"

I said no and, "Yes, it is all we have." Father Baldoni's eyebrows furrowed. He flipped the page upside down and then back. Then flipped it over, as if the long-lost secret code were handwritten there. It had happened many times, so he said. How many times had he told me, "This is a simple job. Humans are straightforward, and their art is, too. There is nothing new under the sun."

Except, from the way he was looking at my paper . . . maybe there was?

Baldoni walked over to a high table and flipped a switch which illuminated the surface. I followed, with Konnor at my back.

"Here." Baldoni placed the paper on the light table and pointed at the naked top of the diamond. "We would expect more rays here, if this symbolized a sun or a flower of some sort. Perhaps a navigational compass, a directional tool."

"The lines are similar to those used to represent a holy power," I suggested, remembering what I learned ten years ago, right here in this study.

Father Baldoni nodded. "True, yes. Such as the Holy Spirit. Although, generally, in a symbol, that would be quite clear. A cross or some other religious icon would be included. This . . ." He made a very Italian gesture at the horizontal diamond. "This is nothing."

He flipped the paper ninety degrees so that the diamond was now stretched along the vertical plane. "Now this. This is much better."

Konnor leaned down into my ear. "What is he saying?" I held my hand up, inadvertently brushing his cheek with the back of my fingers. The contact sent a warm flush through my body. Damn body. I was at the house of a respected Vatican academic. This was no time to get distracted by thoughts of how Konnor's beard felt soft against my skin.

I had almost missed what Baldoni said, but as soon as he turned the design ninety degrees I saw it, too. "A heraldic shield, perhaps?" I suggested. It was the shape of thousands of coats of arms across Europe.

Father Baldoni nodded. "Yes, exactly." He pointed at the lines now stretching from the left side of the diamond. "But what are these? Spears? Arrows?" He looked at me as if I had more information, but all I could do was shake my head.

"As far as I know, they are just lines." I reached out and rotated the paper back. "And it looked like that."

Baldoni pursed his lips. "It must be incomplete. It looks unfinished."

I repeated the words softly to Konnor, translating them into Driedish, mostly to be polite. Then I added, "Perhaps the tattoo wasn't finished?"

Konnor looked back at the design. "And if the lines went all the way around, what would that mean? What is it, then?"

I repeated the suggestions Father Baldoni had made earlier. "A sun or a flower, he says."

Konnor shook his head decisively. "That's not Christian."

Father Baldoni looked up at that response. "Christian?" He echoed, misunderstanding the word and interpreting it as a Franciscan priest would. "No, this is no Christian symbol." He scratched his chin and tilted his head, as if he saw it in a new light. "Perhaps . . ." he mumbled to himself as he moved toward a bookshelf.

"Giovanni!" He shouted his clerk's name, and the young man reappeared so promptly I had to assume he had been waiting just outside the office door. Father Baldoni asked for some reference items and then started paging through a text he had selected from a shelf. "There." He motioned toward a page he had found.

"Pagan runes?" I guessed, looking at the page of assorted lines and triangles in various configurations. The priest confirmed that I had guessed correctly.

He pointed at one, a diamond, but again it was vertical. "But it is the wrong direction. If you are correct," he said, with the distinct insinuation that he believed my description of the symbol was wrong or incomplete.

Giovanni returned with several more books, and the two of them began discussing various cultures around the world. I heard the names of Native American tribes, African civilizations, and more, but when I met Konnor's eyes I knew he had been right. None of this fitted with the Christian Fraser-Campbell we knew—the one with the starched shirts and shiny shoes, the one who had been engaged to a princess. Maybe I had misinterpreted the tattoo. Maybe it had been only the first round of what was going to be a far more intricate and obvious design.

"What are they talking about now?" Konnor asked, clearly getting frustrated at a debate he couldn't decipher.

"They're discussing Egyptian hieroglyphics," I muttered under my breath.

"Right." Konnor's mouth made a grim line as he snatched my sketch from the light table and pounded it on the table under Giovanni and Baldoni's noses. "This has nothing to do with Africa. It would be something connected to Drieden, or Scotland, or a fucking huge amount of money."

Giovanni apparently knew enough Driedish for his eyes to go round as he looked between Konnor and the design of Christian's possibly incomplete tattoo. I went ahead and translated for Father Baldoni—leaving out Konnor's crude choice of vocabulary, of course. I didn't think it was appropriate to talk like that to men of the cloth.

After a beat, Father Baldoni nodded slowly. "Yes. I think you have solved the puzzle." He then began to walk to another bookshelf.

"What'd he say?" Konnor asked me.

When I saw what book Father Baldoni pulled off the shelf, I could tell Konnor truthfully, "You may be right." I nodded at the symbol on the cover of the book Father Baldoni carried. It was the square and compass that had represented Freemasons for over a thousand years.

Father Baldoni placed the book next to the piece of paper and he, Konnor and I compared them. The Freemasonry symbol was not a closed diamond, like the one I thought I had seen on Christian's chest, but it was more horizontal than vertical. We continued looking through the illustrations and, when we found the symbol of the open eye that had radiant beams extending from it, the combination was the closest thing we could find to what I had drawn from memory.

"I am not as familiar with these symbols as others," Father Baldoni finally had to admit. "The church and Freemasonry . . ." He made another quintessential Italian shrug that said it all. "However, I have a colleague at the University of St Andrews who has researched the society extensively." Father Baldoni picked up the paper. "May we make a copy to send to him and get his opinion?"

After Giovanni had scanned my drawing and written down Konnor's phone number and my email address, we prepared to leave. Father Baldoni kissed me on the cheek then took me by the upper arms and said, "I was so devastated to hear about your loss. I prayed for the soul of your husband."

"Thank you," I said.

"And this one," Father Baldoni's eyes flicked up to Konnor's stony face. "Be careful with this one. He looks at you like a tiger would watch his prey."

Of course, I didn't translate that for Konnor. I wasn't sure I'd want to hear his opinion on that.

fourteen

KONNOR INSISTED ON RETURNING TO THE APART-
ment right away, and I agreed reluctantly. Rome was a beautiful,
ancient city, but it was also full of thousands of international
tourists, many of whom might recognize me, even with my unflatter-
ing dark hair. My goals to discover the truth about Christian would
only be hampered if I attracted the attention of every European
paparazzo.

I paced for a bit in the apartment, wondering what my next move
should be. Would Konnor let me go now that I had done my part
in helping him decipher this one clue? I could let him keep my
email address and the link to Christian, I would give him the password and everything. But even then, I had a feeling that Hugh
Konnor would need more persuasion. He'd always been stubborn
around me, more than most of the palace bodyguards. It was a lot to
handle.

He was a lot to handle.

I caught a view of him in the parlor, leaning back on the couch,
one arm hooked around the back of his head. In that position, it
was impossible not to notice the girth of that bicep, the length of

his torso, the way his shirt pulled up to reveal a tiny sliver of taut skin.

I must have made a noise because he looked up from whatever he was reading on my tablet. *My tablet!*

And I must have made a face because he looked unimpressed with me. "May I help you?"

I flopped into the nearest chair. "Have you heard anything?"

"No." He redirected his attention back to my tablet.

"What are you reading?" I asked.

"*The Driedish Times.*"

It was a more liberal newspaper than the professional staff generally read, featuring more salacious articles about reality stars and gossip about my family than the other national papers. "Anything interesting?"

Konnor looked back up at me with a thoughtful expression. "There's a bit of news about some of the upcoming celebrations."

"The jubilee?" I asked. My grandmother's anniversary of taking the throne was coming up in a few months.

"That, too."

It was a strange response. "Is there another celebration I should be aware of?"

Konnor avoided my question by reading aloud from *The Driedish Times*: "Remains found in newly dedicated Jubilee Park believed to be those of fifteenth-century king."

"Which one?"

He read silently, then answered, "Fredrik."

I thought about that for a moment. My sister was the amateur historian in the family. I wasn't sure whether fifteenth-century King Fredrik was one of the important ancestors or one of the ones who had been ineffectual or riddled with leprosy or died at birth. I had always classified the branches of the family tree into two categories: useful knowledge and not so much. When one was a princess, one had to be practical about such things. Some monarchs had universities named after them. Some were buried under car parks. One had to know which was which.

The thought of Theodora made my stomach ache a little. All this talk of her presumed-dead and supposedly dangerous ex-fiancé, yet I had not spoken with her in over nine months.

"Is she . . . doing well?" I asked.

"Who?"

"My sister. Princess Theodora. Your boss?"

"Yes." Konnor's eyes met mine. "You could be in Drieden by tonight, you know. Ask her in person."

I pushed out of my chair. "No, thank you. I don't intend to return to Drieden any time soon."

"May I ask why?"

The question should have been impertinent. Palace security guards did not presume to ask why a member of the royal family was doing anything. They were dutiful, respectful of their boundaries. But I wasn't a real princess anymore. And I had blown past so many boundaries with Hugh Konnor, I couldn't object to his question.

But I didn't have to answer it either.

"Sure," I said, avoiding his eyes and crossing to the far wall, ostensibly to get a better look at the Ardesque painting in an overly large gilded frame.

"Why did you not return to Drieden after your husband's death?"

"Why would I return?" I asked. "My grandmother disowned me. Most of my titles had been stripped. I had nothing to return to."

"I think we both know that's a lie."

I spun on my heel and crossed my arms, ready to show him exactly how much disowned princesses enjoyed being called a liar when a tell-tale *ding* came from my tablet.

A new email.

"What does it say?" I crossed the room, hoping hard that the

Scottish expert referred by Father Baldoni had provided us a firm
explanation of what Christian's tattoo might symbolize. If we had
some direction to start looking for Christian, we could get that done,
and then Konnor would leave me alone to live my life in peace.

"Fuck." Konnor's face darkened after he opened the message. I
sat down next to him—practically in his lap, as the man wasn't indicating that he was going to spin the tablet so that I could read whatever
it was that had made him so mad.

Then I saw why Konnor had used profanity. The email wasn't
from a scholar of ancient Freemasonry in Scotland.

But it was from a Scot.

TO: Cavalleta@villacavalleta.iy
FROM: 1717vx7171@eulink.eu

Re: Re: Varenna Rental inquiry

Hello Caroline,

 I would very much like to set up a meeting to discuss your
future. You always struck me as the one with the most sense.
The responsible one, I think Thea once called you. I have
been hoping that you would help me clear up any remaining
misunderstandings.

 Further, we could discuss our mutual friends in London at
The Times. Please respond within twenty-four hours to arrange
a time and place.

 Perhaps a location between Varenna and Rome?

Yours,
Steading

PS It does seem like you will not be returning to your home
in Varenna. Pity, as the view from your veranda is really
breathtaking.

"Caroline." Hugh's rough voice grabbed my attention. Then I realized he was vibrating. Or rather, that his pocket was vibrating. I had leaned in to him to read the newest electronic missive and now it appeared I was preventing him from answering his phone.

"Of course," I murmured as I slid away on the couch, tablet in hand. Konnor rose and answered the phone in Driedish.

"What happened?"

The urgency in his voice made me look up, and I saw his posture completely change as he heard whatever news was being reported to him. His weight shifted forward, his shoulders drew back, like a gladiator entering the Coliseum.

He looked over his shoulder at me, and I saw something dark and focused in that gaze. Something that would have a lion in the ring running scared.

"I need a team of ten asap." He rattled off the address of our location, then paused. He didn't like what he heard. "Fuck protocol. Do you know who I have with me?"

I didn't stop to think. I launched myself at Hugh Konnor. Or, more accurately, his cellphone. And even though he outweighed me by fifty pounds or more, the element of surprise worked in my favor and my flailing arm was able to knock his phone out of his hand, send it flying in the air.

I scrambled past him to get to the phone first, and perhaps he was slow because he was pondering the exact level of crazy I was exhibiting at that moment. But then he recovered. Caught my shirt just as I lunged to the floor, where the cellphone had landed. A rip of cotton filled the air and I felt a breeze on my back, but I was single-minded. A survivor.

And there was no fucking way Hugh Konnor was calling the palace guards on me. My hand wrapped around Hugh's cellphone just as a wide palm wrapped around my middle. He was larger than me, sure. A professional trained in the art of bringing people down and busting psychopaths. Fine. Could he throw me over his shoulder and carry me all the way to Drieden without breaking a sweat? Quite possibly. But he was not getting this cursed cellphone from me without my permission.

A split second before he hauled me backward, I did the only thing I could think of. Literally, my last recourse. A line I knew Hugh Konnor would never cross.

I shoved his cellphone into my underwear.

Konnor tugged on me a little too hard, my socks slipped on the hundred-year-old marble floor and down I went, like a piece of toppled Roman statuary. His arm was still around me and, somehow, he landed on top of me, one thick arm somewhat breaking my fall but potentially shattering his elbow.

Are you all right? I bit back the words. This was war. He took me on, took his chances; he had to suffer the consequences.

"Ufph!" was all he said, but his glare was intense. A lesser woman might have meekly tried to apologize right about now, but I was a former princess who had put up with a bully for far too long. There would be no forthcoming "I'm sorrys."

"Are you insane?" Konnor growled.

"You were calling guards here—"

He spoke right over me. "Your house in Varenna was firebombed an hour ago. I was calling them to get to Varenna. Last night there was an attempted break-in."

I gasped and pushed against the concrete chest that was now pinning me down. "Elena and Signore—"

Konnor knew what I was asking. "They were out. No one was in the house."

I relaxed only a little. "If something had happened to them . . ." I broke off.

"If something had happened to you!" He glared at me, furious at the idea. "This is why you need round-the-clock protection behind twenty-foot gates."

"Or you could drive me to the airport and let me buy a ticket to Montevideo." Once again, it was a reasonable counter-offer. "Leave me alone and we both get what we want."

His eyebrows snatched together. "What I want? You think this is about what I want?"

Just then, I became fully conscious of the rest of my body. His body. His weight pinning me down. His thigh between mine. I struggled to take a deep breath. Probably because I had two-hundred and twenty pounds of solid muscle on top of my lungs. Sure, we'd go with that.

It had nothing to do with a mad crush I had on the man a decade ago. Or how this was pretty much exactly all of my teenage fantasies come to life. Hugh tearing my shirt off. Tackling me. Telling me exactly and explicitly what he wanted.

"What do you want?" I had to ask. "Do you want to catch Christian, or do you want me . . . to be safe," I finished lamely. Had I imagined a flicker of something *more* in his eyes when I asked? Was it wishful thinking, or had he seemed to shift his weight subtly over my hip?

Is that a cellphone in my pants or are you glad to see me?

"Both," he admitted roughly. "Now give me my phone back so I can do my job."

"I don't know where it is." How I said that with a straight face I'll never know.

He glared but didn't move. I guess he thought I'd run if he let me up. Okay, he was right about that. A back part of my brain was already calculating whether I could outrun him to the servants' elevator. The rational part of my brain had already concluded that no, I could not.

So I had to negotiate. "There's only one way for you to get your phone back."

"If you say I have to call it from a landline, I think it qualifies for some sort of workplace-harassment charge."

I bit back a smile and not a little bit of mortification. God help me. If his damn phone starting vibrating right now, I'd never live this down. Suddenly, I felt helpless. Small. Under Hugh Konnor, in the face of his stubborn ferocity, what choices did I have? What kind of power could I wield?

Once again, I faced the stark truth that I was not my mother. I couldn't flirt my way out of this. And I wasn't my grandmother, with all the inherent authority of her birth. I couldn't order Hugh to leave me alone.

There was one thing I hadn't tried yet. My one last, humbling option.

"Please." My voice was throaty. I closed my eyes so I wouldn't have to face the pity that would surely be on his face, just inches from mine. "Please, Hugh. I just want to be left alone. It's the only way to protect everyone."

He shifted, gently pulled the arm out from beneath me and braced himself over me. I could still feel his looming warmth, but he was no longer pinning me down. *For my own safety.*

"Someone tried to break into your house. Then they tried torching the place. Christian's email proves he is connected to those people." He paused. I opened my eyes and met his straightforward gaze. "If you were me, would you let Princess Caroline go?"

You let me go before. I wanted to say the words, but of course I would never. I had a tattered sliver of pride left, if one ignored the fact that I had recently shoved my bodyguard's cellphone into my underwear.

But he made an excellent point. The Hugh Konnor I knew would do the right thing. Always. Even if that meant giving up the search for a presumed criminal to personally escort me back to the royal palace.

"Fine," I said, propping myself up on my elbows. "I'll give you back your phone. Do you want to take it out or will you allow me some privacy in the bathroom?"

Konnor pulled up to his knees and I scrambled to my feet. He wasn't looking my way when I tucked my tablet underneath my arm and headed quickly to the master suite.

fifteen

KONNOR GAVE ME TWENTY MINUTES OF "PRIVACY" in the bathroom. I knew he'd be a gentleman like that.

And when he pounded on the door, I had expected that, too. "Caroline!" No more *Your Highness*. I smirked at myself in the mirror facing the deep, tiled bathtub where I was currently perched. "Are you . . . okay?"

I saw a low-battery icon flash on my tablet. Then the bell of an incoming message. I knew it wouldn't take long to get a response and now I had only a few minutes to charge it before we needed to leave.

I flung open the door to the bathroom, promptly handed over Konnor's phone and side-stepped around him. "I need to go and plug this in," I said, as nonchalantly as I could, even as I mentally counted down the seconds . . . *one . . . two . . . three . . .*

"What did you do!?" I didn't turn around. What was the point? I knew he'd follow up with, "*It's not working!*"

"I flushed the memory card down the toilet," I informed him crisply. "That way, no one can track us without us knowing."

I hadn't flushed the card down the toilet. I'm not a complete idiot. It was safely stashed in my bra—another place Hugh Konnor wouldn't deign to root around in, stupid man that he was. But I knew he'd buy my story.

"Track *us*?" Konnor said, in a voice composed of ground-up nails and gravel. "Where do you think you're going?"

"Us, Hugh. Collective pronoun. Come on now. Since you said you wouldn't leave my side, we'll just get my usefulness out of the way."

I plugged my tablet into the charger and went to pack my few belongings back into my small bag. There was no reason to leave without my hairbrush, after all.

Konnor snatched the tablet and read what I had left open on the screen. I mentally counted down the seconds . . . *one* . . . *two* . . . *three* . . .

TO: 1717vx7171@eulink.eu
FROM: Cavalleta@villacavalleta.iy

Re: Re: Re: Varenna Rental inquiry

Christian,

This is all becoming quite tiresome. You and I both know that your proposition won't fix anything with Thea. As for our friends at *The Times*, I don't think they should be dragged into anything, to spare everyone embarrassment.

But as a gesture of nearly familial goodwill, I will meet with you. As it happens, I will be arriving at my mother's Tuscan estate later this evening. As I just saw you in Varenna, I'm sure you're not out of the country yet. Please let me know when I can expect you.

– C

PS If you had anything to do with the vandalism of my Varenna house, I will expect reimbursement. I love that veranda.

TO: Cavalleta@villacavalleta.iy
FROM: 1717vx7171@eulink.eu

Re: Re: Re: Re: Varenna Rental inquiry

Dearest Caroline,

    I am so pleased to hear from you. I'll take it as a yes to what I asked you in Varenna. If we do this correctly, Thea will never have to know about how I convinced you to help me. And, if you agree, there will be ample funds to repair your little flat.

    I will meet you at Felice's estate later tonight—9 o'clock. Please ensure that we have a private meeting.

Eagerly yours,
Steading

Konnor's dark eyes were bright with anger and I automatically took a step back. "I'm giving you what you want. What you've been searching for. He'll meet us tonight, and you can nab him then and this will all be over. You'll never have to spend another tortuous moment in my presence again." He was still a seething knot of emotion, but he hadn't blown up. He was listening. He was considering what I was saying.

"What am I supposed to do with you, then?" Konnor ground out the words between a clenched jaw. An image of his hard body pinning me down on cool marble jumped to mind.

I swallowed hard and mentally shoved the almost-dirty thought back into my overactive subconscious. "There's the village a short distance away. After I meet with Christian, you can drop me off there. I'll catch a bus, head to my next destination." *Wherever that was.* "You get what you want, I get what I want. We're all good." I swiped my hands together. Pfft, pfft. "Done."

Konnor looked at me for a long moment. Maybe he was weighing up his options. Maybe he was wishing he'd never turned me away when I was a nubile innocent, before I'd gone mad and cynical besides. Hey—a woman could fantasize about a man regretting his choices.

"What did he ask you in Varenna?"

I avoided his eyes, went to double-check the zip on my bag. "Exactly what I told you. He wants me to help him talk to Thea," I lied.

"And your London friends? At *The Times*?"

Crap. I'd forgotten about Christian's oblique references to Clémence and Cordelia. "Royal reporters," I said. "Reputable ones. I think anything with Christian should be kept out of the papers, don't you?"

"He's not a good man," Hugh said softly. "He tried to take the Queen down."

"I'm not calling you a liar," I said evenly. "But whatever damage Christian did to the realm, it's clearly been dealt with." I waved a hand. "My grandmother still reigns and statues are still being erected."

"He's done terrible things to your family."

His mention of my family was like an uncomfortable bedspring popping into my back. "They're no longer my family," I reminded him, trying hard for breezy and unconcerned. "It's in the first chapter of the disownment manual. Now. Are we going back to Felice's or not?"

Finally, he nodded, and my knees softened like melted butter. I had to reach out and grab the bed post to steady myself. I hadn't realized I had locked them into place while I was confronting him and acting oh-so-tough.

"We'll leave in thirty," he said. Then he gave me a pointed look. "And I'll take this," he said, snapping the tablet's cord from the wall and slipping the tablet underneath his arm.

*

SEVERAL HOURS LATER, WE WERE ON THE DARK ROAD leading to my mother's villa. Hugh was driving, and pulled off into a dirt lane that seemed to go nowhere.

"What are you doing?" I asked as he got out of the car. "We're not there yet?!"

He popped the trunk and withdrew something from it. "Konnor?" I asked in vain, somehow knowing that his plans and mine were probably not going to align. "What are you doing?"

I opened the car door, scrambled out and saw exactly what I feared—the glint of a gun barrel in the last rays of sunset. "Konnor—we had this worked out. I told Christian in the email that I was going to meet with him . . . alone."

He looked at me like I had suggested that the Driedish national football team retire en masse and take up ballet dancing. "In what world do you think that's going to happen? Let me remind you, Your Highness, that I don't have to do anything Christian Fraser-Campbell suggests." He gave me a pointed glare. "Or you."

"Wait." I was confused. Was he conceding that I was no longer royal—and thus it was no longer his duty to protect me? Or was he simply saying that he could ignore me if he wished?

I had to admit, I found that I did not care for either possibility, which was a tad concerning, if I thought about it too long.

Which I wouldn't. Because I had yet another battle of wills to win with Hugh "Tough Stubborn Guy out of a Fifties Hollywood Movie" Konnor.

"I don't want you to use a gun," I said, thinking that was fairly diplomatic of me. A nice starting point for negotiations, really.

"Too bad," he snarled.

"No guns." I added extra emphasis this time, for clarity's sake.

Konnor made a show of looking down the barrel, off into the distance, checking . . . something . . . out. What, I wasn't sure. I wasn't the sportsman that my father was, nor the royal marine that my brother was. Guns were completely foreign to me.

"Please." My voice broke. "Just—"

Konnor didn't let me finish. "This is how it's going to be. You made this arrangement your way, so I'm going to take it from here and do it my way. Against my instincts, training and plain good common sense, I brought you here to meet with Christian. But there's no way you're taking one step onto your mother's property without me checking it out first"—he waved the gun in his hand—"my way."

I swallowed. Of course, I had always known that my bodyguards were experts, had always respected their training and acumen, but there was also always a tension in the relationship. They were in charge of my safety, yes, but I was in charge of . . . well, had it been the eighteenth century, I would have been in charge of their country. The power balance always tended to tilt in the royal family's favor.

And here we were. This is what it felt like when the power tilted back. When the employee refused to defer. When the subject refused to bow.

There was nothing to be done about it. How many times had I insisted to Konnor that I wasn't a princess anymore? Wasn't even a royal? Now, I would demand his obedience?

It would be ludicrous, and I wouldn't be so pig-headed. No, if I wanted him to treat me like an independent adult, I had to return the favor. We were a team.

. . . a team.

Hugh Konnor and I.

What the hell had happened here?

He was glaring at me, with a gun in his hand. A man who was ready to do violence, who wasn't buying any of my bullshit. Well, not tonight. Maybe I should have been intimidated by him, by the threat he could represent.

But . . .

The word "team" had quickly planted roots in my mind. It seemed as solid and true as a hundred-year-old oak. And I liked the idea of Hugh and me joining forces. Fighting crime. Building something together.

"Okay," I said softly. "You go in first. Tell me what I need to do."

He cocked his head. His eyebrows scraped together. "No fucking around, Caroline. I'm serious. You stay where I tell you, when I tell you, until I tell you to move."

Caroline.

First-name basis. Like partners.

I nodded. "I got it. I want this to work, truly I do. I'll listen to you, I promise."

There was a deep disbelief in Hugh's expression, so of course I had to address it. "Look, I don't know why you don't believe me—"

"It's hard to figure that one out," he scoffed.

"Your sarcasm is unnecessary," I informed him. "I'm not a willful child. I'm a grown woman who can make her own decisions—"

"Like eloping with a man-child race car driver."

Huh. Someone had an opinion on my marriage. Join the club with ten thousand members. "I make my own decisions," I repeated. "And tonight I'm deciding to do as you wish."

He tilted his head, as if trying to comprehend the strange words coming out of my mouth.

"Call it a . . . truce." I crossed my arms, as if that could protect my heart from further rejection by Hugh Konnor. "Let's try it. One night where I listen to you and you don't despise me."

"What . . ." He stopped, then started again. "Whatever gave you the idea that I hate you?" His voice was a low burr and his expression was indecipherable. "Because I . . ." Another pause, a brief press of his lips. "I don't."

"Oh," I said, more of a breath than a sound.

A flash of something bright crossed his face—something like the interest of the opposite sex—and then it was gone. Which meant it was surely a trick of the fading light or lingering echoes of my own teenaged delusions. "Good," he said shortly, then he motioned at the car. "Get in and lock the door."

"Where are you going?"

His eyes were defiant. "To kill Christian Fraser-Campbell."

sixteen

I WAS OBEDIENT FOR NEARLY FIFTEEN MINUTES.

In my defense, the car got stuffy. And my former bodyguard—now teammate who didn't hate me—was heading off to murder someone.

MURDER.

Was I supposed to be calm about that? Accepting? I don't know about non-royal families, but in mine I was not brought up to sit idly by while a murder is committed. What, exactly, I was supposed to do about a murder threat was never covered in Royal Princess 101, but I was fairly certain that waiting in a car on a remote Italian lane was not remotely effective at stopping anything.

So I started walking through the grass, tracing the route up the hill, taking care to be as quiet as I could. The sun had set now, the light was fading fast, but I saw a few lights on in the main villa, ahead.

What would Felice do?

That was a strange thought. My mother? My mother, Lady Felice Sevine-Laurent, would not be walking through the dirt and dry winter grass, that was for sure.

No, she would sashay into her own villa, call out Christian's name and declare that she was parched. Do be a dear and find some champagne.

It was tempting. But I would never possess the self-confidence of my mother.

Also, Hugh Konnor would have my head if I so blatantly disregarded his instructions.

There was another alternative. A nearby loggia, built into the hillside next to a swimming pool that was currently covered for the winter.

It was the perfect spot for a lookout, I thought as I ducked under the tiled roof. Exactly where a good partner would station herself, to keep an eye on her buddy's six. Whatever that was.

I partially stood behind a stone column and had a clear view of the house below. For a few minutes, there was nothing but cold wind and a half-moonlit landscape.

And then.

I heard them first. Low, rumbly voices.

Speaking in Driedish.

Out of the shadows came five of the burly policemen I had seen at the train station when Hugh had tried to double-cross me.

Every muscle and fiber in my body went tense. I wanted to scream. But what? To whom?

I gulped deep breaths. Focus, Caroline. Why was I here?

Why were they here?

We'd come to meet with Christian Fraser-Campbell.

Hugh had come to murder him.

Simple goals, if a bit violent.

So why the entourage?

The crew tried the door, as if they were expecting it to be open. One said something about checking out the back and then they split up.

I was so intent on trying to make out the figures in the dark that

I didn't smell the cigar until it was too late and the man was right beside me.

I froze, terror whipping around me. "Christian?" I whispered, but my brain knew it wasn't the man who had been my sister's fiancé.

He was stockier, darker, somehow more ordinary and more malevolent both at once. Of course, that could have something to do with the high-tech rifle he had slung over his shoulder.

"No," the man said out of the side of his mouth, with a Slavic accent of some sort. Russian? Ukrainian? "But I have something from him." His hand extended, a shadow draped in black. "Go on," he urged. "It won't bite."

A chuckle. Like the gun-wielding man hiding in the dark thought this was funny. It wasn't funny. The very opposite.

Don't do it. Hugh's voice in my head. *Run*.

But we were so damn close . . .

I took the item from the man. It was a disposable cellphone.

"He's waiting," he said.

I held the phone up to my ear. "H—he—hello?"

"Caroline? Hello again. It's been too long." It was Christian. He spoke Driedish with his Scottish accent. It was charming, almost disarming.

"Where are you?" I moved my head cautiously around, not wanting to take my eyes off the Ukrainian who was now casually sighting his weapon, giving it little strokes and pats, like it was his pet.

"I'm afraid I've been delayed a bit. Once my colleague Sergei there informed me of the Driedish police who were camped out on your mother's beautiful lawn, I felt it was unwise for me to show my face."

"I didn't know they were coming," I promised, suddenly aware of the danger I was in. But whether the danger was greater from the cigar-smoking assassin or from the Driedish police officers, I wasn't sure. "I wanted to meet with you, find out your story, just like we talked about."

This was true, I realized. As much as I had been begging and wheedling Konnor to leave me the hell alone, I was also now thoroughly invested in whatever this mystery was. I wanted to know why I had been dragged into it. How I could bring it to a conclusion.

"Yes, perhaps you didn't," Christian mused. "After all, I was the one who invited them to the house."

I didn't understand. "But you said you wanted to talk in private."

"Oh, I do. That's why Sergei has given you this phone. So we can chat whenever we want."

"But—" I swung round as a loud *ch-chuck* came from Sergei's rifle. He was pointing it at the house. "What are you doing?" I demanded, either of Sergei or Christian.

The Ukrainian ignored me. Pulled the trigger.

Maybe I screamed. It was hard to tell with the blast echoing under the loggia.

I dropped the phone. Spun toward the villa. Squinted in the dark. How could the Ukrainian see? It was all shadows and specters down there.

Was that a body slumped next to the door? "No . . ." I breathed.

More figures, running out into the night. Slow motion. Spinning. Metal glinting. There.

They see us.

Bang!

Stone splinters around me.

Bang! Right in my ear.

Rat-tat-tat. Like a distant nail gun at a construction site, but the rhythm and pitch were all wrong.

Dust and dirt sprayed over me.

I clutched my hands over my ears right before another spurt: more shots. My heart was in my throat. Clogging my airway, choking the scream that was desperate to be let loose.

The Ukrainian had ducked behind another column. Taking a rest, my brain interpreted. A moment of silence, I dared to hope that the violence was over, but there was another *rat-tat-tat*. Then Sergei pulled something out of his pocket. Glanced over at me. I will never forget what happened next. In the shade and horror, he winked at me. Then a brilliant burst of a fireball reaching into the rural Italian sky. The explosion swallowed my mother's villa in one single cloud, leaving nothing in its wake.

I was on my knees. Landed hard, I didn't care. Stunned. Not believing I was seeing this. Refusing to believe that he could be gone.

Him.

Hugh.

Where was Hugh?

But there was only crackling and hissing from the fire. Smoke and ash in the air. No movement except from flames and the tumbling of debris.

The Ukrainian gave me one cold once-over then methodically started to check his weapon. Was there one last bullet for me?

I pulled myself up to my unsteady feet. Not ready to die on my knees—not here.

"You're going to pay for this," I said in a shaky voice. "You won't get away with murder."

The Ukrainian lifted his eyebrows, like I had surprised him. Like he was scared of me.

Good.

Then he was shot in the neck.

The shot had come from behind me.

Sergei crumpled, an expression of incredulity on his frozen face. He hadn't been scared of me, he had been scared by a ferocious Driedish bear.

I turned, stumbled and headed straight into Hugh's arms. Instantly, he locked them tight around me, giving me exactly what I needed. A safe, sturdy place to land. I felt his hands glide down my back, his face pressed against my hair. He murmured something incomprehensible and tightened his grip on me.

And I felt again.

The doors unlocked, the gates opened and it all came flooding back. Pain, panic, fear, rage, lust.

The explosion on the thirty-second lap of the Slovenian Grand Prix. My mother's house in a fireball. A terrified sob broke from me. This was what happened when I dared to step outside of my prison. Destruction. Death. Chaos.

My nose buried into Hugh's chest. I took a shaky inhale to steady myself, but it had the opposite effect. The scent of him—sweat and smoke and cedar—made my head spin, my heart flip like a kite on a stormy day. Here was the one man in the world who wouldn't have me, and he was the center of everything for me at this moment.

Here, Hugh made sense. Here, there was protection. There was . . .

An anchor.

I had never been ultra-adept at following commands, but if an archangel had fallen from heaven at this point and ordered me to stay in Hugh Konnor's embrace for the rest of my life, I would have readily agreed.

But all good things come to an end. And before I knew it, Hugh was shifting his weight, as if he was readying himself to pull away from me.

I clutched at his jacket. "No." It was a woman's pitiful plea. His hands caught mine, overwhelming them, soothing.

"Caroline," he said gruffly. "We can't stay here. We have to leave."

I knew he was right. *Run! Go!* My native survival skills were screaming at me right now. But first.

"What about him?" I asked about the lifeless man on the ground.

Hugh looked over my shoulder, and his mouth set. "Right. I should tie him up."

He squeezed my hands one last time and pulled away, going toward Sergei.

"You mean, he's not dead?"

"No. It was a dart." Hugh plucked a tiny needle from Sergei's neck. "I'm not going to kill a man until I know what I can get from him."

"Oh, of course. Naturally," I said as I plucked Christian's cellphone from the ground, taking advantage of the fact that Hugh's attention was distracted by the zip ties he was putting around the Ukrainian's hands. Then he started patting the man down, before ripping his vest and shirt open.

It was dark, we were both probably shell-shocked, but there was no denying that the tattoo on Sergei's chest was an identical twin to the one I had seen on Christian's.

I swore. So did Hugh, but then I noticed he was flinching, holding his side. I swore louder. "You're hurt," I said as I went to him, tried to help pull him up.

"I'm fine," he said through gritted teeth.

But I was searching for his injury, and when he hissed, I demanded, "Were you *shot*?" I weaved. No. This was not happening.

"I'm fine," he repeated, and to be fair, I was the one who was clutching at a stone column and gasping for air. I didn't do well around blood. It was why I hadn't gone to medical school. Also, having a princess for a physician would have probably made patients uncomfortable.

I tried focusing on something else to take my mind off . . . Hugh's possible gunshot wound.

Yeah, my mother's still-smoldering villa was not exactly calming, and it made me ask, "The authorities . . . will they be coming?"

Hugh took a deep breath, not an easy one, either.

"And those police officers down there . . ." I waved at the ruins. "Are they—"

"Gone," Hugh bit out. "They were all inside."

The sky seemed to tilt. Good thing I still had this column to lean on. "This is . . ."

"War," Hugh finished, with a grim, gravel edge to his voice.

I saw it all so clearly then.

"I'm an idiot," I said, shaking my head.

"What?"

I didn't want to admit out loud that I hadn't taken Hugh seriously. Okay, yes, he'd said all the words describing how Christian had become a bad guy, but I had still been in my princess bubble. *Surely*, it wasn't as bad as he said. *Surely*, this could all be cleared up with minimal fuss and a polite conversation over a civilized cup of tea.

Clearly, watching my husband die in front of me wasn't enough to destroy all my illusions of a fairy-tale world.

Now, five of Drieden's finest had been sacrificed, because I'd been too stupid to listen to a reasonable grown-up.

Just like before.

No, I had to listen to my heart and elope with Stavros.

No, my parents couldn't just quietly behave and live separate lives.

I was being dragged into some palace craziness again, this time amplified to the nth degree. And I was going right along, surfing on the crest of the wave. Why? Because my sister's psychopath ex-fiancé was playing dead and had sent me a few emails? Because my so-called first love had shown up and said he had to protect me?

"Caroline?" Hugh reached out, offered a steady hand against my arm.

"Nothing," I muttered, and pushed away from the column. I knew what I had to do.

"Do you have your phone on you?" I asked Hugh.

He narrowed his eyes at me. "The one you took the card out of? The card you flushed down the toilet?"

"Yes."

"And what, pray tell, are you going to do with it?"

"I should call my mother. Tell her that her house has burned down."

Hugh looked concerned. "How? With magic?"

I reached into my bra. "Some call it that."

seventeen

KONNOR TRIED TO ARGUE, BUT HE HAD LOST BLOOD, and when I swore on my sister's tiara that I was taking him to my family for medical care, he finally gave me the car keys.

The trip should have taken six hours, but we were there in five. I had been married to a race car driver, after all. I knew how to drive fast.

Konnor passed out outside of Florence and woke up about an hour inside the Swiss border.

"I thought you said we were going to your family."

"We are," I said vaguely.

"Are we driving all the way to Drieden, or do you have a plan?"

I avoided his question. "You need a doctor. Someplace safe. We're going to deal with that first."

In the loggia at my mother's smoking villa, I had realized that I had lost my way. The path that I had started on after the death of my husband had veered off onto a dangerous detour.

I had opted out of the crazy life of a European royal. I had purposely decided to live a private, paparazzi-free existence. But somehow, they had dragged me back in. And once again, people had died.

After I had arranged for medical care for Hugh, in a secure location, I was opting out again.

This time for good.

But all of it hinged on being received at the compound I was now pulling up to, high in the Alps.

Part castle, part fortress, the stone edifice was bleak and chilling even against the landscape of snow-covered mountains. At first glance, the iron gates were old and rusted, but I knew that they were probably equipped with the most up-to-date technology and reinforced with modern materials.

Konnor peered up at the imposing walls looming over the valley. "Are you sure this is a safe enough place?"

I only made a *hmph* sound before I rolled down the window and pressed a button on the discreet box at the gate.

Beep. The box chirped. There was a long moment before someone answered with "Hello?"

I swallowed hard, resolving to ignore Konnor's wise-ass remark that was sure to come after what I would say next.

"I'm seeking sanctuary for two people."

"Are we hunchbacks?" Konnor muttered.

The box asked, "Your name?"

I paused, discomfited. It should be so simple, really. A name is given to a child at birth. Maybe it morphs into a nickname. Possibly a woman will adopt a husband's surname. But it doesn't have to happen. Generally, your name is your name. *Finis.* The End.

Except I wasn't sure of what my name was. Not this year, certainly not today.

Finally, and before I could respond, the speaker clicked on.

"Greetings are extended to Caroline Aurelia Marie of the House of Sevine. You may enter."

There was a loud buzz and a *clack* and the gates rolled open.

"House of *Sevine*?" Konnor asked, his voice low from exhaustion or caution or both. "Don't they mean House of Laurent?"

"No, they don't," I said as I pulled the car slowly through the gates and up the last bit of the winding, narrow drive.

A beat. "Where are we?" Another beat. "And don't say Switzerland."

"This is the former Convent of St Felicitas the Martyr."

Konnor sighed and rested his head back on the headrest. "Of course it is."

I ignored him.

"Is there an oil well behind the castle?" he asked.

Poor man. He had been shot not eight hours ago. He didn't know what he was talking about. "It's not a convent now," I explained, in case he had some sort of confusion about that. "It was converted into a private property in the early nineteenth century."

"You really know your real estate."

"I guess it runs in the family." I paused. "Look, we needed a safe, quiet place to get you looked at. This was the most secure location I knew of within a day's drive."

Out of the corner of my eye, I noticed Konnor staring at me. "Why do I feel like this is a trap?" he finally asked.

"I don't know." It was an honest answer. "I can't pretend to know how or why you think in the twisted ways you do."

"Who owns the convent now?" Konnor asked, with resignation in his tone.

I bit my lip. "My grandmother."

Konnor jerked himself upright. "What?"

"Not her," I said. "The other one."

*

MY MATERNAL GRANDMOTHER GREETED ME IN A COS-
tume that brought to mind medieval knights. A loose tunic, wide-legged
pants, a brown leather corset belt and a sword strapped to her back.

Yes, I said sword.

She was as tall and fit as she had ever been, her skin tawny from
outdoor exercise and fresh mountain air and her lush snow-white
curls piled up in a regal knot on the top of her head.

"Caroline!" she shouted with a smile, before noticing Konnor
limping in behind me. "Your guest?"

"Needs medical attention, as quickly as possible, please."

Lady Astrid Decht-Sevine, the Dowager Duchess of Aronberg,
strode directly to Konnor's side and called a name. "Fetch the doctor,
if you will." She peered into Konnor's chalky face, and then to his
shirt, where a dried-blood stain was once again glistening. "A hunting accident, I presume?"

Konnor's mouth slid slyly. "Sure."

Astrid barked a laugh. "Good man. We'll get you patched up in
no time."

Sure enough, a man in thick glasses and a very practical navy
sweater came rushing into the entryway, followed by two younger
men in what might have been some sort of martial arts uniform.
Astrid instructed them to examine the guest and then paused. "I'm
sorry, I didn't catch your name."

"No, you didn't," Hugh replied.

Astrid blinked and smiled faintly. "If you are staying in my fortress, I'll have your name."

"I'm in your granddaughter's service. Isn't that enough?"

My grandmother thought it over briefly then nodded and waved
off the men. One reached to help Konnor, but he looked at me instead,
his feet seeming to plant themselves into the centuries-old stone floor.
"Don't go anywhere."

I opened my mouth and shut it without promising anything.

Konnor's lips tightened in a tense line and then he turned to follow the doctor and his assistants.

Astrid waited until they were gone before she faced me again, a bemused expression on her face. "I expect you'll tell me everything?"

I grimaced and said, "I'll need a shower first."

"Excellent," Astrid said. "Ravi!" she shouted at an incredibly handsome man with jet-black hair standing by the door. "Show my granddaughter to her rooms." She lifted a dramatic eyebrow. "The suite in the tower should do nicely."

I dutifully followed Ravi through a side door but then stopped and spun on my heel. "Oh, and, Grandmother?"

"Yes, dear?"

"Will you do me a favor and call my mother to tell her that her villa in Tuscany was bombed?"

Astrid's brows clicked together. "Oh God. Which one?"

"She has more than one villa in Tuscany?"

Dear Grandmama simply shrugged. "At the prices these days, it's only smart to stock up." Her lips pursed. "In case one gets bombed."

FROM THE OUTSIDE, THE CONVENT OF SAINT FELICITAS the Martyr seemed cold and forbidding. But inside . . . the guest quarters were warm and luxurious. The suite that Ravi had brought me to was as elegantly and comfortably appointed as any presidential (or monarch's) suite at the finest hotels around the world. I was up to my chin in a giant porcelain tub of scalding-hot water. Steam had condensed across the marble floors and the gilt-framed mirrors and fogged up the air, creating an otherworldly, relaxing atmosphere that I desperately needed after the past few days of running from vague threats of violence and then, the real deal.

I closed my eyes and tried to forget, for just a few moments, the hellish scene at (one of) my mother's villa(s). I tried to tell myself that I was back on track. That after a brief pit stop at my grandmother's isolated Alpine convent-fortress (what—doesn't everyone's granny have one of those?) I would be able to fade back into obscurity. Back to privacy. Independence.

"You're using up all the hot water."

I gasped, startled out of my skin, nearly jumping out of the tub. Water sloshed onto the floor.

"Stop sneaking up on me!" I cried through gritted teeth. Seriously. Hugh Konnor was built like an ox but snuck around as quiet as a house cat. *How* did he do that!? Through the steam cloud, I saw his large figure enter the bathroom. Then he closed the door behind him.

"Why are you in here?" I shifted in the bath, but I didn't think he could see anything. I'd left only a candle burning and it would be hard to make out anything more than my outline in the water, with the candlelight and steam in the air.

"I had to see you. Make sure you were secure." He leaned against the wall, and did I detect a note of exhaustion in his voice? He had been shot, I had made him travel half a day to get to a place where *I* felt comfortable. Guiltily, I asked, "Did the doctor examine you? Are you okay?"

"He did," Konnor said. "I am."

"I'm glad," I said, because I was. I really was.

If something had happened to him . . . the thought of it . . . And just like that, a wave of overpowering emotion knocked me over. I started to cry, for no good reason. "Oh fuck." I heaved and pulled my knees to my chest. It felt necessary to cry, vital to let out . . . whatever this was.

It was because of me. Stavros. Hugh. Those burly blond men bearing sidearms and creeping into my mother's house. Hell, even Sergei wouldn't have been in that loggia if it hadn't been for Christian trying to contact me.

They were hurt because of me.

Sobs wracked me. I curled my head into my arms, resting them on top of my knees. My own little sweat lodge, wrenching every useless emotion out of me. The exhaustion, the confusion, the elation, the suspicion.

"Caroline . . ." His voice was nearer. I looked up and saw that he had approached the tub. "It wasn't because of you." Had I said something out loud?

"You had a bullet in you," I hiccupped.

"Look."

I looked. Big mistake.

He had unbuttoned his shirt. A bandage covered his lower side, right where a crest of muscle crossed over his left hip. I saw a bloodstain.

"It passed right through," he said, like that was going to reassure me.

Yeah, no. That didn't.

I went faint, and since I was in the bath it might have been fine, but Hugh swore and jumped, his palms catching my head as my face splashed into the water.

He lifted my face, cradled in his strong palms. "You're really not good with blood, are you?"

"I just don't like seeing it," I said, which caused him to chuckle.

Fingers caressed along my cheek, back behind my ears. Gently. I leaned into his palm, the sweet dampness of his skin cool on my flushed face.

"I'm glad you're okay . . ." I murmured, another sob tearing through my throat as I said the words. If anything had happened to him because of me . . .

I couldn't finish the thought.

"Caroline . . ." My name between us. My real name. Maybe the only true thing we'd ever share. He hushed me, stroked my hair.

Hands moved to my neck, my shoulders, rubbing, teasing the tension out of my muscles in strong, long strokes.

Slowly, my tears subsided. But he didn't stop. Kneading the line along the top of my shoulder, drawing a thumb along the curl of my spine. I started moving with him, subtly indicating where he could press harder, deeper.

I let out a soft moan.

He stopped. His voice seemed to cloak me like the cooling steam. "I can't let you go," he said, all arrogant authority.

I dropped my head further into my arms, stretching out the back of my neck, before lifting my suddenly exhausted head. "Do you know why I dropped out of sight, after Stavros died?"

"No."

"I didn't want my life anymore. I knew what they would do to me. I'd be recast into a tragic figure. I saw what they've done with Mother. The press, the drama, the never-ending circus of it all. I didn't want to be *that princess*."

Silence from the strong silent type behind me. Go figure.

I continued. "I don't want whatever is going on with you and Christian either. It's not my business, it's not my . . ." I faltered over the word. "War," I finished, using the word he had used earlier. "There's no good ending to me staying involved in this melodrama."

Finally, after one last touch that might have been an afterthought, he said, "Finally. One thing we agree on."

eighteen

FOUND MY GRANDMOTHER IN HER LIBRARY, SURROUNDED by research and folders of every kind. Maps hung all over the walls, ancient cartography symbols mixed with modern satellite imagery.

She looked up when I knocked a massive carved bookcase. "Ah, Caroline. Settled, are you?"

"Yes, thank you. For making room for me—"

"And your servant."

"Yes. My . . . friend."

Astrid gave me a knowing look, tossed a pen on to her desk and settled back into her over-sized leather chair. "I presume there must be something highly unusual going on to make you emerge from your hiding spot and return to your people."

"Oh, no." I shook my head. "I haven't returned to anything. In fact, as soon as I take care of a few things, I will be returning to my hiding spot."

"Really?" She smirked. "Which one?"

I shifted my weight from side to side. No one knew better than my grandmother Astrid about a Sevine women's hidey-holes. She had led by example—wresting this convent nearly forty years ago from her brother's inheritance (a story that was nearly legendary in high-flying European nobility circles) and collecting other, less notable properties as well. And I'd sought her advice years before when I started investigating discreet, efficient ways to invest in real estate.

"Sit, Caroline." She indicated the chair on the other side of the messy desk. "And tell Grandmama everything."

I sat and then began to pick my way carefully through the story. "I'm not really sure where to start," I began. "And I'm afraid I don't know all the particulars," I continued. "But it has to do with Christian Fraser-Campbell."

Astrid drew back. "That wretched man who abandoned Thea on her wedding day?"

"Yes."

"And then killed himself, rather than face her?"

"Well . . . about that. It seemed that perhaps he didn't. Or perhaps he has a twin or an impersonator who found me and is really quite insistent on meeting with me, for some reason."

"A twin? An impersonator?" Astrid coughed a laugh. "Darling Caroline, always trying to make excuses for people. A born mediator, that's what you are. I see what's happened."

"I'm glad one of us does."

"Your *other* grandmother lost control of a situation." Glee lit her face. "Aha! You know what they say about the chickens coming home to roost. Aurelia always thought she could manipulate people better than she actually could. She probably tried to buy this man off, make him agree to disappear, rather than continue to shame the royal House of Laurent, and now he's reneging on the deal."

It was possible . . . but based on what Hugh had told me, not probable. But I didn't want to correct Astrid, since Hugh's version of events dealt with some very serious treasonous accusations.

I went ahead and described the violence that it seemed Christian was sponsoring—to my house in Varenna, to my mother's villa.

"And when Hugh was hurt, and needed medical attention, I could only think that this was the best place."

"For both of you," Astrid pointed out.

I avoided her too perceptive gaze and tried to focus on a map of Jerusalem on the wall to my left.

"You're not returning to Drieden, then?" she asked.

"Why would I? What's left for me there?"

"*She* did strip your HRH, didn't she?" Astrid said it like she had just remembered that factoid. But I knew my mother's mother. She kept everything locked up in her brain. I imagined it like the royal vault under the palace. Walls of reinforced steel, heavy, thick locks, a thousand years' worth of secrets and scores to settle.

Like this one. Astrid wasn't particularly status-conscious, but only in the way that the most connected, well-to-do nobles are. A descendant of a branch of the Sevine family, she married back into the main family, then her second daughter married into the royal family. She certainly had the privilege to retreat from society, live on an Alp and devote her days to her deep-dives into archeology and cultural studies.

For instance, for the past twenty years or so, Grandmama had become one of the world's leading experts on the Crusades, the Knights Templar and the search for the Holy Grail. Think of her as an elegant, female version of Indiana Jones's father. Before that, she roamed Nepal and China, even followed Marco Polo's travels, as far as the Soviet Union would let her.

She was obsessed with ancient history, which is why it probably shouldn't be a surprise that she had some ancient history with my Big Gran, the *other* grandmother, Queen Aurelia of Drieden. "That woman," she muttered. "First she was a vindictive bitch to your mother. And then to you. And for what reason? To protect her precious blood line?" Astrid scoffed. "Don't get me started on the Laurents' bastards back in the eighteenth century."

"I . . . won't . . ." I murmured.

"Receipts. That's what I have." She waved dramatically at the stuffed bookshelf behind her. "We all know, all these Morganatic assholes, how they manipulate the laws and the titles to protect their fortunes." Here, Astrid used air quotes around "fortunes." Between that and the fact that she kept "receipts," I had to respect her up-to-date knowledge of modern lingo, even as fascinated as she was with the past. "The Laurents were always trying to keep up with the Sevines in that department. That's because *we* embraced things like technology and commerce and weren't content to wallow in the feudal system for an extra useless century."

"Anyway," I said, merely to interrupt this train of thought. I knew from experience that it could all too easily devolve into an hour-long rant about the superiority of one half of my family tree. With the long-standing ill will between the two families, how anyone thought my mother and father's marriage would last forever was beyond me.

"Like I said, I have no reason to return to Drieden. I have no role in the family business. I've probably become a total outcast in the past year, and I don't wish to become a tabloid sideshow like . . ." I cut off when I realized what I was about to say.

But Astrid knew. "Like your mother?" she said drolly.

It was true. My mother, Felice, had embraced a life of frivolity and fancy after her divorce from my father. She remarried twice (or was it three times? There had been another fiancé, I remembered, an Australian media mogul, but perhaps he had never successfully wrangled Mother to the altar), she traveled the world, hopping between her homes in Argentina, New York and the 6th arrondissement. She posted fabulous photos of herself on a yacht in Sardinia, sat at the front row of fashion shows next to Carine Roitfield and Anna Wintour, was even a guest judge on a drag-queen reality show for a bit. That, I really enjoyed, even if Big Gran nearly blew a gasket when she heard that Felice had worn her wedding tiara on the show.

"My mother lives her own life," I finally said. "But I'm not interested in all of that."

Astrid nodded in understanding. "Sevine women, we each must find our own way." Her expression darkened. "It's what distinguishes us from the Laurents, am I right?"

"Enough," I warned her. "You're talking about me and my sisters."

My grandmother was unconcerned about any accidental insult. "Yes. And I did notice that your sister Thea is just over there." She pointed at a mountain outside the window. "I read that she'll be attending that conference in Davos this week."

"Yes, speaking on some sort of education initiative, something with technology and girls."

Astrid smiled. "Someone keeps tabs on her family."

"I do," I said evenly. "How better to know when I need to duck for cover?"

She laughed, her signature joyous bark. Another sign of the aristocracy—the complete confidence to let every emotion out if one felt like it. See, also, e.g., my mother. Astrid reached for her fountain pen, flipping it through her fingers. "I had thought to send her a note, invite her for a visit   "

"*No!*" My answer was firm and loud. Loud enough to drive my grandmother's eyebrows up.

"Are you on the outs with Theodora?"

I covered my face with my hands and sighed. How could I explain that I wasn't on the outs with my older sister, that I simply felt extreme guilt over us losing touch, that I wasn't sure how I would be received and—oh yes—that her once-pretend-dead fiancé was possibly stalking me and threatening me with some sort of . . . persistent yet unclear threat.

"It's complicated," I mumbled.

"You two probably have a lot to discuss," Astrid said vaguely, pulling up a pad of paper to scribble some thought down that had just occurred to her. But I couldn't be worried about whatever she was writing because the thought of my sister had reminded me of Christian and the memory of Christian's phone, and that he was out there . . . somewhere . . . and that he really, really wanted to talk to me about . . . something that I had no business being a part of.

I was opting out, I reminded myself. As much as the story of Christian's disappearance tempted me, I knew this was going nowhere good. I was leaving. Just as soon as I could.

"Since we're talking about Sevine women finding themselves . . ." I started, knowing Astrid wouldn't be able to resist that lure.

Sure enough, Astrid's attention was diverted from her personalized stationery. Her clear blue eyes rose to meet mine. "Yes, my dear?"

"Do you happen to have a secure internet connection I could use?"

"You mean, an untraceable IP address from which one could access travel reservations, bank accounts and private emails that self-destruct within thirty minutes of opening?"

Errr . . . "Yes?"

Astrid gave me a conspiratorial smile. "Let me give you the password."

nineteen

JUST AS GRANDMAMA HAD PRODUCED A NEW, ULTRA-sophisticated-looking laptop for me to use, the door to her office flew open, which was really impressive, since the door was four hundred years old, solid oak and about five inches thick.

"Oh my," Astrid said under her breath at the sight of Hugh Konnor barreling into the room. "Can I help you?"

But Konnor only had eyes for me. Those intense, serious bodyguard eyes that made a girl forget that she was merely a task on a list of job duties. "There you are," he growled.

"Safe in my grandmother's loving care," I said, irritated that I had let him get under my skin again. That I had, even for an instant, thought he was concerned about me for other, more intimate reasons. "How are you feeling today?" I asked, for good manners' sake, as well as to remind him that I had put his care first, after all. I didn't just leave him in an Italian ditch, like I could have done.

He held out something in his hand. His fingers uncurled and I saw a cellphone.

For a moment, I panicked. I thought it was the one that Sergei had given me, the one presumably from Christian and the one I had kept secret from Konnor—until I knew exactly how to execute my escape plan.

But no. I recognized the phone as being the one that Konnor had used in Rome, before I hid the memory card in my bra and rendered it useless, for a short time only. "What about it?" I asked.

"We got a message. From St Andrews University. In Scotland."

Hello. Yes. This is Professor James Fergus McIntosh. I received an inquiry from Father Baldoni in Rome, regarding your curious symbol. I must admit, it was a head-scratcher at first, but Father Baldoni's direction was helpful and led me to the text—let's see— ah. Here we are. Oh, it's frightfully old. Funny, it was released from the Vatican's secret archive, which is ironic, isn't it? Because Father Baldoni is in Rome and, oh yes. The symbol. I do believe I have an impression of it, not a lot of information, but it's yours if you want it.

I made a noise of exasperation then glared at Konnor. "Really? That's what you came in here for? Did you call him back?"

He glanced briefly at my grandmother and then said, "Father Baldoni was your friend, and the message was for you. I thought you might want to return the call."

My fingers clenched around the phone. Out of frustration, and resolve. No. I was not being dragged into this anymore.

"I am not going to call him back," I informed Konnor. "This really isn't my business now."

"Not your business?" Konnor repeated the words back slowly, as if he was having a hard time understanding me. "Not your business, after the way that Christian has targeted you? After he keeps bombing buildings to get your attention?"

"That's not fair," I said. "I never asked to be involved."

Konnor snorted. "I wonder what it must feel like."

"What are you talking about?"

"To be a princess and have so much fucking privilege that you can just walk away from terror and injustice."

My mouth gaped open. I felt like I had been slapped in the face, but I knew he was right. I had tremendous privilege, advantages that allowed me to hire a private jet, fly to Cape Town, escape into the bush and never be seen again. If I wanted to.

"I still don't see why I have to be the one——"

"Because, for some fucking reason, you're the one that Christian fucking wants to talk to."

"Watch how you speak to my granddaughter, sir," Astrid warned from across the room.

Konnor barely spared her a glance. "He's obsessed with you. So whether you or I like it, that makes you the key to catching him."

Guilt flared in my chest as I remembered Sergei's cellphone. Maybe that was a key, but it was also my last bargaining chip for freedom.

"Fine," I bit out. "I'll be on the call to this professor. But I'm not flying to Scotland to look through his secret Vatican papers or anything."

A *tut-tut* sound came from Astrid. "I'd like a shot at them, if you don't."

I rubbed my forehead and wished Konnor hadn't brought all this up in front of my religious-history-fanatic grandmother. Poor Professor James Fergus McIntosh would probably be receiving a visit from the Dowager Duchess of Aronberg in the near future. She lived for Vatican secrets.

Yes, sometimes I wondered what it would be like to have two grandmothers who liked to knit and make cinnamon streusel cakes. It must be so lovely not to have eccentric, strong-minded grandmothers who didn't try to control one's life . . . and troves of secret Vatican papers.

Case in point: Grandmama Astrid had flipped open the new laptop she had been about to lend me and started typing something in. "We can use my secure IP to video-call the professor," she said, demonstrating more tech savvy than my regal grandmother. "This way I can be on hand, in case you need my expertise," she added helpfully.

Konnor shot me a confused look. "Grandmama is the former Duchess of Aronberg and also a Crusades scholar," I explained. "She talks to professors all the time."

Konnor didn't look overly thrilled to have her included, but I'm sure he thought her harmless.

It was almost like he hadn't met the women in my family before.

PROFESSOR JAMES FERGUS MCINTOSH ANSWERED WITH A jolly, Scottish-sounding greeting. I introduced myself, my "colleague" Hugh Konnor and my grandmother, Astrid Decht-Sevine. After that last name, Professor McIntosh's eyes grew round. "Madame Decht-Sevine? Of the Decht-Sevine-Solomon-Basilica Papers?"

Konnor and I turned to gape at my grandmother.

The professor continued, "Oh, well, yes, of course. This makes sense, why Father Baldoni reached out, then. Thorough research into these topics is so very difficult, wouldn't you say?"

Grandmama smiled serenely. "But that is what makes it so satisfying." She leaned toward me and muttered in Driedish. "What the hell are you researching, Caroline?"

"You asked about the symbol," Professor McIntosh said, holding up a copy of the drawing we had done for Father Baldoni in Rome.

Grandmama reached for her glasses. I nodded. "Yes, your message said you knew what it was?"

"Well, I wasn't sure, at first. It looks incomplete, as you noticed. But since Father Baldoni suggested that it could be an early form of Masonic heraldry, I decided to start with my very oldest texts. Sure enough, as I said in the message, I believe I found an impression of it, in the Chinon Parchment."

"I am not familiar with this." Grandmama sounded accusatory.

"It is a papal document from 1308, signed by Pope Clement, recounting the interrogation and absolution of seventy-two Templar knights. Believe it or not, it was misfiled in the Vatican Secret Archives and was not discovered until several years ago. The only reason that I can think of as to why Father Baldoni didn't look there himself is that there are no actual drawings in the document and he, as you know, would have been primarily concerned with illustrations."

"But you said you found the symbol in this . . . scroll." Konnor waved his hand about as he searched for the right word.

"Yes, the parchment. Well, the facsimile of the original parchment."

"How? When there aren't any pictures?"

"The document goes into great detail about the interrogation of the knights. What they wore, what they said. It's practically a court document. Well, it is, in a way."

Hugh interrupted the academic discussion before the professor could fall into a hole of fourteenth-century Inquisition history. "What did you find?"

"Ah, yes. There's a description of four of the knights." Professor McIntosh picked up a paper and began to read, as if he were translating as he went. "These four souls, hereby attested to the following, that they had no name, no family and no other loyalty than to their fellow companions. They lived, fought and died as mere shadows, giving voice to the supreme will of God on Earth."

Professor McIntosh paused, seemingly caught up in the details of a seven-hundred-year-old story.

"But what about the symbol?" I pressed.

"Oh. It goes on to describe it, you see. Here." He pointed at the page. "The four shadow souls dressed in the garments of peasants, barefoot and threadbare. Upon interrogation and searches, they were discovered to have marks on their breasts, identical all. The four-sided closed eye of Vox Umbra."

"Vox Umbra . . ." Grandmother murmured.

"The Shadow Voice," I translated.

"Quite," Professor McIntosh agreed. "The paper further describes this symbol accurately, Your Highness. The lines from below and the horizontal direction of the diamond. And once the author called it a closed eye. I saw it then, didn't you?"

He held up my drawing into the range of the camera and he was right. The horizontal diamond with lines extended downward did resemble a closed eyelid.

"The Shadow Voice . . ." I repeated. "Vox Umbra. Have you heard of this phrase before? What do you make of it?"

Professor McIntosh hesitated. "I am a scholar of Masonic history, but it is a secretive society. What we don't know about the Knights Templar, about the secret societies that ruled Europe for nearly a thousand years, would fill yet another secret archive under the Vatican."

"Or maybe it already does," Astrid drawled.

The good professor chuckled. "Spoken like a true skeptic, Your Grace."

"Have you done any other research on this, Professor?" I asked, but as soon as I produced the words, my grandmama clapped a hand over my wrist.

"Oh, he's done too much, Caroline. Academics like Professor McIntosh have their own scholastic pursuits. Please, dear sir, do not spend another moment on this favor you have done us. We do truly appreciate your time and expertise. Tell me, what can I do in return to repay you for your trouble?"

As my grandmother and Professor McIntosh took turns humble-bragging and complimenting each other, I saw Konnor had taken Astrid's fountain pen in his hand and was scrawling the symbol from memory in the margins of a newspaper.

Even with the information that the professor had just shared with us, I wasn't sure that it did any good. Which is what I said as soon as Grandmama hung up on the video-call.

"I don't even know what to do now. Our only lead is from a secret parchment that was buried under the Vatican for the last thousand years."

Grandmama smiled benevolently. "Those are my favorite kind."

I sighed heavily. "We're not researching the Crusaders, Grand-mama. We're looking for a possible sociopath who left my sister at the altar. Two entirely different pursuits."

Konnor lifted his eyebrows at me. "We?" he said, a low, careful rumble.

I pressed my lips together. It had been an accidental use of the word. "For the time being," I said reluctantly. "Until tomorrow, at most." After all, I hadn't figured out where I was escaping to next. South Africa? An island in the Indian Ocean? Maybe an anonymous flat in Chicago or Atlanta. Some place where no one kept up with the everyday exploits of younger siblings of European royal families.

He said nothing else, but that was because my grandmother had just cursed out Christian Fraser-Campbell. "He's not worthy of a Sevine woman," she said, with a glare in my direction. I lifted my hands in innocence. I had made a lot of bad decisions in lovers, but agreeing to marry Christian Fraser-Campbell had been all my per-fect big sister's decision.

"Your Grace," Konnor addressed my grandmother. "What do you know about all this business that Professor McIntosh was going on about?"

"The Knights Templar, the Masonic societies and the Vatican?" she smirked. "What don't I know?"

I threw my hands up again and left the room. Konnor had opened this bag of worms. I was going to let him have it.

twenty

OVER THE YEARS, THE CONVENT OF SAINT FELICI-
tas the Martyr had been used for many purposes. Of
course, it had been a convent, but it had also been used as
a hospital, a training center and, now, under my grandmother's own-
ership, it was half an academic center for study and retreat and half a
stately and luxurious aristocratic estate.

I was in the chapel, which some Sevine ancestor had turned
into a cozy den. The pews and kneelers had been replaced with
overstuffed chairs and couches in sumptuous velvet and the walls
were draped with rugs and tapestries and, curiously, a mishmash
of art, ranging from cubist sketches to sensational almost-nude
portraits. Probably a great-great-grandmother had sheltered starving artists in the last century, and I imagined the resident ghosts
of medieval nuns had been shocked by the licentiousness of the
commune.

The collection of art pieces reminded me of the apartment in
Rome, another Sevine family holding. Growing up as a princess, naturally I knew a bit more about the royal side of my lineage. It was part
of my education, along with that of my brother and sisters. We had

tutors on Driedish history, royal genealogies and, of course, the ever-essential etiquette and protocol rules.

But lounging in the chapel-cum-den in Grandmama Astrid's Swiss convent and after my second—or was it third?—glass of the exquisite Château Margaux Astrid's housekeeper had produced for me, I pulled my feet under the Hermès cashmere blanket and began thinking deep thoughts about my Sevine side of the family.

Or as deep as they came after three glasses of wine.

Maybe Astrid was right. There was something in the blood line. Something that made the women in our family different. After my mother's infidelities and the divorce and the reality shows and tabloids, we—my siblings and I—had become estranged from her. How could we not be? We were princesses (and a prince) of a royal house. We had all the privileges and burdens that came along with that. When my mother threw a metaphorical glass of champagne in the face of the House of Laurent, we had no choice, really.

Years went by, I was a good princess.

Until I wasn't.

Until I defied the Queen and she taught me that both the privileges and the burdens that came with my birth were only mine because *she* allowed it.

And now who was I? A princess without a title, sure. A woman with a comfortable amount in Swiss bank accounts, absolutely. I was intensely aware that so many women would love to be in my shoes.

Freedom.

I had it now, didn't I? Exactly what I thought I had wanted when I demanded to be granted permission to marry Stavros.

But freedom is so very . . . free. Wild. Uncontainable.

After a lifetime of constraints and rules and dictum, I saw now that maybe freedom didn't settle on me as comfortably as I'd imagined it would. It was a silk Pucci kaftan after a lifetime of tweed

Chanel suits. It was going barefoot on the sands of Bali after only wearing Louboutins on slick marble.

Of course, it was going to take a while for me to get used to the feeling. To the *lack* of expectations. That was all this was, really. Quite understandable that I was having a hard time saying *no* to Hugh Konnor and his continued insistence that I stay safe by his side. I had spent nearly twenty-nine years doing exactly that, obeying my Laurent side.

It would take some time to grow into my Sevine side.

I closed my eyes and tried to imagine it. Openly saying, "Fuck you," to the House of Laurent, to the courtiers and politicians. To not hiding anymore.

Because really, hiding? My last six months of solitude in Northern Italy? Hadn't that been another concession to the royal princess playbook? To not make a fuss, to hope that people averted their eyes and ignored my indiscretions?

What if . . .

What if I were more like my mother?

A distinct feeling of discomfort skipped through my veins.

Or maybe that was too much, too soon.

Baby steps, maybe?

And then, as if the universe had heard me . . . and then laughed . . . who came stumbling into the room but Hugh Konnor.

"There you are," he said, pulling his head back as if he was seeing me for the first time in ages. Giving me a look that a man does right before he says something like, "Done something new with your hair?"

Except he didn't say that. Hugh Konnor would never *not* notice a change in me. He noticed everything, didn't he? If I darted my eyes, if I shifted my weight. I had always felt like a pinned butterfly specimen when he was around. As if I was only there for him to study. To amuse him.

The thought was arousing in a sneaky way. I always thought I hated the idea of being pinned in place by Hugh. But then, as the image sat with me, as the feeling grew solid, made my limbs loose and languid, I discovered I quite liked it.

It probably was the wine talking.

Liar, the wine said.

He shut the door behind him. "Free at last," he mumbled, walking with a slight jerkiness toward me.

"Hugh Konnor!" I said in shock. "Are you drunk?"

He collapsed on the other end of the sofa I was curled up on and he seemed to give his answer some consideration. "Yes." He raised an eyebrow at me. "Your grandmother has excellent taste in schnapps."

I lifted my wine glass in a toast. "She has excellent taste in everything. Welcome to Astrid Decht-Sevine's world."

"You."

"Excuse me?"

"It's your world, as well."

And wasn't that an echo of my deep thoughts? I shifted uncomfortably, but stopped when Hugh's hand landed on my ankle.

It was still underneath a blanket, sure, but the weight—the heat—of his hand sent sparks scurrying up my leg, circling my hips, waist, skittering across my skin.

The image of a pinned butterfly came to mind again.

I did not pull my ankle away.

He rubbed a thumb haphazardly, whether it was against the cashmere of the blanket or against my skin, I didn't know.

And I didn't mind.

"Your grandmother is a very smart lady," he said, his working-class Driedish accent thickening under the influence of excellent schnapps. "She knows the dates this tower was erected, the name of the priest who gave last rites to a king of Jerusalem, the cost of a jug of ale during the French Revolution." He glared at me. "I see where your sister gets it from."

I couldn't help but chuckle. He was right. My sister Theodora was a history buff who tended to talk people's ears off with random Driedish history facts whenever she got nervous. I hadn't put the connection together with Grandmama Astrid before. Another example of the Sevine bloodline sneaking through the House of Laurent's walls and gates.

He kept rubbing my ankle, and I remembered the way he had reduced me to a puddle of suds and steam with a simple neck massage earlier. Experimentally, I stretched out my foot. He wrapped his fingers around it.

On purpose.

Catching me.

My gaze snapped to meet his. Oh yes, he knew exactly what he was doing.

To me.

The thought ignited a long-hidden spark of anger in me.

"That day in the barn," I started. "When I was nineteen."

He froze. Every other time I had brought this up he had avoided the topic. Moved away. But right now he was staying exactly as he was.

I slowly extended my other leg, nudging my left foot against his thick, denim-clad thigh as I picked my words carefully. "Did you know that day? What you had done to me? The spell you had cast over a young girl?"

My question held the edge of resentment I had carried for so long, and I hadn't meant to say the word: *spell*. It was too magical, too sweet, for what I had come to understand in the intervening years had been just a simple hormonal reaction. Young pretty female + strong virile male = sexual attraction.

But as I said it now, Hugh didn't dismiss it. Or mock me.

Instead he started moving his hands deliberately—God, the man was a demon with his hands—circling my toes, stroking my ankles, lightly brushing up my shin.

"I would like to know the same," he said, his voice a low rumble in his chest. "Whether you knew what you did to me." He pulled his eyes from my legs to my face.

"I was a child," I said defensively. "I didn't know what I was doing. And clearly, you hated me."

His full lips twisted in a half-smile. "I hated that you were a child. I hated that I would get fired or worse for even thinking of you that way."

Oh, this was bad. He was halfway drunk. Hell, so was I.

I also carried the Sevine gene for bad-decision making. So anything that happened wouldn't be entirely my fault. I was simply pre-programmed to slide, nestle down deeper into the burgundy velvet upholstery. "I can't fire you now," I breathed.

It was an invitation which Hugh accepted. He stretched and began climbing down the length of the couch, hands skating along the outline of my body, covering me exactly as he had in all those girlish fantasies of what exactly a good bodyguard should do.

He took his thumb and drew my bottom lip, as if it were a precious, fragile jewel. "My lady." It was the hottest thing he'd ever said to me. Until the next thing. "May I kiss you?"

The sweetness of it melted everything away that wasn't my essence. I was no longer princess, child, Sevine, Laurent, I was simply Caroline. *His lady.* I nodded and he pressed his lips against mine.

A fairy-tale kiss. A prince and a princess under a wonderland bower. A moment in time to be treasured in glass, in a museum.

And then, as quick as a flash, it changed.

We changed.

A girl grew up. A man became feral. We clicked. Hormone— chemical—heat—fire.

Roaring in my ears. Hands on skin, ripping blankets, seeking under, over. I clenched at his shoulder, nipped at his ear. He gripped my ass, teased my nipple. Schnapps meets Château Margaux. Proletariat rebellion smashing the castle walls.

Years of pent-up frustration, lust masquerading as hate, it all exploded right then and there. His hands were peeling down my pants, his tongue stroking along my collarbone. I was kneading the back of his head, lifting my hips to assist his efforts to undress me when, distantly, my brain alerted me.

To a rush of cool air. The sound of my name coming from someone who was not the man I was in the process of seducing.

"Caroline!" A pause. "*Hugh?*"

We froze.

Hugh dipped his head, his weight on top of me still and heavy and beautiful for one more moment, before he said, with both reluctance and obedience in his voice: "Your Highness?"

twenty-one

"WHAT THE HELL ARE YOU DOING HERE?!?" I yelled at my older sister, her Most Perfect Royal Highness ever, Princess Theodora of Drieden, as I pulled up my pants.

Because of course. All this time, all these years, she was still cockblocking me in our grandmother's house.

For her part, she seemed to be recovering from shellshock, looking at me and then at Hugh's straight back. He had jumped to attention and faced a corner as he tried to calm down from our super-hot-almost-sex-makeout session that had been so rudely interrupted.

"Excuse me!?" I snapped my fingers at her, and she jerked, as if she was offended by that small act of disrespect. Whatever. What about me? I felt *hugely* disrespected right now, after her barging in like she had. "What are you doing here?" I repeated slowly and clearly.

Thea seemed to take in the room again, and then she recovered, like Ms. Perfect always did. "Well, hello again, dear Caroline. So lovely to see you, after all these months," she said pointedly. "I've been so worried about you after your husband's passing."

I silently called her a very bad word. "Thank you, dear Thea," I replied, echoing her regal, distant tone and flawless diction. "I did so appreciate your thoughtful notes after I lost said husband."

She smoothed a hand down the front of her precisely fitted wool jersey dress. Theodora of Drieden was always elegant, cool, calm and predictable. I could read her like a book. Even now she was reaching into her formidable royal bag of tricks and was about to play a princess card that was so indisputably well mannered that no one could possibly find fault with her.

"It is good to see you," she said. "Even while you're putting the moves on my bodyguard."

Oh. Kill. Me. Now.

Where was a good Swiss sinkhole to swallow you up when you needed one?

I bit my lip and tried my hardest not to look at Hugh. Or Thea. Or anywhere except the portrait hanging above Thea's left shoulder. There. If I concentrated hard enough, I'd be able to get through the supreme awkwardness of this night.

"How did you know I was here?" I asked, once I had regained my composure. "Did Konnor call you?"

"It's Konnor now?" she murmured.

"No." That was Hugh, now turned and transformed back into stern bodyguard mode. There was no trace of the passionate man who had kissed me so recklessly just a few minutes before. "I didn't call her," he said, looking only at me, which made my heart leap awkwardly into my throat. Yeah. I wasn't sure how to handle this situation at all. I focused back on the portrait behind Thea, of a woman. Mid- to late-sixteenth century, from the dress. Pale skinned, honey brown hair pulled back and adorned with a coronet of pearls and rubies, sitting in a salon of some sort. I had no idea who she was or why she was hanging up here in the tower. Did they run out of room in the official gallery? Was this a punishment of some kind? Had she been a particularly nasty mother-in-law?

The artist had painted her coat of arms behind her—this I did recognize—the Sevine coat of arms. It was on my mother's formal stationery, had probably been on other items in our house while I was growing up, and it was everywhere here, too.

So of course I knew it, the quartered shield featuring a cross and a fox and leaves of laurel. But my royal tutors had always focused on our Laurent heraldry, impressing upon us those symbols and consigning the Sevine insignia to the forgotten corners of my mother's inheritance.

That was why I had never spent a single moment thinking about the significance of the fourth quarter of the Sevine shield. I had never wondered what that bold horizontal diamond meant, or why there were gold rays extending from only the bottom half of the design.

Hugh reached out and steadied me with one hand on my waist. "Caroline? Are you okay?"

Thea turned to Hugh. "And what a surprise to find you here. Especially as you haven't checked in in several weeks. Do you have any updates for me?"

He glanced at me again. "Possibly." He seemed to hesitate for a second before saying to my sister, "Actually, if you could give Lady Caroline and me a chance to finish our conversation, I can brief you afterward."

"No," I said suddenly. I was aware of both of them turning to me in surprise, but I could only stare at the portrait.

When I studied art history, professors had remarked how I saw paintings differently. I would comment on the obscure parts, or a technique or some significance that few others pulled out.

And now, it would seem, I had done it again.

"I have to go," I mumbled as I broke from Hugh's grasp and went to find dear old Grandmama.

WHEN I ENTERED THE MAIN HALL MY ATTENTION WAS caught by the Sevine coat of arms etched into the stone floor. Then by the tapestry hanging high on the wall opposite the door, where an older version of the same insignia was embroidered in gold and red.

All those horizontal diamonds. All hiding in plain sight. It seemed bold, daring, reckless, even.

It was the Sevine way, I guessed.

The handsome Ravi showed me back to Grandmama's practice room, as she called it. There were two fencers in the middle of the piste, their epees flashing like Christmas tinsel. Upon our entrance, they paused and one pushed back their mask. It was Grandmama, wearing sporty eyeglasses. "Caroline, what an inconvenient time to visit."

"You lied to me."

She showed no response to my accusation other than to shrug. "No matter, I'm losing terribly. Now I have an excuse to defer this game to another time." Her partner took off his helmet and ran a hand through his sweaty dark hair. Like Ravi, he was an exceptionally handsome man. Clearly, my grandmama had refined and specific tastes.

After the two men left us alone, Grandmama went to a nearby table and poured from an insulated pot. "Herbal tea?" she asked, and I declined. Still, she poured two cups.

"You haven't asked me why I've come," I observed as she took a sip of tea. I didn't wait for a further response. "It's about Vox Umbra.

You're connected to it somehow. And Christian. He has a tattoo of something in your own crest and you lied to me about it."

"Darling, we were in the middle of a conference call."

I sputtered. "Were you going to tell me? He's a madman. He's blown up your daughter's house, he kidnapped your granddaughter, he threatened your Queen!"

Grandmama set her teacup down. "Well, that last bit's not that bad. Aurelia deserves it."

"Did you tell him where to find me?"

"Do you want to know the truth about yourself, Caroline? About your heritage?"

The sudden, direct twist startled me. "I know everything about my heritage," I said bitterly. "You forget what type of education a princess must endure."

Astrid pinned me with her ice-sharp gaze. "Your *other* heritage. We're Vox Umbra. It's an organization the Sevines have been involved in for a long time."

"This is real?" I asked, remembering Professor McIntosh's evidence about fourteenth-century Inquisition documents. "This has been going on for nearly a thousand years?"

"Isn't it fascinating?" Astrid closed her eyes slightly, enraptured at the thought, and I saw what had stimulated her passion for archeology.

Then she continued, "It's simply a small group of influential people, bound by blood to ensure that the will of God is done on Earth. Historically speaking."

"You're religious zealots."

My grandmother chuckled. "Perhaps in the past. In this century, we consider ourselves peacekeepers."

"You're powermongers."

"We bring stability and prosperity to our nations."

"By keeping a small cabal in authority."

Grandmama was not bruised by my accusations. Instead, she looked almost . . . amused.

And I understood why. I raised my hand. "Okay, fine, I get your point." It was ironic that I, raised in a palace, given all the princessy titles, would be shocked at such things as cabals that kept power in the hands of the few.

"But why would you bring Christian into all this? He's running from the law!"

Grandmama pressed her lips together. "Throughout the centuries, a small group of families passed leadership of Vox Umbra among themselves. One by one, they would take a turn. Some were successful and some . . . well, we don't speak of them anymore. Christian claimed his hereditary membership shortly before his engagement to Theodora." She lifted her hands. "Who knew he'd turn out to be one of the rotten apples?"

None of this made much sense. "But if he's Vox Umbra . . . why would he try to destroy the Driedish monarchy? You just said the organization is interested in stability and peacekeeping."

Now Astrid's smile had faded. "That is what we're wondering. He's a loose cannon, obviously, but he's clearly found asylum with some other members."

"And he's blown up buildings, and kidnapped people, and he knows—"

I broke off before I shared too much.

But this was Astrid Decht-Sevine. "What does he know about you, Caroline?" she asked softly.

"He knows what I've done."

Her eyebrows lifted slightly. "Ah." She let silence do the pressuring for her.

Finally, I had to admit it. "For years, I've published newspaper stories under pen names." I paused. "Some of them were stories about my family."

If Astrid was shocked, or disgusted, I couldn't tell. "What were these names?"

"Cordelia Lancaster. And Clémence Diederich."

She frowned a little and then shook a finger at me. "The Formula One series in the British paper. I wondered how the reporter knew so much about Stavros's team."

My stomach twisted. Trading in secret insider information never stayed secret, did it?

"How does Christian know of all this?" Astrid asked me.

How indeed. I shook my head. "I don't know, but Christian will tell everyone all the things I've done if I don't help him put his story out there. To publish it. Let the world know it."

Astrid straightened, as cool and as dangerous as her epee. "We cannot let that happen."

"Which part?"

"All of it, darling. You're one of us," my grandmama continued. "You'll just have to help us stop him."

I cursed softly. Being dragged into more drama was not my plan. Which is what I told her. "I thought I'd go to Patagonia next. I've heard it's nice," I finished.

Astrid was not impressed with me. "This is not who you are. You are a Sevine woman."

"Mother ran away," I said, a little like a toddler, if I'm honest. But of course, Astrid ignored that.

"What if Christian was threatening your sister Sophia? What would you do to stop him from hurting her?"

The surge of anger, the rush of violence, caused my fist to clench. "To protect someone I love, there's nothing I wouldn't do," I said quietly.

Astrid smiled warmly. "Well, then, welcome to Vox Umbra, Caroline of Sevine." She extended a hand to me. "Now, let's catch that bastard."

*

HUGH FOUND ME ON A BALCONY.

The night air was cold, and I now knew from experience how warm I'd find Hugh's embrace.

But I couldn't go to him.

Astrid and I had concocted a simple yet effective plan, but in order for it to work, I'd have to lie to everyone involved.

It had been surprisingly easy to agree to this. After all, I'd been lying to the world for a very long time, it seemed. No one knew the real me; no one knew my secrets or my dreams.

The only person who had been able to unlock that door recently was Hugh Konnor.

And now I had to slam it shut. Lock the bolt.

Which was fine.

He didn't want me, not really. And I couldn't have him. Not without destroying his life. Which wasn't a very polite thing to do, now, was it?

So. I would lie. Hide in plain sight. And ensure the safety of my family, the stability of my country and the secrecy of an organization whose existence I'd only just discovered today.

Not bad for a Tuesday.

"You shouldn't be out here," he said, in a bossy bass. "It's freezing."

"I'm a native Driedener," I said, with a rueful smile at the dark shadows of the Alps around us. "I laugh at cold wind."

"Hmph," was all he said as he draped a blanket around my shoulders.

My heart twinged a little at that gesture. This was why I went gaga for him at nineteen. Because he did these things that a body-guard did and I always misinterpreted them as something more intimate, more meaningful.

"We need to talk," he said.

Another heart string pulled. Nope. I wasn't falling for it.

"You'll be happy to know that Astrid and I had a long talk. She's convinced me to go back to Drieden."

Hugh pulled back, his face filled with skeptical surprise.

"I'm not staying," I told him sternly. "I . . . can't. She simply has some business that she might need some assistance with."

It was the truth. Astrid was convinced that a Vox Umbra member in Drieden had helped Christian. She felt that if I was in the country, and if Christian wanted to meet with me, he'd feel more confident coming forward and we could potentially catch him, and identify his protector at the same time.

"Have you told your sister?"

I shook my head. "I haven't seen her. Not since we were . . ." I let that drift off, uncomfortably reminded about all the places Hugh had placed his hands—and lips—just a while ago.

Our gazes locked. He looked down at me with a molten golden stare and I got the distinct impression that he was thinking about the same things.

"We can't," I started.

"No," he agreed quickly.

Too quickly. I felt the familiar resistance, the old wound of his rejection, that he found me ridiculous and repulsive, but I remembered. His fingers, his touch, the way he greedily tasted me.

My inner princess was now offended. "Why can't we?" I demanded. "A lot of men think I'm attractive. A lot of women, too," I added, for good measure.

A tense sigh tore out of him. "I know."

"You know that I'm attractive, or you know that a lot of other people think I'm hot enough to . . ." My voice tapered out under the undeniable heat of his gaze. "Kiss," I ended lamely.

"You don't want to be with someone like me," Hugh said, almost kindly.

"Someone like you?" There was my alter ego, Awkward Repeating Robot, again. "Are you gay?" I asked him.

"No."

"Impotent?"

His mouth slid to one side. "No."

I wracked my brain for other possible reasons why I would not want to be with this tall, handsome, extremely competent man with intense eyes and clever hands and a loyal heart and . . . oh. Crap.

"You're married."

"No."

"Otherwise attached?"

Another frustrated sigh. "No. I'm a fucking street kid from Koras who joined the army simply to get food and a roof over my head. I'm a government employee with cheap suits, tattoos, a government pension that starts in two months and absolutely no knowledge about expensive wine or the Crusades or the fucking king who got himself killed in that supermarket car park." Suddenly, Hugh was much closer, practically looming over me.

"Wait. You think you're not good enough for me?" I laughed. Oh, irony was delicious. "You know I'm not a princess anymore, right?"

"So you keep saying. But all I see is the daughter of the next king of Drieden."

I held his gaze for a long moment. "Liar," I finally said.

"What did you call me?"

"You heard me. I called you a liar. If all you saw was an untouchable princess, then you wouldn't have done what you did."

"It was a mistake."

"Not on the couch," I said. "In the stables. When I was nineteen and asked you to take my virginity. You know what I think?"

"I couldn't possibly guess."

"I think you were tempted to take me up on the offer."

"You were a child."

"I was nineteen. You were—what, twenty-five?" I shook my head. It wasn't an unheard-of, insurmountable age difference. "You saw me as something else."

"You're right."

"See?"

He leaned in, inches away from my face. "I saw you as trouble."

It all clicked then. Hugh's fundamental nature, how he took his job so seriously. He'd said it in Italy, hadn't he? He thought his job was to protect me from my own bad decisions.

Even if my bad decision was *him*.

"Fine," I said, even though it most definitely was not. I backed away and regarded him solemnly. Like a giant jar of candies that held a prize, if only I could guess the correct amount inside. "You win."

Strange how Hugh didn't seem happy about that statement. "What do I win?" he asked, as if he was already regretting asking the question.

"You think I'm trouble, you don't want us to be involved. Fine. You win. We'll go back to Drieden, I'll keep doing my thing and you'll never have to see me again."

"Like hell you will."

I smiled. I saw what he was about now. "Then you'll agree to my terms."

twenty-two

THE FIRST RULE WAS SIMPLE: DON'T TELL THEA anything.

Hugh didn't like this rule, but he didn't like anything I suggested. Ever. I could suggest getting some chocolate cake for his mother's birthday and he'd probably tell me his mother would die from an acute chocolate allergy and I was a horrible person for even suggesting it.

"Once Thea finds out, she'll have her creepy security detail all over me," I explained. And that would make it much harder for me to get close to Christian. Astrid had agreed with my theory that Christian had approached me because I was the one outside of the palace walls—metaphorically and literally. I was easier to approach if I was all alone.

"I'm her creepy security detail," Hugh said evenly.

"Exactly." I smiled sweetly. He did not seem won over by my charm. Strange.

And so the lying began. I shook off any vague discomfort that was creeping up on me. Like I said, my hunch was that I could lure Christian in if I was more accessible, but every time I told Hugh that

I was offering myself up as bait, he got all weird about it. And if he got weird about it, then I could just imagine Thea getting equally weird and protective about it.

But my older sister was the intelligent one in the family and she immediately guessed I was hiding something when I found her to tell her that I would be accompanying her on her flight back to Drieden.

"What are you not telling me?" Her eyes focused on Hugh, correctly identifying him as the weak link. He'd probably crumble under her skillful and adept interrogation, which is why I wasn't telling him anything of my plan.

"Don't speak to him like that," I snapped at her.

She looked shocked. "He works for me."

"Are you saying I don't deserve a bodyguard?"

"No," she said instantly. "Of course you do."

"Are you asking him to betray my confidence?"

"No, but—"

"You and I both know that a good security officer has to also have a certain trust with the person they're charged with protecting."

My plan was working perfectly. Thea was completely distracted from pressing Hugh on details and was not totally focused on me. "Yes, I agree," she said reasonably. "But I found him on top of you, with his hands under your shirt and his tongue down your throat. That's a level of trust that I've never reached with my security staff."

For some reason, Hugh coughed just then, and Thea's cheeks colored in response. "Wait," I said abruptly. "Have you two . . ."

"*No!*" they said in unison.

"Good," I mumbled uncomfortably.

"You two . . ." Thea looked between us, shaking her head. "I'm worried. I heard about Mother's house. What happened with the team there was a horrible shame. And Grandmama said you were wounded . . ." She said this to Hugh, but once again I jumped in. To save him from my sister's tricks.

"A different incident," I told her. "I did it to him."

"You?" She looked confused, for some reason.

"Yes," I said. "He keeps jumping out of the dark and surprising me. I had to protect myself."

"You. You shot Hugh?" she asked.

"Is it so hard to believe a princess might carry a gun?"

She looked discomfited by that question and I realized my mistake. "Of course, my apologies. I didn't mean to presume. It's simply a habit to refer to myself as a princess in such a way. Especially when I'm around my family." I was embarrassed. Even though I had been liberated from my royal family, a breach of protocol inferring that I had a title which I did not have was awkward, to say the least. Would I ever get used to it? Not being a princess? Feeling like an outsider?

I was scared I wouldn't.

"It's all right . . ." Thea paused, started again. "We should probably talk about that. There have been . . . developments."

Her cagey way of describing insider family matters only made it worse, underlining that I had not been in the inner circle for the past six months, nor would I ever be again.

"It's fine," I said, trying to cut her off before either of us said something we would regret. "It's fine," I repeated, in case she didn't believe me the first time. "I'm going back to Drieden City. Tonight, I think. I have some old friends to meet."

Thea's smile was one of relief and delight. "Oh Caroline, I'm so glad to hear it. We've been worried about you, all by yourself, alone, with no one around."

"You don't need to make it sound so pathetic," I said. "It's what I wanted. What I still want. I just need to take care of a few things, that's all."

My response was curt enough to make her press her lips together for a moment. She looked at Hugh and for a brief instant I wondered if something more passed between them than an innocent glance. But then she spoke again. "And Hugh will be going back with you? To Drieden City?"

It felt like a trap. It smelled like a trap. But for the life of me, I couldn't figure out how to sidestep it.

The best I could do was, "If he likes."

It was not a good way out of whatever trap Thea had just laid for me. She turned to him then, a funny little smile on her face. "Hugh? Will you be accompanying my sister to Drieden City?"

Hugh must have smelled the smell of trap, too, because his jaw tightened and he just nodded in response.

Thea smiled broadly. "Excellent."

EVEN IF I WAS GOING BACK TO DRIEDEN, HUGH WASN'T going to get his wish of tossing me behind the palace gates and throwing away the key.

He'd been working for the royal family long enough to realize that wasn't quite how it worked.

A person had to be invited into a palace, after all. And as I was not officially part of the royal family, I couldn't simply walk up to the door and use the key hidden under the fake rock in the garden.

(Just kidding. Officially, THERE IS NO PALACE KEY HIDDEN UNDER ANY FAKE ROCKS IN THE GARDEN.)

(It's hidden in a fake soda can.)

So when we landed at the private airport outside Drieden City and the pilot asked us where the limousine should take us, Hugh was only half frustrated when I told him, "The Hotel Ilysium."

Hugh got that look on his face that said he was about to argue with me, and I had to shut that down quickly. "It's where my mother always stays when she is in the city. They have excellent security— you probably know it well yourself."

"Caroline." He used my name to make me stop blabbering on. I complied. "I'm on sabbatical."

"On leave?" I clarified. "From palace security? Since when? You didn't tell me this before."

He shrugged. "You're not the only one who can keep secrets."

I put my fingers on the window as the fields and houses of Drieden flashed by. How long had it been since I'd seen my native land? The last time I'd driven this route I was on my way out of the country, catching a plane to meet Stavros, tears streaming down my face.

"I don't have so many secrets," I sighed. "All I did was fail to give the world a change of address card after Stavros died." And a few other things. But really, in the grand scheme of things, my secrets were few. Ish.

When Hugh didn't reply, I turned to him. "But you found me. In Varenna. I wasn't such a good secret-keeper after all."

His face was still and serious. "I didn't find you."

"Right." I leaned back into the seat, closed my eyes, embarrassed again that I had inferred that Hugh had cared for me at all, or had bothered himself with a search for me. "That's right. You were just following Christian, who supposedly stumbled into my path."

Hugh's eyes flicked toward the soundproof glass between us and the driver then back at me. "I still don't feel like you are taking this seriously."

If he only knew.

Hugh's jaw flinched. "I tried to find you."

I felt frozen. "When?"

"A few weeks after the funeral, when no one had seen or heard from you."

"I don't understand . . ."

"Whatever accounts you set up, your holding corporations, they worked. I couldn't get through. I couldn't trace your steps."

A lovely liquid warmth started melting my ice. *He had looked for me.*

"So when I tell you again that Christian had the ability to find you and I did not, please get it into your head that this means that Christian Fraser-Campbell has the contacts and a network to uncover more than I, a member of the Driedish national police with the full authority of the Royal family, do."

My lovely warmth curdled in my stomach. "Oh."

"He has friends in high places. If he found you in Varenna, he can certainly find you at the Hotel Ilysium."

"Fine," I said dismissively, because wasn't that the whole point of me coming back here? To lure Christian in? To find who his friends in high places were? "If he finds me in my suite, it'll make it that much easier for you catch him. You could always stay with me." I smiled guilelessly. "Unless you don't think you're up for the job."

A glint of gold flashed in his eyes. "I think I could handle the challenge, my lady."

twenty-three

HUGH DISAPPEARED ALMOST AS SOON AS I HAD dropped my few belongings in my suite. The hotel was used to royal and celebrity visitors and I had forgotten that there was a central location where security personnel could monitor the comings and goings of their clients without being too intrusive in their rooms.

So that was how it was going to be, then. He was going to stay close enough to keep an eye on me but not close enough to hold a conversation or do anything else.

I still wasn't sure exactly what I wanted to do with the man. Hitting him and throwing him out of my life still seemed a viable option. But then I would remember the sparks we made on that burgundy couch in Switzerland and I would shiver.

Go.

Yeah.

Remember what happened last time.

I fell into a mad, passionate affair with Stavros, and that had ended in literal flames. No mere man could survive my reputation at this point. Hell, the best way for me to punish Christian would probably be to start a relationship with him. Right in public, where everyone could see. Then he would . . .

No, I'd learned my lesson. Any relationships from this point on would be strictly physical, with firm rules and guidelines. Nothing passionate. Certainly nothing public.

And . . . ?

I pushed the thought away as the hotel manager greeted me. He was glad to have another member of the royal family staying with them, he told me.

After I made a quick call to my former personal shopper in the city (I was getting tired of the same jeans and sweater) I made a call on the other relative on the top floor of the Hotel Ilysium.

"Hello, Mother."

She hadn't aged a day in the last fifteen years, thanks to the best surgeons and dermatologists in the world. Her blonde curls framed her face in an artfully youthful way, her clothes were feminine and sporty. My mother, Felice, the Duchess of Montaget, everyone.

She lit up. But she always lit up. "Indefatigably perky," a news reporter once called her. "Caroline! My angel!" She reached for me, pulled me into her thin embrace. "My doll, just look at you." Her fingers smushed my cheeks. "You've gained . . . no. Lost weight. No." She cocked her head. "Have you stayed the same? After all the soap opera of the past year?" She tutted. "To stay in such control, in the face of heartache and drama! Oh, don't tell me, are you your father's daughter after all?" Her laugh tinkled through the air like the chinking of champagne flutes. The idea clearly seemed ridiculous, that I might exhibit characteristics of my paternal DNA, rather than my maternal genes.

"How are you, Mother?" I asked, partially to distract her, partially because I truly wanted to know. We hadn't seen each other since Thea's aborted wedding weekend and we all knew how insane that had been, trying to put the right faces on in the middle of a royal crisis.

Felice rolled her eyes. "Wonderful, naturally. Everything is simply divine. I was at the Beyoncé concert in The Hague last week."

"You were?" I asked politely, even though *of course she was.*

Her fingers brushed my arm. "Backstage with old Tommy. You know what fun that can be."

I had no idea who old Tommy was.

"And then the afterparty." Her tinkling laugh again. "You'll never guess who we ran into."

"Beyoncé?" I asked.

"No."

"Elton John?"

"My God, no. Caroline, do be serious. Why on earth would I tell you a story about Sir Elton in the Hague?"

Right. Silly, silly me. "Who did you run into?" I asked patiently.

"Henry!" She half screamed with delight. "Didn't you know?" I shook my head. I hadn't spoken to my twin brother since my elopement, either. He had offered to fly to Monaco and walk me down the aisle. I declined because I hadn't wanted him to also incur the wrath of our Queen. One of us was enough.

Felice continued, "Oh my, I had never felt so old. My own son, at the Beyoncé afterparty, with a pretty little thing on his arm. A barely dressed American actress, I believe, but is there any other kind? I swear, they're crossing the Atlantic in droves, all of them, hunting for a prince to marry. He looked dashing, of course, my sweet boy, and no one could *believe* I was his mother." She lifted a self-conscious hand to her right cheek, as if testing its youthful elasticity.

"And now here we are," she said as she grabbed my hands again. "Both shacked up in the Ilysium, royal outcasts like us. Two single, gorgeous women who know a thing or two, wouldn't you say?"

"I don't know about that . . ." I murmured. Outcast? Check. Single? Check. Gorgeous? I held my own, that was for sure. But a woman who knew a thing or two? I was currently feeling quite hopeless in that arena.

"Champagne!" my mother exclaimed as she picked up a leatherbound folder from the nearby desk and extracted the room service menu. "Why don't we have champagne? Darling, where is that assistant of yours? We must have champagne and something else . . . what decadence are you craving for our reunion?"

"I'm fine, really. And I don't have an assistant."

Felice's head snapped my way. "Caroline, what happened? Did she try to steal your jewelry?"

"I don't . . ." My voice gave out. It was exhausting—no, *she* was exhausting. "I haven't had one since before . . . I married Stavros."

"Oh God." The room service menu fluttered to the floor, as elegant and dramatic as my exhaustingly sophisticated mother. "My dove! I had forgotten you were still mourning your husband." She placed a hand to her breast. I counted an at least five-carat gemstone twinkling on every finger. "Your poor, sweet broken heart. Oh, how I understood you. It was truly inspiring to see how you disappeared, only to re-emerge when you were ready to take on the world again. Like a gilded rainbow butterfly." She nodded wisely. "I did the same thing after I left your father."

"You ran off with your horse trainer, Mother."

"Exactly. I needed to find myself. Rediscover who I was as a woman, if you know what I mean."

I bit my lip and looked up at the ceiling. It was at times like this that I felt a bit more religious than usual, praying for intercession or a timely strike of lightning to save me from further parental awkwardness.

"But you have it so much better," Felice assured me. "You're still young, you'll be able to start over, unfettered by children."

Ouch. Either Mother noticed the look on my face or realized the carelessness of her words. "I didn't mean——"

"I know you didn't," I said quickly, before she stuck her foot any deeper in her mouth. "It's fine. I mean, the children, they weren't meant to be."

"Caroline."

I recognized that tone. My mother might play the part of aristocratic showgirl to perfection, but she was quite capable of being solemn and businesslike if she wanted. "Are you quite all right? Medically speaking?"

Felice looked serious, which was really saying something. "I had a few . . . complications after you and Henry were born." She let out a small, bitter laugh. "Consider yourself lucky. When you're bearing possible future heirs to the throne, they examine every square inch of you to determine if you're fit to bear another child. Ridiculous. Like they think they own your uterus."

The idea of it made me sad for my mother. No woman should be treated like a broodmare. "But you had Sophie," I pointed out, and I couldn't help but smile at the thought of how adorable my little red-headed sister had been as a child.

"Yes. Sophia. My baby. My little miracle." My mother lit up again, as bright as the fireworks on Queen Elsa-Marie's birthday night. Whatever her faults as a mother, I had never doubted that she adored all of us. Maybe she hadn't wanted to be faithful to our father, maybe she hadn't wanted to attend school functions and spend week nights with us, but she loved us in her quintessential Felice way.

She reached down for the room service menu. "Now. Champagne. Two bottles, I think, because I have so much to tell you about. Old Tommy had the most interesting gossip about a certain Singaporean country club and one so-called Manhattan billionaire—you'll die when you hear it."

*

I RETURNED TO MY SUITE SEVERAL HOURS LATER, exhausted but also, somehow, rejuvenated. Being around my mother had that strange effect on me, as I could see the parts of her that I wanted to emulate . . . and the parts that I wanted to ensure I never did.

The lights came on automatically, at a low level, which was a nice touch at a hotel of this caliber. Therefore, I wasn't completely terrified when I saw a woman sitting in the middle of my king-sized bed.

She looked at her watch. "Where have you been?" my elder sister asked.

I looked around for something to throw. "I am getting really sick of people letting themselves into my rooms!"

"Who else comes into your rooms?" Thea asked, understandably concerned.

I sighed loudly, also understandably. "*How* did you get in here? Five-star hotel penthouses should be difficult to get access to," I grumbled.

Thea gave me an arch look. "I'm Princess Theodora. You're family." She shrugged, as if it was a foregone conclusion.

Of course. "Here in Drieden City you can probably leave and enter every building at your whim. You have a whole country at your disposal," I said, only slightly sarcastically. This was the twenty-first century. Princesses didn't automatically get *everything* they wanted, after all.

I was proof of that.

"Where were you?" Thea asked again.

I decided that I might as well tell her. Or else she'd dangle a hundred euros at a hotel clerk to have him access security footage for her. "I was in Mother's room."

I'm not going to lie, it felt good to tell Thea something that she didn't know. "*Mother is here? Our mother? The Felice?*"

"Her Grace Felice Sevine-Laurent, the Duchess of Montaget and formerly Her Royal Highness Princess Felice," I replied, letting all those titles and noble names roll off my tongue as easily as a strand of pearls slipping through my fingers.

Thea still looked alarmed. "Why is she here?"

Now I shrugged. "You're the royal with unlimited access to information. Why don't you tell me?"

She slipped a very modern-looking cellphone out of the pocket of her trousers and looked at it thoughtfully before putting it back. "I came here to talk to you," she said bluntly. "I'll deal with Mother later."

"You came down from the palace to talk to a commoner in a hotel room?" I feigned an expression of shock. "You do remember your position, right? A princess does not go to the people, the people go to you."

Thea's shoulders sagged and she looked at me as if she'd had about enough of my attitude. "Is that what this is all about? Your title?"

"My what? No!" I objected automatically but couldn't help but notice the unease that had crept into my stomach. It was the same feeling I had experienced at Grandmama's convent in Switzerland. I was inexplicably angry at Thea. I was inexplicably uncomfortable with her, as well.

She swung her legs off the side of the bed and stood, hands on her hips. "You can have it back. I'll make you a princess again."

"Ha!" The nerve of her! "*You?* You're not Queen yet, Thea." I held up my hands. "Oh, sorry. Your Royal Highness. No, I took all the same regal lessons as you, and I certainly remember that you've got a queen and a crown prince to go through before you have the power to reinstate my titles again." The spiky prickles of anger rose up my spine, across my shoulders. Anger that came out of nowhere.

Right?

"You're mad at me," Thea said.

"No." *LIAR*.

"You should be mad," she said evenly. "You were treated horribly."

"It's fine." *LIAR*.

"Gran shouldn't have disowned you. You were just trying to find happiness." She stopped, stilted; tears shone in her eyes. "I wanted you to find that. Even if it meant that you left all of this—all of us— behind." She shook her head. "It's all so fucking sick and stupid. But please, Caroline, you were happy, right?"

I paused. "Yes." Mostly. But I would never admit to being otherwise. Because then, what was it all for?

Thea must have suspected the truth. Because while she smiled slightly, a polite princess smile, her eyes stayed sad and cautious. A bubble of silence grew between us until she finally pricked it like the well-mannered royal she was.

"A lot has happened since my wedding day." She seemed to pick her words as carefully as plucking a needle through a piece of linen. "There's a lot that you probably need to know."

"I don't want to know," I said automatically, raising my hands. "And technically, I'm not even part of the family anymore. Perhaps I don't have the clearance to know."

Thea gave me an oh-please look. "You'll always be part of the family."

"Not according to Big Gran," I couldn't help but point out. "You can minimize it all you want, but we both know that my lack of a title remains a Big Fucking Deal."

"That's part of what we need to talk about. A lot of things that were a BFD are not anymore. A lot has changed in the past year. For me, for Big Gran . . . and I suspect for you, too."

"What does that mean?" I asked, alarmed at what she might suspect. There was no way she could know what I was planning . . . was there?

She nodded a little at something behind me then met my eyes with a gotcha sisterly stare. I knew what the issue was before I turned around.

I just didn't expect Hugh to be dangling my hotel room key from his finger quite so distractingly.

But she recovered with the grace that only a princess could demonstrate. "Good. Now I can invite you both."

"Where?"

"To Perpetua."

twenty-four

PERPETUA? I SHIVERED. "WHY IN THE WORLD WOULD you have to go back there? Did you do something wrong?"

Thea gave me a quizzical smile. "Sort of. Maybe."

"That doesn't make sense."

"Come with me," she said suddenly, clutching my hand. "We have so much to catch up on. And there's someone I'd like you to meet."

"On Perpetua? The drafty royal residence on an island in the North Sea that we're only sent to when Big Gran wants to get us away from civilized society?"

Thea nodded.

"Anyone you want me to meet on Perpetua is probably a hundred years old or the biggest son of a bitch Drieden has ever seen."

"You're half right," she said, with another mysterious smile.

AS THE HELICOPTER LANDED ON THE ISLAND, I COULD tell there had been recent activity on the grounds. The lawn looked a tad less windswept and barren and perhaps a coat of paint had been applied. It was hard to say for sure when everything was a bleak granite color, even the sky. And the water. And the freezing sheet of rain that pelted us as we ran toward the door.

When we were inside the old building, I shivered and pulled my down jacket around me. It had been cold in Drieden City—it was February, so of course it was cold. But here, with no trees or wind breaks or sunshine, it was devastatingly frigid.

"Wasn't this a convent as well?" I asked, trying to remember the history of the place as I followed Thea through the corridors. "Like Grandmama's?"

Thea laughed. It bounced in between the walls but if I wasn't mistaken, she also seemed . . . happier? Lighter? Here on this rock? Strange. "Yes, now that I think about it. So many convents around Europe, hundreds of years ago. All built in order to give women some meaning to their life."

"And to lock them away, control their sexuality and force them into unpaid labor for the rest of their lives."

Thea paused and gave me a wry look over her shoulder. "That hits a bit close to home, mmm?"

Mmph, was the best response I could come up with. I had never drawn those connections before, between modern palaces and medieval cloisters, but Thea was right. It was a bit close to home. Too close.

"Anyway, welcome to Perpetua," she said sunnily as she punched a code into a security box by a reinforced steel door. "The new and improved twenty-first-century version." The door swung open and we stepped into what seemed like a large glass box. Sleek aluminum bars and ancient weathered beams framed skylights and a panoramic view of the dark, cold ocean. But what had just minutes before seemed gloomy and threatening from the helicopter now seemed exciting and mysterious. The clouds of anthracite and silver swirled, blanketing inky, restless waves. In the far distance one could just make out the skeletal silhouettes of oil platforms and ships skating across the horizon.

Once I tore my eyes away from the spectacular oceanscape I started noticing that things were, indeed, very different from the last time I had been sentenced to Perpetua. Several people sat around at desks, quietly doing . . . desk-type things on computers. What they would be doing here, I had no idea. Two men with more military bearing stood in a corner. One was the blond buzz-cut type I regularly associated with Driedish police or military, but the other man was dark and scowling, with a face that looked like it had gone a round or two in a dark alley filled with pissed-off wolverines. And I didn't doubt that this man had left them all in his dust.

He looked up, over at us, and his posture subtly changed. His shoulders went back, his chin lowered in acknowledgment of my sister. And my sister . . . oh. Wow.

She absolutely transformed. More than lighting up, she seemed to blossom with a sensuous, powerful energy that made me want to look away.

Because ew. That was my sister.

And that man was clearly her lover.

The man murmured something to the officer he was talking to and quickly made his way over to us. They didn't touch. They didn't need to. Even I could feel the magnet that drew them together, something stronger than any brush of skin or mere handshake.

"Caroline, I'm pleased to introduce you to Nicholas," Thea said.

"So proper," he said, with an accent that I didn't immediately place, but it made Thea blush.

"Nick," she amended. "And Nick, this is my sister, Caroline."

"Pleased to meet you, Caroline. Thea speaks of you often." He extended a hand to me and of course I shook it, even as my latent princess brain was noting the lack of formality in this exchange. There was no "Your Highness." He didn't even bow his head—at me or my sister. And he called her Thea, something that only her closest friends and family did.

And then, only after my brain had finished categorizing all the evidence that this man was clearly intimate with my sister, did I realize something else vitally important.

"You're Scottish?"

"I am," Nick answered shortly, but there was a very slight wary energy that popped up in both his and Thea's expressions.

"Interesting," I said. "Seems like your compatriots are taking over the world. Everywhere I go, I run into a Scotsman."

Thea and Nick now exchanged a meaning-filled glance. "I haven't told her," Thea replied to his unsaid question.

"Would you like me to?" Nick asked.

"Tell me what?" I let out a half-laugh. "This sounds so dire. Are we at war with Scotland suddenly?" It was a joke, but neither Thea nor Nick laughed along with me.

"War is a very interesting way of putting it," came a familiar voice behind me.

I jumped, spun and snapped at Hugh, *"Would you stop sneaking up on me?"*

THEA, EVER THE PROPER ONE, WAS THE ONE WHO SUG-gested we retire to a conference room, which seemed like it had been decorated by newly-weds, each intent on bringing their own hobbies and interests to their first home.

A framed football poster squared off with a signed treaty from some Driedish war (a reproduction, possibly, or not, knowing the way my sister could sweet-talk the old timers at the national archives).

Black leather couches were in a circle around a flatscreen TV at one end of the room and a mahogany dining table surrounded by six Lucite chairs was at the other end.

But it wasn't the decor that surprised me, it was that, once again, none of this had been on Perpetua the last time I'd been here.

"What is going on here?" I asked Thea, aware that she'd not only allowed Hugh and this Nick person to enter the room with us but that they seemed completely at home here.

"I don't know where to start." She frowned at a small pad of paper on the table. Moved it three inches. "You heard about Christian's suicide."

Hugh met my eyes across the room. His brows lifted in a silent question. Somehow, I knew what he was thinking. *Time to tell your sister about Christian?*

"Yes," I told Thea. "I was devastated to hear the news."

Nick coughed, a dry, harmless sound, but by the way Thea looked at him I suddenly felt like the two of them also had their own secret language. Hugh looking at me. Me looking at him. Thea and Nick practically blinking in Morse code . . .

"This is ridiculous," I broke out. "We're in some sort of secure room, I think we can all stop speaking in code and say what needs to be said."

Nick barked a laugh and Thea broke into a relieved smile. "There you are. My blunt sister. Always trying to fix things for people."

"You think I'm blunt?"

"Straightforward," Hugh interjected. Thea turned and gave him an appraising glance.

"Exactly so, Hugh."

"Well, let's be straightforward, then," I said, wondering whether being blunt, or straightforward, was a character asset or defect. I turned to Nick. "Who are you, and what are you to my sister?"

Nick's warm eyes didn't seek out my sister's this time. "My name is Nicholas Fraser-Campbell. And I'm the man who's devoted to your sister."

At that declaration, my heart melted like a chocolate ice cream on a July afternoon. And then I realized . . . "Your name. You aren't . . ."

Nick's lip curled. "Yes. He's my younger brother."

"Your—" I broke off as I considered all the consequences. "Well, that will make it awkward at your next wedding."

This time it was Hugh who laughed inappropriately, while Thea and Nick had the grace to blush and stammer. "I guess you two haven't quite made it that far," I said, trying to salvage the moment.

"I suppose from that statement that you know that Christian isn't dead?" Thea asked delicately.

"She knows," Hugh said. "Because he showed up on her doorstep. In Varenna."

"The fuck?" Nick growled, taking a step forward—to where, I had no idea. Thea put a hand on his arm.

"Why didn't you immediately let me know?" she asked Hugh.

He crossed his arms. "I was busy."

"Since you don't have him on a rope behind you, I guess you couldn't get your hands on him."

Hugh let Nick's insinuations roll off without a reaction.

"It was because of me," I said. "Hugh didn't capture Christian because of me."

Hugh's head was already shaking vehemently. "No—"

But my sister had already turned her attention to me. "Did he hurt you? What happened?" She had her hands on my shoulders, her eyes roaming over me, looking for some kind of injury.

"I'm fine. It's my house that got firebombed."

Thea gasped. "My God. Before or after Hugh was shot?"

"What the hell happened in Italy?" Nick asked.

"It's a long story," I began. "But I had the most perfect view of Lake Como from my veranda."

THE STORY STARTED AND ENDED WITH A SCOTSMAN.

"What about this Sergei fellow?"

Nick looked over at Hugh. "Have we checked with the local authorities? Did they pick him up when they were alerted to the fire at the villa?"

This was new. I hadn't even thought about whether Sergei was in custody somewhere in a small Tuscan village.

Hugh shook his head. "They didn't find him. Either he slipped my knots or he got out with help."

"Maybe it was Christian," I said. "Maybe he'd been close all along."

Thea frowned at me. "What makes you think that?"

I fumbled. I hadn't told anyone about the cellphone Sergei had given me, and I certainly didn't plan to. Not yet.

"His emails. I'll give them to you. He made it sound like he was going to meet us at Mother's house."

Thea looked at Nick then. "We should talk to Sybil about the Italian police records."

Oh, no. "Sybil?" I asked warily. "Not . . . *our* Sybil?"

Hugh frowned, and Nick looked amused. "Let me guess. You have a complicated relationship with the fortune teller."

"She's not—" Thea started to say, but I interrupted her.

As a matter of fact, I had a very complicated relationship with the psychic/tarot reader who used to serve all of the ladies in the court, but I didn't want to get into those details right now. Besides, it was ancient history. And private. But still I had to make sure. "That Sybil?

She's here?" My voice raised. "What the hell kind of place are you running here, Thea?"

"She knows more about this country than anyone," Thea informed me. I noticed that she sidestepped answering my question directly. "And she, like everyone else, is a valuable part of this team. Right?"

"Fine," Nick said reluctantly.

"Sure." Hugh grunted.

"See? Everyone is going to work together," Thea said pointedly to the men. She picked up a phone on the conference table, punched a few keys and gave an order to someone. After she had hung up, she told Hugh and Nick that they were expected in the lab. "They have the Italian inspector's number as well. You'll be able to speak with him directly."

Nick nodded, and his hand and Thea's brushed as he walked to the door. Hugh stopped and spoke to me before he left. "You're okay here?" he asked me.

"For heaven's sake," Thea sighed. "She's with me. Behind a security system you designed. On an island!"

Hugh didn't respond, but the heat behind his hazel eyes made me think that there was nowhere that I would be safe from him.

twenty-five

ONE OF THEA'S UPGRADES TO THE FACILITIES ON Perpetua had been a steam room, powered by the thermal springs that bubbled up in a cavern under the island.

We were sitting there, enjoying the heat and smell of menthol and eucalyptus, as she described how she had discovered the cavern. "I found it when I was running on the beach. The tide was low, and there was this opening between the rocks. It's really amazing down there. A hundred feet high, all carved-out rock and mineral water."

I blotted my face with a cool towel that smelled of peppermint and faced my older sister. "Thea, that's fascinating, but what the actual fuck is going on here?" I asked in the most reasonable tone I could muster.

"What do you mean?" She tried to avoid my eyes, but I knew her better than almost anyone.

"The upgrades to the island, the fact that you and Nick seem to live here at least half of the time, and that the dining room feels like a mess hall and you're talking about police and technology like you're running Interpol from your bedroom."

She bowed her head and took a moment. Finally, she spoke with confidence. "I'm going to be Queen."

"Oh, okay. Is this a newsflash to you?" After all, she was the eldest child of the eldest child of the Queen. This wasn't exactly a complicated math problem.

"This year, I'll be Queen," she replied.

Now that did throw me. "What do you mean? This year? Is Gran sick?" Of course, my brain immediately jumped to the death of my grandmother. That's how sick this monarchy business could make you. One only gets a promotion if someone dies. It's like something out of a dystopian young-adult novel.

"No," she reassured me. "And it's quite a long story but, due to some political pressures, Gran has decided to step down and name me the heir."

"Skipping Father?" Our sweet but absent father was never cut out to be king. But that didn't mean he wanted to be ignored, I didn't think.

"It's for the best."

Her confidence in that fact was surprising. Not that Thea was an unconfident person. She was a self-assured, intelligent woman. But she also took the monarchy very seriously, always had. Perhaps long stories and political pressures had convinced her the line of succession needed to be altered, but I didn't need to be convinced. After all, I wasn't a part of the family anymore, which is what I said, in the most factual and diplomatic of ways. That she could assure me so resolutely that a sudden shift in monarch was in the best interests of the country said a lot about whatever "political pressures" our country had faced in the last year.

Political pressures that were so intense no whiff of them made the newspapers that I regularly reviewed.

Obviously, something had gone down behind the scenes, which pushed all my native curiosity buttons. My fingers actually moved, like they wanted to type. I wanted to know, but Thea wasn't being forthcoming.

Just like me.

"And do the rest of our family know about your imminent rise to the throne?" I asked lightly, as if the answer didn't matter to me.

As if the answer wouldn't hurt when I found out that I was the only person in the family who hadn't been told this important news.

Thea shook her head, though. "Gran and I will make the announcement soon—to family first, then the government. It's perfect, actually," she said, brightening. "Now that you're back. We'll all be together again, a united family."

A mix of emotions rumbled through me. A selfish pleasure that I knew this secret before my brother and sister. A concern for my father. And yes, that dingy, damp hurt from being excluded from the family in the first place.

"I'm not sure 'united' is quite the word to use," I said, as diplomatically as possible, referencing my removal from the family line of succession.

But apparently, not diplomatically enough. Thea made a noise of frustration and reached down for her own cool towel. "It's unacceptable," she declared, sounding pretty queenly already. "I'll have you know that I intend to find a way to undo Gran's disinheritance of you as soon as I am crowned."

Hearing those words made me uncomfortable, like I'd eaten a bad bowl of mussels. "It's fine. I knew the consequences when I ran off to Monaco with Stavros."

"One should never have to choose between family and love," Thea said vehemently. "This is the twenty-first century. Love is love is love is love."

I had never heard my sister defend love so vigorously. Even when she was engaged to Christian, she mostly spoke of duty and lineage and "making good choices."

"This doesn't have anything to do with a certain battle-scarred and grumpy almost-brother-in-law, does it?"

"Hugh?"

I coughed. "No. Nick!"

Even through the steam I could see her resolute expression. "I won't give him up. Even when I'm Queen. People will just have to get used to the way I lead my life. And you, as well."

"What do I have to do with you and Nick?"

She gave me an enigmatic smile. "You'll be another new type of royal the country will have to become accustomed to."

"A new type of royal?" I echoed. "A disgraced former royal living in exile, you mean? I'm sure we've had a few of those in Drieden before."

This being Thea, and given her love of history, I was mostly expecting her to pick up that line of thought by expounding on various members of the family tree who had, indeed, been disgraced and exiled to Italy or Ireland or India.

But no. She went in a different direction. "You, my darling Caroline, will be the undisgraced, re-titled royal, picking up exactly where you left off—and where you belong."

There was the curdled mussel stew stirring in my stomach again. Hearing her say these words should have empowered me, delighted me. At the very least, I should have felt vindication.

"I don't think we can do that," I said instead. "I'm not an ingénue."

"Boring!"

"There will be so much gossip about Stavros, about his death and where I've been."

"So?"

"So, you'll be a new queen, with all the politics and pressures that will entail. You don't need to kick off your reign with something controversial and lurid headlines in all the tabloids."

"The people will be behind me," Thea said confidently, and when

Thea spoke like this, who could argue with her? "Especially if we get started now."

Oh, no. That didn't sound good. "We?" I echoed. "Pray tell, what do *we* need to start?"

"You're back in Drieden and I need help with some things."

"Thea, I don't think—"

She cut me off with a hand. "We'll start with something small, something discreet. Nothing official, just you behind the scenes, doing important work on my behalf with my blessing."

Her cheeks were rosy, her eyes bright. She loved me enough to brave the wrath of our grandmother and the machinery of the national press. How could I say no to her?

I sighed. "Fine. We can try something behind the scenes. Something short-term. Temporary."

But I could tell from her expression that wasn't good enough. She wanted something more.

"Was there something else?" I asked, dreading whatever she was about to suggest.

"You know I love you."

"And?"

"I'm only saying this because I'm your sister."

"Okay . . ."

"And I know how irritated I would be if someone said this to me—"

"Spit it out!"

She grimaced. "Your hair. It's horrible."

I started to giggle. She joined me.

It was like we were girls again. If only it could stay like that forever.

twenty-six

WITH A NAME LIKE KARL SYLVAIN VON FALKEN-burg, I didn't know what to expect. Knowing he was supposedly a billionaire didn't help either. In my experience, billionaires were extremely underwhelming people. They often drove very old cars, had terrible taste in pleated pants and were quite dreary conversation partners at dinner parties.

I couldn't quite place the nationality of this Herr? Monsieur? Mr.? von Falkenburg. On first blush it seemed that he was probably one of those trans-Euro new-money mutts, but the von Falkenburg name was also a very old aristocratic one. Or at least, it probably was. I wasn't an expert in the genealogies of Europe, like my Aunt Beatrice.

But Thea had asked me to take this meeting with the biotech billionaire whom she had met in Davos at their panel on science and engineering education, and as it was supposed to be private, I didn't mind. Too much.

During the hair appointment with Thea's personal stylist, who had come straight to my hotel suite (it was divine; thanks, sis!), I reviewed what material I could find on Mr. Karl Sylvain von Falkenburg. According to several magazine articles online, he had inherited

a smaller set of corporations and turned them into a vast conglomer-
ate that had its fingers in every facet of health technology available.

Thea told me she wanted to see where there were opportunities
for partnership in education projects or research initiatives. I was no
expert in these areas, but I felt reasonably confident in my abilities to
ask and take notes. No one expected more of me, anyway.

Through a series of assistants and phone calls, Karl was scheduled to
meet me in my suite, in the breakfast nook. Both this and the adjoining
bedroom faced the north of the city and had a particularly lovely view of
the Comtesse, the major river that sliced through Drieden City and connected the fertile plains to the North Sea. Today was a dreary February
Driedish day and I grew a bit homesick, thinking of my picturesque
Lake Como view, which led me to wonder where Elena and Signore
Rossi were.

Whether they were safe from Christian Fraser-Campbell.

Whether I had done the right thing by coming back to Drieden.

Whether I should return to my original plan of completely opting
out of royal life.

Whether I should even speak to this von Falkenburg person.

But the door opened and it was too late for any second-guessing.

Hugh, who had emerged from his closet when he heard I had an
appointment, showed him in and Mr. von Falkenburg was . . . nothing like I would have ever expected.

He was tall. Extremely tall. Taller than one expects from a vaguely
aristocratic European of undefined nationality.

Younger than a billionaire had any right to be.

And . . . well, I'm not blind. Dead sexier than the name Karl Sylvain von Falkenburg suggested. If this was a movie, he would have
been named "Thor" or "Blade" or another one-syllable word that
evoked dangerous masculinity.

His head shot down instantly, a sign of extremely good manners,
no matter how rich or how entitled one was. "Lady Caroline." It was

a permissible—and politic—form of address. It showed the man had done some homework. To call me "princess" was likely to offend. To call me Mrs. DiBernardo was also risky. Lady Caroline straddled the lines, as it were.

I envied people who found a middle ground so easily.

"Mr. von Falkenburg. Thank you for meeting me. My sister sends her apologies. An urgent matter has prevented her from being here."

"It is my pleasure. To get to meet not one but two of the Laurent sisters in one month is something that has all the eligible men in Europe seething with jealousy."

His flattery was delivered with such a friendly, frank manner that I liked him instantly. Those words could have been too flirty or too oily but, once again, I had the distinct feeling that von Falkenburg strived to be just right.

Like me.

"Would you like something to drink?" I asked. "Some tea or coffee?"

He declined, as I suspected he would, and I asked him to tell me more about the subject matter that he and Thea had discussed in Davos. Twenty minutes later, I knew more about the low availability of women graduates with STEM university courses than I ever thought I would.

It was fascinating. More importantly, it was something that I could change. *If* I returned to Drieden permanently and worked with my sister on projects like this.

Which I wasn't. *Was I?*

"Can I tell you something? Something I don't tell every princess I meet?"

That made me laugh, even though I was sure that a man who ran in his circles had ample opportunities to meet princesses. There were more of us than people usually thought.

"I think we could be very good friends, Caroline Laurent."

That threw me for a moment. I replied honestly, though. "Friends. Princesses don't have many friends. Let alone good friends, Karl von Falkenburg."

"I would like to invite you on an outing." He stood, checking his watch—it was a very expensive watch, I noticed, but then again, Karl Sylvain von Falkenburg was a billionaire. "Would you be available tomorrow evening?"

Wait. "An outing?" I had to ask. "Is that like a date?"

Karl smiled charmingly. "If you wish. We could also call it a field trip. An excursion. A business meeting in an alternative location."

He must have sensed that I was about to turn him down. "I apologize. I was under the impression that you had a bit more freedom than your sisters."

Freedom. It was precisely the only thing I had that my sisters did not. Why not enjoy that? Exercise the privileges that came with my non-nobility?

I lifted my chin, letting any shame or embarrassment drop off my shoulders to the floor, like a sodden coat. "I would quite enjoy an outing with you."

"Excellent."

"But we must go today." *Before anyone tells me no.*

I HALFWAY EXPECTED KARL TO SAY NO. AFTER ALL, HE was a busy man. Billionaires didn't become billionaires by taking afternoons off to escort princesses around the city.

But if he had any scheduling conflicts, he was too much of a gentleman—too sincere a new friend—to let me know. In five minutes, we had ridden down in the elevators to the underground parking garage and were in the back seat of a large black Mercedes SUV with the windows tinted darker than midnight.

My pulse raced. This was not what I had expected when I woke up this morning. Eaten my eggs and toast, read my newspapers, dutifully dressed in a new businessy outfit of pants and blouse and a Hermès scarf that I had borrowed from Mother's suite.

"Are you cold?" Karl asked as he reached to adjust the seat warmers. Such a gentleman.

We talked of simple things: the weather in Drieden, his house on the coast of Spain, how he planned to travel to London next month to see his friend Harry from Eton. He'd grown up there, in England. His mother's family was English and, to prove it, he switched back into a flawless English accent, which amused me.

Before I knew it, we were on the western outskirts of the city, a suburb that had once been a village and, before that, a wilderness on the edge of the marshland. "Where are you taking me?" I asked, and for the first time I wondered if perhaps I had jumped into this so-called outing a tad too quickly with a man I had just met.

The SUV pulled into a commercial district—a high street, Karl's English side would call it—and then we pulled up to a city park next to a grocery store.

"Here we are," the driver said.

Karl looked excited to show me what I saw now was a construction site in the park. "What is this place?"

"The Battlefield of Langůs," Karl said, as if I should know what he meant.

"You have the wrong sister," I told Karl. "Once again, I apologize that she's not here to geek out with you about . . . that." I waved at the construction in the park and the grocery store car park, which seemed to have been torn up with jackhammers, and a nearby temporary building.

"The Battle of Langůs was the definitive battle that gave your ancestor—I believe it was Fredrik II—the Driedish crown. Didn't you have to study this in your special school for princesses?"

It was, in fact, all coming back to me, if a bit slowly. Like I always said, I was not the historian in the family.

"Let's get out and look," Karl said. "You'll see the important bit next."

We left the warm confines of the SUV, and the wet Driedish winter wind whipped through my bones. I had not put on a decent coat when we'd swept directly from the Hotel Ilysium's underground parking garage into the waiting car. It was perhaps naive of me, but I had not expected an "outing" with Karl would entail being, well, out in the weather.

Once again, he was attentive, and noticed my shivers as we walked closer to the dirt piles between the park and the store. He offered me his jacket, which I accepted, and wrapped an arm around my shoulders. I had just met him, and this would have been extremely forward coming from anyone else . . . if I were still a princess. But I wasn't. So I had the freedom to accept this man's gift of warmth and chivalry.

What I had immediately thought was a construction site I saw now was more an excavation. Flags and ropes and other markers circled the entire area in intricate patterns that would require a key to understand. Then, in a flash, I remembered that I did know something else about this place.

"I read about this. In the newspapers. They were building a monument for my grandmother's Jubilee and they found an archeological site." I looked at Karl. "Is this it? They were building it here, at the Langûs battlefield?"

He nodded enthusiastically, clearly someone who enjoyed his Driedish history. "I believe it was to celebrate not only your grandmother's reign but the uninterrupted bloodline. Five hundred years since old man Fredrik died there." He pointed at the park, which had presumably been dedicated to the ancient battle. "But they found this when they were digging for the sewer." His finger pointed at the excavation site.

It was so very cold and windy, so that was one reason why I was starting to lose interest. I thought of the blissful heated seats in the car and the privacy that those dark windows afforded . . . and I had an idea.

But I needed to get back to the car first. "It's so very inconvenient, I suppose," I said, as I observed the piles of dirt and rock that looked like they had been carefully separated through a sieve. What an awful job, I thought. Sorting pebbles during a Driedish winter. "And this is your . . . hobby?" I finished, not finding a better word to call his interest in history. "Do you go to many battlefields?" I had heard of men who dressed up and re-enacted key historical military turning points. Perhaps that's what billionaires did in their spare time (which only reinforced my opinion of the vast majority of billionaires, to be honest.)

"No . . . not my hobby." Karl looked intently down at me. "My business."

"You're in construction?" That made sense. Men also often took a surprising amount of interest in big trucks and tall cranes.

He shook his head. "One of my companies is a genetic testing enterprise. We're bidding on the bones that were found down there."

I remembered the news articles about the discovery of my ancestor there and grimaced at the hole in the ground he was pointing to. "Who would be interested in a pile of dusty, dried bones?"

"Only every genetic lab in Europe. And them, of course." He nodded toward the temporary trailer parked next to the site and the group of people coming out of it. Half of them carried recording equipment—I could spot a boom mic and a camera a mile away. One of them was the journalist Chantal Louis.

"Why are they here?" I asked as a strong tremble made my legs and spine shake. It wasn't just the cold, I knew. I was caught. In the open. In the daylight. The prey in front of the predators.

Karl chuckled. "I think the press is interested in any royal story these days, Even the almost forgotten ones." He looked across the pit. Smiled politely. Said blandly, "Oh, they're looking over here. Do you think they'll take our photograph?"

And that was how the press caught me. The last time they saw me I was standing in a mourning veil at Stavros's graveside. This time, I was standing at another grave with one of Europe's most eligible bachelors by my side.

twenty-seven

LIKE A CORNERED MOUSE IN THE MIDDLE OF THE night, I turned my head into Karl's shoulder. A natural, understandable impulse.

Go.

The next impulse. To run from the cameras. Give them the chase they wanted.

It was what Stavros would have done, grabbing my hand, or my head, forcing it down under a coat.

Thrilling. Awful.

My heart started to race, anticipating the adrenaline rush. But then I realized, this was not as awful as it seemed.

I whispered Karl's name. "Do you mind terribly if I go back to the car?" I smiled a little, hating that it would be analyzed and discussed all over the internet shortly. "That will give you a little more time to look around without all the fuss."

Karl glanced at the photographers, massing at the side of his beloved dirt pile, and promptly said, "Whatever makes you comfortable. I won't be long."

"Take as long as you need," I murmured.

The back seat was warm and as private as I was going to get these days. I wasted no time, reaching into my handbag and taking out the cellphone that Sergei had given me in Tuscany. Miraculously, it still had a good battery charge. I hit a button and returned a call.

Ring.

Ring.

Ring.

"Hello."

Scottish-accented English.

"This is Caroline. How are you feeling?"

"Much better, thank you."

I kept an eye out of the car window. Karl was walking around the archeological site and heading toward Chantal Louis. Free publicity. I hoped he appreciated my gift.

"I've been worried about you," I told Christian.

"You've always been so kind to me," he said.

"I'm in Drieden now," I explained.

"I know."

I shivered, despite the heated seats. "About your proposition . . ."

"You're still considering it?"

"Of course. It's the story of the century and I need a gig."

He chuckled. "Don't we all."

"How are we going to do this?" It was an aggressive tactic, but intuitively I felt that Christian would appreciate that. One disgraced person to another. "I'll need to interview you thoroughly."

"You can do it now. Over the phone."

Astrid and I had discussed this. "No," I replied easily. "No newspaper or magazine will take a print interview like this without photo proof that you're alive. They'll consider it a hoax. If you really want Clémence Diederich to broadcast your story, you'll have to meet with me and we'll take a photo." I drew a deep breath. "Together."

That kind of publicity would be irresistible. At least, that's what Astrid and I were counting on.

"I'm talking to other reporters, you know."

"I doubt that anyone is taking you seriously. You're dead, Christian. And if you want anyone to believe otherwise, you need a reputable journalist and photographic evidence."

There was a long pause. I saw Karl had finished his conversation with the bunch of reporters and was walking back toward the car. My phone call would have to wrap up soon.

"You really want this?" Christian said, with a hefty dose of suspicion in his voice.

"I don't have a life anymore. What else do I have to look forward to?" I asked.

"Meetings with billionaires?" he suggested. I gasped. How did he know? "I won't be double-crossed," he warned. "Remember, I can send proof of your columns about Thea and Felice and Albert out at any time. Your family does not handle betrayal well. You'll be back out on the street if they find out what you've done."

My gut twisted at the truth of his words and a wash of doubt poured over me. What was I doing, consorting with the enemy this way? Risking everything?

But then I remembered that I really had no choice. If Christian truly had this information about me, then he could release it whether I played this game or not. I might as well do it for a good reason. Karl was six feet away from the SUV. My time was up.

"I'll call you back with a place to meet," I told Christian. "But I won't keep chasing you. That's not the way this is going to work."

Then I hung up to the sound of my heart racing as fast as a Formula One car in the final lap of the Monaco Grand Prix. There were only two options for me at this point: crashing—or winning.

twenty-eight

THE RIDE BACK TO THE HOTEL WAS A BLUR. I'M SURE I was polite enough, probably made small talk. I'm really excellent at small talk, you see. Making other people comfortable, assuring them all is well and fine. Those had been my specialties before I had dared to step outside the gilded box.

But inside, the adrenaline kept pumping. I felt like I had just poked a wasp's nest with a short stick. Like I was standing on the bridge with a bungee cord wrapped around my ankles.

All the things good princesses weren't supposed to do, I had just done them. I had deliberately teased the press. Suggested I put my secret alias out in front of the world. Offered to aid and abet the enemy.

Oh, I knew better. Even though it had been impulsive, disappearing after Stavros's funeral was the most reasonable, most clear-headed decision I had ever made. To go small. To go underground. To listen to my head and not my heart.

And now look what I had done. Yes, maybe it wasn't my fault that Christian Fraser-Campbell had barged into my life and caused so many problems. But if it wasn't for Hugh Konnor reserving my rental apartment, I wouldn't have been with a single, sexy billionaire entre-preneur at a historical excavation in front of the nation's press.

I wouldn't be *feeling* all these *feels*.

And that made me mad.

Even though I had managed a polite, easy farewell from von Falk-enburg once we returned to the safety of the underground garage at the hotel, one angry thought was coursing through my brain: *This is all Hugh's fault.*

I knew what would happen when I reached my rooms—Hugh would be there. Waiting.

What I didn't know . . .

Was my mother would be, too.

If I hadn't been so angry—at myself, at Hugh, at the world—then I would have found the scene amusing. I came through the door to my rooms. Hugh, with his arms crossed, glaring at me. And my mother, Felice. "*Darling!*" she cried, her arms raising for some sort of victory hug, "You've done it! You've reclaimed your womanhood. And in my Hermès scarf, as well!"

It was enough to make me want to throw the scarf over my face and suffocate myself with it.

"How did you two get in here?" I cried, with not a small amount of exasperation. When were people going to stop barging into my spaces?

Felice was unashamed. "He let me in." She pointed at Hugh. "He's been waiting up for you." She lowered her head and said in a stage whisper, "I think he's miffed you didn't call."

My eyes fell on the smartphones that were in both of their hands. "How bad is it?" I asked, to whatever goddess out there cared about the poor plight of princesses. Er . . . ex-princesses.

"It's wonderful!" Felice exclaimed.

Hugh's expression begged to differ.

"Karl Sylvain von Falkenburg!" Felice continued to gush. "Rich, handsome, not royal, but distantly related, you know, so even my mother can't complain."

I was distracted by the anger on Hugh's face and wondering what on earth he could be upset about.

"And I'm guessing the media know about it?" I asked, trying not to wince.

"They've posted photos of what you were wearing and your location and what sort of car you arrived in," Hugh said, his voice so even and businesslike he sounded like the royal bodyguard he was.

"Oh. That's not so bad, then."

"Not bad?" Felice echoed. "Oh, my dear, it's wonderful. I'm ever so pleased for you."

"Anyone could have found you," Hugh said pointedly.

I rubbed my head.

"Oh, darling, do you have a headache?"

Yes. It's a five-foot-four headache with wild blond curls and excellent taste in scarves. "Yes," I said with a miserable nod.

"I have the most precious little pills that my friend Dr. Ashton in Los Angeles gave me. I'm sure they're legal here," she added, with her trademark Felice confidence.

"I think I just need to lie down and rest."

My mother nodded understandingly, came to me and gave me a little squeeze. "You're truly my daughter, aren't you?" she said in my ear, before patting my hair and retreating to the door.

When the door clicked behind her, I turned on my heel and marched to the suite's bedroom. The bed, piled high with pillows, the deluxe view over the lazy Comtesse. It was the perfect place for me to dive in and ride the next six months of media speculation out.

What my mother was excited about—the gossip potential of a made-in-the-headlines glamorous romance with a billionaire—was exactly what made me want to run far, far away.

But first. The heavy-footed grumpy bodyguard who followed me.

"No," I said firmly. "*Out!*"

"Car—"

"You don't get to be angry with me!"

"I'm—"

"I was doing perfectly fine, living a safe, normal, boring life until you and your vendetta came charging into my rental apartment!"

"That wasn't—"

I ignored him. "If you wanted me to be locked up and far away, you would have left me alone in mother's villa. Or in Rome. But no. You kept insisting you knew what was best for me and now I have to deal with *all this* again!" I made wild arm circles at my city, my country, the *planet Earth*. "And I don't want that! I didn't want that! I didn't want to be *her*!" Now I pointed at the door. That led to the hotel hallway. And down the hall to my mother's room.

"Oh," I breathed. I realized I was a bit dizzy from all the yelling and arm gestures. I sat on the edge of the bed and tried to quickly blink away the tears that had formed.

"Oh," I said again as I processed what I had said. What I had said about my mother.

Hugh stood quietly, waiting for something else to erupt from my stupid mouth.

"It's not fair for you," I said. "That you have to stand there and listen to all my tantrums."

"I could leave."

"But we already know that you won't," I said ruefully. "You know too much about me, Hugh Konnor."

"Believe it or not, it's interesting."

I laughed at his dry sense of humor. "You know about me," I said, deciding to be boldly honest. "It really isn't fair, you know. That all these years, you read about me, you watched me and knew absolutely everything about me and I know hardly anything about you."

Hugh pulled his hands back from my shoulders and shifted back on his heels. Now he was the one looking a little uncomfortable in the spotlight, but still he said, "Anything you want to know?"

I considered it. What could I ask? What was important?

I considered him. Standing just an arm's length away. His jeans slung on his hips, an oft-laundered sweater with sleeves that pulled tight as he crossed his muscular arms.

"What's this for?" I asked, pulling up his right sleeve. Slowly, I ran a fingertip along the long line of numbers and degree symbols along his forearm. His skin prickled as I brushed the sparse auburn hairs on his arm.

"It's there to remind me of where I come from," he said.

"They're coordinates, then?"

He nodded, a quick jerk of his head. "Of Koras."

The working-class neighborhood he'd grown up in was one I had visited only a few times before I was an adult, always on some sponsored appearance at a charity for economically disadvantaged youth or a job-retraining center.

His fist clenched. I couldn't help but notice and, for some reason, it wounded me, that closed hand. That he was trying to keep something from me didn't seem fair when I was a perennial open book to him.

I reached for his left hand, then, untangling it from where he held it tight and pushing the sleeve up. Another tattoo, the length of his forearm, this time not numbers but words. In the scrolling calligraphy, the phrase wasn't easily legible at a distance but, this close, I could read it. Latin. *Amor honorem.*

"Honor above love," I translated softly. This time I chose not to trace the letters or touch him further, lest I face another gripping, frustrated fist again. "When did you get these?"

He kept his gaze lowered to the black ink stark on his skin. "In Buenos Aires," he said.

Argentina. That meant . . .

"The week I joined your mother's service."

I swallowed. The week after he'd left mine. My stomach twisted tight and knotted. Did this mean . . . something? Anything? Or was it just coincidence? A good exchange rate with the Argentine peso? A hard night of drinking on the town and a convenient tattoo parlor?

No. These designs were too intentional to be the product of some jet lag and overabundance of cheap Argentine wine. He had gone in with his numbers researched; the precise place of his birth plotted out with a pin. And as for the other . . .

He was a hard, strong man but still, the thought of him willingly subjecting himself to thousands of needle pricks in this sensitive location affected me.

Scared me.

But I had run from my fears too many times. Hidden from the awful pain of adulthood, of vulnerability. I was tired. And I didn't want to hide from Hugh anymore.

"Tell me about this one," I said, rubbing my thumb over the Latin phrase and tucking my other hand into his. If he was going to squeeze his hand shut, it was going to be my hand he was holding.

My chest hurt as he took his time, staying silent before he looked at me. Amber eyes met mine, clear and bright. Honest. True.

"It was meant to remind myself that I couldn't have you."

Truth hurts.

"You wanted me, though." I would always grasp at straws with this man.

A harsh sound. "'Want' is too tame a word, my lady. 'Want' is for a child's tantrum. A shopping trip."

I understood. I clamped my hands around his, closed my eyes and felt that same well of need.

"It wouldn't have done," he whispered. "You were nineteen. And with so much life to live."

My eyes shot open. "And now? I'm still trouble, remember?"

He raised an eyebrow. "And I'm a bodyguard."

Amor honorem. I tapped the words on his arm one more time. Honor over Love.

"I don't know, Hugh Konnor," I whispered. "Things are sometimes more complicated than they seem."

"Like an outing with Karl Sylvain von Falkenburg?" I jumped guiltily and looked up at his face. Did he know what I had done? How?

But there was no indication that it was anything other than an innocent question.

"Outings with any men are complicated," I said wryly. "Like I said, I'm turning into my mother."

Hugh squeezed my hand one more time and left without saying another word. It was annoying that he didn't try to argue with me about that.

twenty-nine

ABIT MADE ME READ THE NEWSPAPERS THE NEXT morning, but I knew what I would find. I girded myself with strong Driedish coffee, an extra shot of farm-fresh Driedish cream- and butter-slathered brioche and began to read the sensational stories about me.

Oh, one could almost hear the heavy breathing of the so-called journalists as they all gushed and critiqued and speculated about my sudden reappearance in Drieden. So many theories were presented as facts, I almost forgot they were talking about me. After all, I sounded utterly fascinating. According to "sources," Princess Caroline (that would be me) was recovering from a complete facelift, a stay in rehab, a monastic epiphany and had been, improbably, carrying on a months-long affair with Karl Sylvain von Falkenburg. All at the same time! It was really quite impressive of me to juggle all that at once. I should offer an on-line course—how to reach spiritual enlightenment, achieve sobriety and meet the love of your life in sixty days. Guaranteed results, no refunds.

Further, Karl and I had been having secret assignations at his country house in Devon, my estate in Botswana and, of course, my friend Ari's yacht in Greece. I did not, as far as I knew, have a friend named Ari. Devon sounded uninspiring, but Botswana was probably lovely in February. I made a mental note to contact a local real-estate broker for more information.

It was as bad as I feared. The photos were clear and unambiguous. Me smiling at a man. My arm tucked in his. His arm circling my shoulders. To my credit, one could hardly tell that it was freezing outside when Karl and I had viewed the battle site or that I had been the dummy who had forgotten a winter coat.

And while the media was concerned with my "ability to love again," they were similarly fascinated with Karl's vast business holdings, his wealth and his corporations. Yes, for every mention of one of my past (and failed) relationships, there was an equal description of Karl's biotechnology "empire" or his business "genius" of identifying genetic sciences as the next health revolution of the twenty-first century.

This, as we all know, was completely fair and balanced. /sarcasm font/

The press would have learned by now where I was staying and that Felice was here, too. Speculation would be rampant about . . . something. I couldn't imagine what new rumor would be concocted next. Mother–daughter facelifts were *so* five years ago. Perhaps she was here to help me plan my next wedding—a beautiful affair in a garden somewhere.

And if this was in the newspapers, it was around the globe. On television, the internet. Elena and Signore Rossi and all the people in Varenna who had treated me like a normal person would all now say, "Aha! That's who she is! I knew she reminded me of someone famous."

And if my photo was everywhere, there was no way it wasn't in the middle of Drieden City. At the royal palace. On Big Gran's desk.

Yes, my grandmother the Queen kept abreast of the news herself, even if it hadn't already been presented to her on her morning breakfast tray. I looked over the edge of *The Driedener* at my own room-service tray. I supposed it wasn't the worst habit to emulate.

So.

What next?

I pulled my computer over and tapped the table idly, brainstorming a few possibilities.

Two, three, four minutes went by and I realized . . . my options had narrowed considerably. The number of places in the world where I could escape public scrutiny had been winnowed . . . again. As for my quiet journalism career as Clémence Diederich, that would be a bust unless I could research and interview in disguise.

Basically, my career options were now limited to professional fashion plate, trophy wife or reality-show judge.

Just like that, I had become my mother.

And when I thought things couldn't get any worse, there was a very officious knock on my door. I tightened the belt on my robe, checked the peephole and saw the unmistakable stern mien of yet another palace official.

After I opened the door, I was handed a note. Written with a fountain pen on cream linen stationery, sealed with a red wax signet ring.

Okay, I'm exaggerating slightly with the red wax seal. Honestly. This is the twenty-first century. Every royal I know would use a vegan soy blend for their signet seals.

I felt a bit sick after the door closed and I was left alone with the note. Yes, I had been accompanied (for lack of a better word) by a palace bodyguard (even if he was on sabbatical) in recent days. And yes, I had seen my sister, even flown with her to a royal residence (even if it was a strange, inhospitable and useless island.) But this physical link to the palace-with-a-capital-P, to the place where I had grown up, made me queasy.

Once they start sending you notes on official stationery via stone-faced courier, the trap had been set. *Zing*. There went the steel teeth snapping around my ankle.

They knew where I was. Hell, *everyone* knew. This time, there would be no sneaking off. Not without some extensive planning and significant bribes.

I settled in, took a deep, calming breath or six and opened the envelope.

It wasn't from my grandmother. It was from my sister.

Caroline,

I was going to call but Lucy reminded me about the phones at the Hotel Ilysium being bugged during Mother and Father's divorce. We'll send someone over soon to check your phone. (Or perhaps we can get you a new cellphone? That would probably be more secure. Nick will bring you one.)

Thank you for meeting with Karl yesterday. I know the attention will be an annoyance—the photographers always are—but unfortunately . . . well, it's something we have to deal with. As soon as they're used to you being here, it will die down, I'm sure. It always does.

I have a meeting with Big Gran shortly. I can't imagine that she won't want to know more about your plans. I'll take care of her—and everything else—in my way. I can't say too much more in a note (is this where I tell you to burn it or it will self-destruct in fifteen seconds? I'm not sure how this should go, only that a note seemed much safer than those phones! Post-trauma from those days, am I right? Remember those Cordelia Lancaster columns? What a nightmare.).

Hugh let me know that you are safe and sound and, as soon as you get your new phone, I'll be able to tell you myself.

(I should probably let the furor die down before I visit again. Lucy always says we shouldn't feed the frenzy.)

More updates coming soon.

Thea

PS Lucy says hello! She's missed you as well.
PPS Sophie's just called. She wants all the gossip. I'll fill her in so you don't have to.

A handwritten note.

Quaint and formal and civilized, practically delivered on a silver plate by a liveried butler from the next Queen of Drieden.

So why was it making me cry?

In the span of the last hour, I'd been detached, amused, appalled, afraid, exasperated and more.

But this simple, stupid note from my sister made me feel all the feels. It was like we were back in grade school, before we were allowed to text or email. The mention of Lucy . . . oh, dear Lucy. Our cousin, and Thea's right-hand woman, who had always been around the family.

And Sophie. My heart swelled. Our youngest sister. It was so like her to immediately hear news and reach out to someone for, as Thea said, "all the gossip." And when I had a new cellphone, she could call me, and we could laugh and share who we'd just seen out at the ballet or in Paris while shopping on holiday.

My sweet family. Imperfect they may be, they cared. They wanted me here, home, in this life with them. Even if I was a disowned, disreputable widow of a princess.

Well, maybe they wanted me. Thea still had to have a chat with Big Gran, after all.

What do you want?

My own voice chided me, echoing through my skull like the

February wind that was currently whipping down the Comtesse River outside my window.

I carefully folded the note. I loved my family. I always had. Yes, even when my own grandmother decreed that I was no longer good enough to be part of the clan. I still loved the rest of them.

What do you want?

I wanted what all women want. Safety. Happiness. Love. The basics.

And those things would be impossible if anyone threatened either of my sisters again.

Whatever type of life I was going to have, it wouldn't be possible until all dangers were met and eliminated.

Which meant I still had to ensure that Christian Fraser-Campbell was dealt with.

Those damn reporters had been damned bad luck. Grandmama and I had believed that Christian had approached me because I was safe but, now, with every photographer stalking me, it had made my goals much more difficult.

But, I realized, not impossible.

I went down the hallway and knocked on Mother's door. After a length of time that could only be explained by the fact that she was likely still sleeping, the door opened. Sure enough, her lavender satin sleeping mask was pushed only partly back on her blonde curls, and matched the lavender and amethyst negligee she wore. "Darling, at this hour?"

"It's nearly ten, Mother," I said as I brushed past her into the room. "And I need your help with something."

"Karl von Falkenburg is just a man, darling, I'm sure you know what to do with him . . ."

I rolled my eyes, as I was fairly certain she was joking. Mostly.

"I need to get away. For a few days. Somewhere private."

"With Karl?"

"No," I said firmly. "That needs to die down. I need to be alone. And I don't have access to royal properties . . ."

Felice smirked. "I know just the place."

AFTER MY MOTHER MADE THE ARRANGEMENTS, I RETURNED to my room and withdrew Sergei's cellphone from my handbag. Guilt flashed through me as I remembered my sister's promise to get me a new phone to protect me from the likes of gossip reporters like Cordelia Lancaster. Little did she know . . . I already had a cellphone given to me by her worst enemy and, well, Cordelia Lancaster was me.

The cellphone still showed a full charge. Technology had gotten truly amazing recently. I carried it next to the window and called the only number that it had saved.

Ring.

Ring.

Ring.

Ring.

Voicemail.

I didn't bother with a message and simply hung up.

Next, I called Astrid with Felice's cellphone, hiding in Felice's bathroom. It felt very cloak and dagger, but after Thea's note about the bugged hotel lines I couldn't trust them again. Strangely, Felice acted like people borrowed her cellphone and made calls from her bathtub every day. "What about your man, your bodyguard? He's coming with you?" Astrid asked me. I told her that I hadn't seen Hugh since he'd left me the day before, that he had been mad about me leaving the hotel with Karl without proper security.

"Not Karl Sylvain von Falkenburg?" Astrid asked.

"You haven't heard the news, then? The press has us married and already on the outs, I believe. We may even be having affairs with other people. It's difficult to keep up."

"Interesting." Astrid sounded distracted, but she probably didn't care about celebrity gossip, unless it involved knights of the Round Table. "When you have a date confirmed with Christian, let me know. We'll need to get my people on it."

I packed quickly. The few things that I'd ordered from my favorite stores in the city barely filled a small carry-on. Then I called for Felice's car and driver. Back to the parking garage; the hotel's security staff had cleared the floor of reporters. Felice's black-windowed Audi waited. When I approached, an arm reached out from behind me to open the door for me. I looked to thank the person and saw a very familiar face.

Hugh.

He hadn't shaved off the auburn goatee but he had put on his dark bodyguard sunglasses. "Hello there," I said, reaching for nonchalance even as my pulse thumped against my skin at the sight of him again.

"My lady," he murmured as he opened the car door.

I slid in the back seat. Waited.

The driver opened the door. The driver got in.

He was broad, solid, and his brown hair was longer than it should be, curling over his collar.

I opened my mouth to say something but found my heart lodged solidly in my throat. Hugh still had his sunglasses on, but as he pulled out of the parking garage I could tell from the dip of his head that he was looking in the rear-view mirror.

At me.

"How did you know?" I asked, lifting my chin. I wasn't apologizing for anything. I was a free woman, and I didn't have to have protection everywhere.

"A little birdie told me," Hugh said shortly. Hm. That was

annoying. But it was the price to pay, I supposed, for staying at the Hotel Ilysium.

"I can help you drive," I offered.

He huffed a short laugh. "No, thank you."

"You didn't complain when I drove you to Grandmama's."

"No, I did not."

Silence. Semi-awkward.

"Do you even know where you're going?" I asked, suddenly aware that maybe he didn't and he'd just slid into the driver's seat and was taking me someplace awful. Like an archeological dig. Or worse. To the palace.

"The Château de Dréuvar."

"Dammit," I muttered, more annoyed now. "Is Stewart fine with you taking the car?" I asked.

"Stewart?" he asked.

I gritted my teeth. "My mother's driver."

Hugh's eyebrows drew together over the sunglasses. "I was supposed to ask?"

I laughed, despite all the warring impulses that rose in my body. To reach out. To make a connection. To break free. To build walls.

To fall in love with this man.

This is what it had been like, when he'd been mine . . . my body-guard, that was.

A gently warming sun. An easy repartee. A keen awareness.

I needed to shake this off. I couldn't let Hugh Konnor break my heart again. He might take his job seriously, but I couldn't misconstrue his devotion to his job as devotion to me.

He had been perfectly clear that all he wanted to do was protect me. More importantly, he wanted to stay close in case Christian Fraser-Campbell ventured near.

And if my plan worked, that would be happening very soon.

thirty

THE CHÂTEAU DE DRÉUVAR WASN'T TERRIBLY GRAND, on the scale of the great palaces of Europe. But it certainly wasn't tiny. What impressed me most as we approached the entrance was the simple beauty of it. A quintessential example of a Northern Province aristocratic estate, its face to the world was a bald, flat visage. Three rows of windows rose above the meticulously maintained garden, each with beautifully wrought cornices and stonework. The house was the color of the flesh of an early-summer peach, which made it glow softly even in the twilight of winter. Twin curved staircases to the double front doors were both an elegant and a showy touch, like an extra dollop of whipped cream on top of a pale custard.

Hugh lowered his chin as if he were about to say something to me, but we were met at the door by a younger couple. The woman had a baby on her hip, which she bounced as she introduced herself and her husband as the caretakers of Dréuvar. As one half of my brain processed the words she was saying, about rooms readied, meal served, the other half of my brain fixated on the child, all chubby red cheeks, freshly bathed and ready for his own bed.

It was the prettiest picture. Two happy parents, working together, a child made from love. And of course, the impressive and historical estate.

But this wasn't some sort of hormonal obsession with the scene. Oh, no.

Well, perhaps. A little.

But this was also a healthy dose of curiosity, like one has at a new exhibition at the botanical gardens or the zoo.

Had I ever seen this little scene before? In person? Up close? A beautiful young family, well adjusted and . . . normal? Grown-ups who maybe, possibly, were equipped to shake hands, hold a conversation, brush their child's damp curls from their forehead and not have anyone lurking in the background to correct them or photograph them.

Stephan and Amira and little Claude showed us to the residential quarters of the house and said they'd be just a quick call away in their cottage on the estate.

Then Hugh and I were alone.

Truly.

Acres and acres of property and farmland surrounded us to the south, east and west. And, if the satellite maps I had pulled up when Mother offered me the house were correct, the sea was just a few hundred yards to the north.

"Are we going to talk about why we're here?" He spread his arms at the high ceilings and the immaculate decor.

"I needed to get away from the press. Get some space." It was mostly true. I walked to the tall, narrow window and looked outside to the grass and reflecting pool two floors down. Disappointing. I had hoped for a view of the ocean. It was suddenly exactly what I needed, now that I didn't have it.

"I'm going for a walk," I announced.

"I'll come with you." Hugh nodded, a placating expression on his face. "After I make some checks of the system and the layout."

Frustration rose in me. This wasn't what I had planned. I needed to be alone to make contact with Christian. And I didn't need an overprotective bodyguard. "You didn't do this at Grandmama's," I pointed out, a bit mulishly.

Hugh paused on his way to the door, shot me a dry look over his shoulder. "Your grandmama met us at the door with a sword, thousands of yards up a Swiss mountain. I was confident she could handle any barbarian invaders."

I made a little sound. I supposed he was right.

He went as if to leave the room again but then stopped and turned to me. "Why don't you come with me?"

His hand extended. This was strange new protocol for a bodyguard. "I've never had security want me to . . . secure things with them before."

Hugh shrugged. "You can tell me all about your plan and why we've come to the Sevine seat for it while I . . . secure things."

"I don't have a plan," I said, but Hugh stepped forward, closed his warm, rough hand around mine and whispered one word to me.

"Liar."

I opened my mouth to defend myself but found no words came out. He shook his head, gave me a half-stern, half-amused look and tucked my arm under his.

It was obvious that arguing wasn't going to get me anywhere. Not with Hugh Konnor on duty.

We found the alarm systems easily enough, in a room off the kitchens. The lights of the monitors glowed back on Hugh's face as he studied the floorplan of the house. After finding it satisfactory enough, he wanted to check on each exit.

"It's similar to Father's house, in Ceillis, isn't it?" I asked.

"Except Ceillis House is about five times the size," Hugh said, with a glance at the painted ceilings in the hall we were now in. "And a bit grander for His Royal Highness."

"Well, he will be . . ." My voice trailed off as I realized what I was about to say—that Father would be King—and how it was nearly a lie. If what Thea had said was true, my father, Crown Prince Albert, would not be king. He would spend the rest of his days, I supposed, ensconced at Ceillis House, fly fishing and reading scholarly journals and doing quiet charity work. The kind that royals without much of a job were relegated to doing.

It could be my life, too.

If I wanted it.

An image of a chubby, sleepy baby plastered itself into my head. Clung there like it was cranky and needed a bottle.

"The floorplan is quite similar," I said, a little too forcefully. I'd talk architecture to avoid thinking about babies, especially with Hugh Konnor holding my hand. "To Ceillis House, I mean. All that money and the grand families of Drieden never wanted to update their houses." There was a note in my voice that sounded like Grandmama Astrid being peevish about the Laurents. Funny.

"To be fair, the Driedish without money never updated their homes much either," Hugh said quietly.

I was instantly shamed. "I'm sorry. I know that, it's that . . ." *I've spent too much time around my family lately.*

Hugh's squeeze of my hand was reassuring. "Come on now, one more floor, and you still haven't told me about why you picked this place."

We rounded a corner, went up a stairwell. "I didn't." This, at least, was the truth. "I told Mother I needed a place to get away. She offered this because I can't go to any of the royal estates anymore and the Sevine family—her family—they collect properties like some people collect shoes or dolls."

Oh, crap. Did that sound tone deaf and overprivileged as well? "Not that there's anything wrong with collecting dolls," I said quickly.

"Who wouldn't enjoy that," Hugh responded graciously, letting me extract my foot from my mouth with ease.

"I think it's because the Sevines were richer than God but weren't aristocratic or noble for so long. They were merchant class, really, so always looking out for good investments. And what's a better investment than beautiful houses and estates throughout Drieden?"

"And the rest of Europe," Hugh reminded me. "Italy, Switzerland."

I sighed. He only knew a tenth of it.

We had come back to our original starting place, the apartments we were assigned. The fireplace was now crackling and emitting a sauna-level of heat.

"So Felice gave you a nice big country house to stay in to get away from the press," Hugh concluded. "It's very kind of her."

"Well, she has some experience in this area," I said.

Hugh and I faced each other now. The sun had set and, at this latitude in February, it was almost black outside. The room had taken on a soft, romantic glow from a single lamp and the steady fire.

After a moment, he was the one to speak first. "And so do I."

"Getting away from the press?" I asked.

He shook his head. "Accompanying you."

"You didn't have to."

"When are you going to understand? I don't have a choice." He sighed. "Especially when you're making a bad decision."

Certainty rocked me. Denial would be useless. "You know, then."

"That you're still trying to meet with Christian?"

I nodded.

"Yes. I'm not an idiot."

Something on my face must have revealed my disappointment at my surreptitious skills because he promptly reassured me that, "Also, before we left the convent, Lady Decht-Sevine and I had a little talk."

My face went hot and it wasn't the roaring fire in the hearth. Once again, I had an overbearing grandmother trying to run things.

"Did you think you were going to take down Christian by yourself?"

If I was honest with myself, no. I shook my head slightly. "But no one else needed to be threatened," I said. "My life's already in tatters."

Then Hugh put something into words, all the fear that I hadn't allowed myself to face.

"People care about you. You don't have to be alone. You're not in exile. Not anymore."

He placed his hand on my cheek and I had to close my eyes. Emotions had not been the plan. Connecting with this man had not been the plan.

But damn, if it didn't feel so, so right.

A little voice popped into my head. *This won't end well.*

And then another one.

Go.

I opened my eyes and found his. Placed my hands on his shirt. Felt the rise and fall of his chest.

Slowly, I slid my hand up around his neck. His skin was smooth, warm. My fingers tangled with the hair at his nape and pulled. Hugh kissed me, let me set the pace and explore his full bottom lip, his beard against my cheek. I felt alive, electric, powerful. He rubbed his hands up my arms, traced my shoulders, cupped my face, brushing softly under my chin and down my throat. Warm, lazy currents awakened inside my body, ones that had lain long dormant.

He was powerful, tight, tense and also incredibly gentle. Those fingers. Those hands. Sure and steady, he stroked under my breasts, sliding down my lower back, the tilt of my bottom. I groaned. He stilled.

"Don't stop," I murmured, and then I parroted the same movements that were working on me. Sliding underneath his shirt, scratching my fingernails lightly down his stomach to the fly of his pants. Where I stopped.

My eyes opened. I met his golden gaze, sought his consent. I had been the one to start this. If he said no—

"Don't fucking stop," Hugh growled. His hands tightened, he pressed me against him and his kiss held all that I needed to know.

We undressed each other, slipping and sliding and stripping until we were skin to skin. He was perfect in my eyes, lean muscle, auburn hair, the tattoos on the arms that cradled me tightly. The fire blazed behind me, reflected in his lion eyes. And even though I had been terrified of having my heart broken by this man, when I gave my body to him I was one hundred per cent certain he would never hurt me. Not like before.

thirty-one

EVENTUALLY, WE MADE IT TO A BED. STUMBLING through the halls of the dark house, clutching our clothes like teenagers trying not to get caught. Hugh curved his body around mine and I fell asleep almost instantly, not waking again until the smell of coffee hit me the next morning.

"I love that you always know where the coffee is," I murmured, still deliciously sore and spent from the night before.

Hugh, wearing only his jeans, which hung low in his hips, handed me a cup, and I sighed with pleasure. *This* was the real fantasy, I thought. Forget being a royal princess draped in couture and rare jewels. All I needed was my mostly naked man and a hot coffee.

"Do you?" he asked, as if he was amused by me.

"I love that you know a lot of things about me," I said huskily as he sat on the edge of the bed next to me.

"I do," he said with a twinkle in his eye. "And a lot more today."

Oh God. There it was. The fierce blush of the pale-skinned

Driedish women. I felt my cheeks burn bright but tried to stay all sophisticated and worldly. I was a woman of twenty-nine, not a child of nineteen, but I couldn't control the blood racing to my skin at the thought of all that I knew about him, too.

He reached out and stroked the back of my left hand, lying on the bed. "I also know that I can't talk you out of what you're trying to do."

I looked at my still-supine body, naked under the blankets, yes, but not trying to actively seduce him at that moment. (#butfirstcoffee). "What am I trying to do?"

"Caroline." He leveled me. Absolutely. With one even, hazel stare. "Because I know you." He slid off the bed and picked up my handbag and set it on the foot of the bed. "You already told Christian you were coming here?"

I sighed. He really did know me so well.

"Can I get dressed first? I don't want to talk to Christian without my clothes on."

"Fair enough." He chuckled. "I can't say that I would enjoy that either."

WHEN I EMERGED FROM THE BATHROOM, FRESHENED UP in a pair of jeans and a sweater, Hugh had also put his clothes back on, which was disappointing. Then I noticed my handbag was open and he was holding the Ukrainian's phone. Wordlessly, he extended it to me.

I had never told him about it, and I didn't know what to say now, especially after we'd taken things to the next level. Finally, I exhaled, determined to face the situation like a grown woman. "That's—"

"The phone from the guy at the villa," Hugh finished.

My shoulders dropped. "You knew?"

He came to me then, cupped my face and kissed me. "Cell batteries don't last that long."

My blush rose again. "I'm not sure I'm good at this."

"You're very good at keeping secrets." He smiled. "And I'm very good at figuring yours out."

My heart thumped hard against my ribs. I had a partner; we were a team. I understood what that was like, now, with this smart, patient asshole of a bodyguard.

I kissed him again. "Let's do this."

TO: 1717vx7171@eulink.eu
FROM: Cavalleta@villacavalleta.iy

Apology

Christian,

I left you a voicemail, but I'm not sure if you received it. I don't know if you have access to the news, but they've done it to me again. I had to leave the city, the press is intolerable. I can't help but think of you, and the wretched way you've been treated. Thea has been . . . Thea, about this whole thing, and I know you probably (understandably) want nothing more to do with this whole family. You've probably given up on our whole plan but I'm sorry you were ever dragged into this wretched circus.

Best of luck,
CL

Hugh and I stared at the screen.

"He didn't answer my last call," I pointed out. "He might be indisposed or injured."

"Don't raise my hopes," he muttered.

"He might be on his way to Australia," I said.

Hugh's head swiveled toward me. "Why would you say that?"

To be honest, it had popped in my head because of all the silly half-truths I had told Signore Rossi. But now I had to explain it to Hugh. "Because it's very far. And he could blend right in," I added, as I realized I might be on to something. "He's Scottish; only his pasty skin would set him apart."

Hugh regarded me with a new look in his eye. "Is that what you thought of? When you ran off to Italy? Where you might blend in?"

I had not expected a question about myself so I took a moment before answering, to give it a thought. "No. I chose a place I loved. Where I would feel . . ." I searched for a word. "Protected."

"You felt protected in *Italy*?" Hugh's question was tinged with disbelief but something more. Was he . . . hurt? By what I said?

I shrugged. I wasn't sure I could explain it. "It's the other end of Europe. And I didn't feel like I would be exposed," I continued. "Not if I put my head down and didn't draw attention to myself."

Hugh snorted.

"What is that for?" I demanded. "You don't believe me?"

"I don't believe for one moment that you, Caroline Laurent of Drieden, would ever not draw attention to yourself."

My mouth dropped and I made a noise of indignation. "What are you saying? I'm a drama queen?"

Now he looked at me like I was crazy. "No," he said. And when that didn't allay my (admittedly low) outrage, he continued, "You're not. You're like . . ." He stopped, as if he couldn't get the right words out. "You're like. You're so—"

Ching!

The email alert.

Our attention swooped to the computer screen.

New message.

TO: Cavalleta@villacavalleta.iy
FROM: 1717vx7171@eulink.eu

Re: Apology

Caroline,

As someone else who has been shunned by the holy family of Drieden, I'm quite sure that you're the only person who could understand what I've been through. You know, as I do, that the stories that are released to the press are biased in only one direction—toward certain queens and princesses who think they truly rule and don't realize that they are merely figureheads.

Of course, you are excluded from that assessment.

That is all to say, thank you for your apology. It does mean quite a lot.

I hope we can remain friends in exile.

Steading

I looked up at Hugh, who had jumped out of a chair and stood at attention just at my right hand. Ready for battle against a digital message, no doubt.

"This is good, right?" I asked. "He wants to be friends?"

Hugh's lip curled.

"Well, obviously, I'm not going to invite him over for mani-pedis. But we can use this."

Hugh didn't look convinced at my positive outlook. "This is going to take forever," he grumbled. "Playing games and kissing his ass to wheedle information out of him."

"Your friends in the police community haven't done any better than this," I pointed out. "We're going to do this my way." Hugh was seriously underestimating my expertise in kissing ass. I had trained for this my whole life, learning the finer points of receiving and giving flattery.

I cracked my knuckles. *Let's do this.*

TO: 1717vx7171@eulink.eu
FROM: Cavalleta@villacavalleta.iy

Re: Re: Apology

Exile friends? That sounds quite Napoleonic. I'm not sure Big Gran would approve. Ha.

XO,
C

I hit send and Hugh snorted.

"You think you could do better?"

"No," he said with a perfectly straight face. "I know for a fact that you're better at making jokes about Napoleon than I am."

"At least you're admitting I'm better at something."

"Of course," he scoffed. "You were born a royal princess, given four names and a polo pony for your first birthday."

The thing was, he wasn't joking. He looked like this was a serious argument for why I was better than him.

Which was as ridiculous as giving a baby a polo pony, but one thing gave me pause.

"Hugh. How did you know I have four names?"

"Because I do."

"Do you know them?" Most Driedeners didn't. Because why would they?

A slight hesitation. "Caroline Aurelia Marie Laurent."

"You remembered that from the convent?" The speaker at the gate had spat out my names, I remembered. That must be why he knew them.

"No. I knew them from before."

"From when you were my bodyguard."

"Yes. It was in your file."

"Ah." Something still wasn't right. "And you know Thea's, then, from her file," I said. "I guess, because she was oldest, they gave her the most ridiculously embarrassing family names."

He cleared his throat but didn't meet my eyes. "Surprised she didn't get teased out of princess school with names like that."

I tried very hard not to smile. Because once again, I had caught Hugh Konnor in a tiny white lie. One that completely revealed more than he wanted me to ever see.

Ching!

Saved by the bell. Hugh's finger clicked before I could reach the keyboard.

TO: Cavalleta@villacavalleta.iy
FROM: 1717vx7171@eulink.eu

Re: Re: Re: Apology

A Napoleon joke? You must be bored out of your mind in that big northern country house by yourself.

It felt like I had dropped off a roller coaster. My stomach dipped. "We got him." Wait. I looked at Hugh. "He thinks I'm alone because you drove. If he had a spy or something, they probably reported that it was Mother's car and driver that left the hotel."

I laughed gleefully. Yes! This was going to be so easy. And even Hugh had dropped his usual skeptical expression and allowed a bit of a hopeful gleam into his eyes. I knew he had different reasons for catching Christian, but he wanted to as much as me, if not more, so when he reached over and closed my laptop I didn't understand.

"Hugh! All I have to do is toss the man a juicy bit of bait. We can reel him in anytime we want."

"You seem to have forgotten that *you* are the bait."

I rolled my eyes. "And you seem to have forgotten that you're a bad-ass royal guard." I reached out and took his hand in mine. "You can end this. Today. Christian isn't the one with power here. We are."

He didn't argue with me and my exceptional powers of (well-deserved, on this occasion) ass-kissing. His jaw tightened, and then he gave me one curt nod.

It was my cue. I flipped my screen open and considered exactly what type of net I should extend to catch this particular fish. A small one, meant for a trout in a stream? A large one that trawled the coast?

TO: 1717vx7171@eulink.eu

FROM: Cavalleta@villacavalleta.iy

Re: Re: Re: Re: Apology

Ugh. You're right. I'm dying out here.

.

.

.

.

And it would really piss them off if you came to visit. ;-)

Château de Dréuvar, Northern Province. I'll have the Scotch ready.

Xo,

Caroline

Hugh shook his head.

"It's going to work," I assured him. "I know him."

"Then it will be the first time in history that one of the most wanted criminals was captured with a winky face."

I caught it then: that glint that I loved—no, that I *liked* so much—was back. I suddenly had a hard time breathing. "We're a good team," I said, trying very hard to sound casual. Chill. Like I had no feelings about him, one way or another.

"A team?" He echoed my word, looking almost confused. "Sure. That sounds about right," he said absently, before muttering something about checking the security cameras and leaving the room.

It wasn't what I had wanted. I was a grown woman, a widow, for God's sake, and I had no idea how to act around the hot bodyguard. Again.

We had made love last night. Or had sex. We had definitely slept together. But I had no idea how to act now.

Go.

The order came from deep inside. Always before, when I'd heard that simple word echoing through my skull, I'd obeyed by running off, doing something reckless. Marrying Stavros, for example. Leaving his funeral in a cloud of crêpe and black tulle. Deciding to hunt down Christian Fraser-Campbell for what . . . a newspaper story?

I saw now that it had never been about a career opportunity. Or protecting my secrets.

I was looking for *more*. I wanted peace and security, yes, but I also wanted sex and laughter and adventure.

A Sevine woman, through and through.

Maybe it was time to accept this side of me. Accept that this bloodline was my fate, even if Thea managed to undo a royal disinheritance. And where better to explore my Sevine genealogy than here? At the ancestral seat of Château de Dréuvar?

This room, for example. It was a beautiful drawing room, with walls painted a deep clover and set with inlaid gold panels. The windows were draped in an emerald-green satin, tied with gold rope the width of my forearm. It was a room that rivalled any chamber of the palace in the city in beauty and decadence, but somehow, it still felt like a family could live here.

A baby named Claude came to mind. Him and his cute toes and sweet, round belly.

What else did I know of the Sevines? My mother grew up here, I knew, but we never visited, even when her parents still lived here, before her father retired to their city townhouse (which officially qualified as downsizing but still took up a city block) and Grandmama to her Swiss convent. My siblings and I were heirs to the throne. Our world rotated around the palace and the grandmother that wore the Jaipur sapphire on her head.

Maybe . . . Maybe this was the place where I could finally be who I was.

With him.

I started walking through the room, touching and lifting little pieces here and there, as if the Sevine family DNA could be amplified through transfusion.

When this was all done, when Christian was caught and I was back on my own again, maybe I'd even return to Grandmama's Swiss mountain convent, settle down in her library and let her teach me the ways of the better half of my family tree and that whole Vox Umbra situation. Maybe it was my Sevine blood running a little faster now, but I could see how alluring a secret organization guaranteeing the stability of the continent could be.

I heard a distant ring of a doorbell.

My stomach flipped. It was time. This was happening. Soon enough, I'd be able to start directing my own life again. Go wherever I wanted to go. Be whoever I wanted to be. With whoever I wanted.

thirty-two

I RAN DOWN THE GRAND STAIRCASE, NOT KNOWING WHAT to expect. Would it be just Christian by himself? Where was Hugh? Did I need a gun?

What I saw in the entrance hall sent my feet stuttering over the marble. Thea and Nick and a team of Men in Black were entering the château with a caravan of shiny black SUVs sparkling in the sun behind them.

Hugh appeared from a side door and seemed to be sliding something into his waistband at the small of his back.

"Caroline." Thea half jogged to me, pulling me into her arms and kissing me on each cheek. Then she turned to Hugh. "You're off this project. Starting now."

Hugh barely flinched, but I didn't like the sound of that. "He's on sabbatical. You can't tell him what to do," I told my domineering sister.

"Sabbatical? He volunteered for the assignment," she said.

"Which he hasn't completed yet," Nick added.

Hugh's jaw tightened and, when he shifted his gaze from his boss to me, I knew.

"You were working with them. You lied to me." Oh, it was a shot through my heart. This heart, which had just started to feel again. It was incredibly bad timing.

"Caroline——" he said gruffly. But I didn't need his explanations. He'd told me he was on sabbatical to try to get closer to me. He hadn't told me about working with Thea because they wanted poor Caroline to believe she was doing something good for her family, for her country.

"Let's go somewhere. The study, perhaps," Thea suggested.

"That makes you, what, a triple agent?" I spat at Hugh. "How very adept you are at secrets."

"The study. Now." Thea used her princess voice, and miraculously, the two hardened, scowling security men next to us looked ready to immediately comply.

Me? I was immune to that royal bullshit now.

"You don't tell me what to do. I'm on Sevine property."

"Caroline."

"I'm not a royal. You don't control me."

"No, I don't," Thea agreed.

"More's the pity," Nick muttered.

"Oh, shut up," I snapped at him. "This is all because of you." I heard Thea gasp, but I didn't care. Sevine women didn't have to bow to the Laurents, and certainly not to their boyfriends. "Christian was your younger brother and you were certainly responsible for his taking your title and becoming prince-worthy material." Bringing up Nick's past disappearance, even if it was because of his service to his country, might have been unfair but it was certainly relevant to the conversation. Everyone had played their part in this fiasco.

"We're just trying to protect——"

"I don't want to hear it!" I shouted. "You were trying to protect me? Where was all this familial protection when I was being cast aside?" Thea looked like I had struck her, but I continued. "All of you have made impossibly bad decisions. But somehow, I'm the only one who gets punished for mine."

My voice shook, my hands shook. I was furious. "What I have of a life has been completely turned upside down and wrecked because of the man *you* were going to marry! I was happy in Italy. For once in my life I could breathe, and then . . ." Hugh had crossed behind me, put his hands on my shoulders. I half wondered if he would stop me if I physically went after Thea. Which princess would he protect? "Then *you* have the nerve to tell me how I get to react when my house, my privacy, my livelihood are threatened once again because of this goddamned family."

Thea had paled, her eyes wide. "Caroline . . . I didn't mean . . ."

But I had had enough of empty royal promises. "I don't want to hear anymore. I won't help, I'll go back to Italy. Just leave me alone."

"You were contacting Christian, a man we've been hunting for months. Of course we want to be involved."

"But I was trying to help you." The words tumbled out of me.

"Help me?" Thea's expression went glacial. "The apprehension of Christian is a matter of national security. I have a team of trained professionals—what makes you think you could send him a flirty email and bring him in when they couldn't?"

My mouth opened. Closed. I felt tears in my eyes. It was all I had ever done in this family. Try to make everyone happy. And it seemed I had finally been told that I was completely useless.

Hugh's hands tightened for a moment, his thumbs brushed the back of my shoulders, but when I pulled away to go back to my room, he didn't come with me.

thirty-three

THERE WAS A KNOCK AT MY DOOR THE NEXT MORN-ing. I had already bathed and dressed and was ready to jump on the next vehicle going south. No one had come to try to talk me out of it, after all. I tried to tell myself I didn't care, that I could go back to Italy and relock all the doors that I had closed after Stavros's death. And whoever was at the door wasn't going to stop me.

When I opened the door, I realized that, yes, somebody could stop me.

Because there was a person that I really, really, did not want to deal with today.

"Hello, Sybil."

She looked freakishly amazing and chic, with a straight black bob and a pale, nearly wrinkle-free face. She even knew how to use black eyeliner to make a perfect cat-eye, which was a bit extra at eight o'clock in the morning but on her looked just right.

She smiled at me, like a favorite aunt. "Care to go for a walk?"

All of a sudden, a walk outside in the cool morning breeze sounded like perfection. I jumped on the chance to explore the grounds of the château and I knew exactly where I wanted to go—the water.

I followed my nose and Sybil followed me and, before too long, we had rambled past the gardens, through the bower of dead roses, and we were on a wide expanse of flat, windblown land that looked out on the North Sea.

I took several deep, cleansing breaths before Sybil spoke. "I came with your sister," she said.

"I figured that out."

"I help her with getting information."

I stayed silent.

"Much like I've helped you in the past."

Another cleansing breath wouldn't help the nerves that just rattled through my body. "Sybil——"

She held up a hand. "I'm not going to betray your secrets. I wouldn't."

"Then why are we even talking about this?"

"Because we received an alert that your personal medical records were hacked," she replied, with as much matter-of-fact concern as if she were discussing a nasty sunburn I'd gotten on one of Sophie's friend's yachts. "Your sister wanted me to get information on who might have done it. And to see what I can do to connect to the evidence you've collected on Christian Fraser-Campbell."

"Okay . . ."

"And I've done it."

"That's great. Well done."

"I traced the address of the hacker, and they'll be receiving a visit from law enforcement shortly." She paused, and I could tell from her expression that the rest of this wasn't going to be welcome news.

"Spit it out."

"While I was in his system, I took a look around at what else they've been looking for." Her face softened. "They were looking for you."

"They found me."

"No. Everything about you. They had a file on you. They knew your Swiss accounts. Your real-estate purchases. They were in your email. They know about Clémence Diederich and Cordelia Lancaster," she finished.

"Ah."

There was a pause before Sybil spoke. "You already knew this."

Might as well be upfront with the family's psychic-slash-computer hacker. It wasn't like I could hide anything from her. "Christian has been low-key blackmailing me with that information since he found me in Varenna."

Sybil brushed her hands, and said, in a very practical Driedish way, "You'll need to tell them."

"No." My answer was automatic. But inside, a tiny nugget of doubt sprang up.

She grew sterner. "Caroline. Secrets only give these bastards power over you. Once you expose all the truths, they can no longer win."

I laughed, a bitter, sharp sound. "Oh, yes. I see your point. Once I tell my family that I wrote a royal gossip column under the name Cordelia Lancaster, it won't matter so much when the bad guys expose me on national television."

"It was almost ten years ago."

"It was the most difficult, brutal period my family has endured," I reminded her.

"You wrote those columns to take control of the narrative. You always had the best intentions."

I shook my head. It wouldn't matter that it had only ever been an impulsive way to try to turn the tide of public opinion back to supporting the family. Any type of unsanctioned involvement with the press would be treated as a mortal act of betrayal. And I'd just now returned to Drieden. Already I'd had one minor scandal, and there couldn't be another. Not with Gran abdicating this summer and Thea taking her place.

It would be the world's worst timing.

I had never been very religious. Oh, I had probably attended church services more than the average Driedish girl, but piety was considered a plus for princesses. But right there, on the cliffs of Dréuvar, I wanted to pray. I wanted to pray for salvation, for a way out of this awful place I'd found myself in. I wanted to pray for vengeance on whatever creepy jerk had sat in the dark and lurked in my private corners only to hurt me. I wanted to pray for grace. That after all the mistakes I had made, maybe—just maybe—I would be allowed a small sliver of peace. Or love. Or both, really.

"If I tell them, that's it." I swallowed hard. "My relationship with my siblings, with my parents. They'll be destroyed."

Sybil raised an eyebrow. "Could it be any worse?"

I barked a laugh at her cynicism, but she was right. Telling them everything would sever the last flimsy thread of connection between me and my Laurent legacy.

Would it be so bad?

My Sevine side had its answer already.

"What will you tell Thea about my forays into tabloid journalism?" I asked.

"I've already given her the identification information. I will also tell her that you have been thoroughly targeted. But that's all for now." Sybil pressed her lips together, like she already regretted keeping information to herself.

"Can you give me some time? A few days, a week?"

Her voice lowered. "And what will you do?"

"Sybil, you disappoint me. Don't you know already?" She was a psychic, an astrologer; she had charts and predictions for all of us.

She smiled mysteriously. "Your cards have always been a little oblique."

When we got back to the château, we entered at the back hall, a high-ceilinged square vestibule where two wide stairs faced each other. Once again, it was similar to my father's house at Ceillis. One stair would go toward the west wing and the other toward the east.

Sybil went up a few steps toward the west and then, when she realized I wasn't following, stopped and turned. "They're meeting in the dining room. I was told there was breakfast."

Even as stressed out as it was, my stomach rumbled. Never too traumatized for breakfast, it reminded me.

"I need a moment," I told Sybil, who seemed to understand and left me with a nod and an appraising smile.

In the center of that entryway, I stood like a statue. Whirring thoughts raced through my mind with such speed Stavros would have been impressed.

Oh, Stavros. Briefly, I wondered what Christian's hackers would have seen of my marriage when they peeked through my digital curtain. It was probably very little, which was ironic. The most scandalous thing I'd ever done hadn't played itself out in black and white, in emails or direct deposits. No, my marriage was all physical. Stolen kisses and cars belching exhaust and a thick black veil that concealed my face in a shadow so dark a photographer's flashbulb couldn't penetrate.

It probably qualified as the most morbid thought of my life, but still I wondered if what I was feeling now was similar to what Stavros had felt in those last few moments of his life. Did he see the crash coming? Did he recognize that he was out of control, that his choices were limited? That no matter which way he turned the wheel, he was headed straight into disaster?

Because that was where I was. No matter what choice I made today, or tomorrow, or twenty years from now, someone out there could have information that would hurt me or humiliate me or drive a wedge between me and my family.

So maybe prayer was the only answer. Maybe a miracle was the only way out. I huffed a laugh, shook my head, looked up at the sky and then saw, out of the corner of my eye, a figure coming down the west staircase.

Hugh.

His steps were sure and fast, his face that so-familiar mix of focus and concern. "Sybil said you were down here," he said when he reached me.

"I hope I didn't worry you," I said, with only a little bit of sarcasm.

He looked quite serious when he said, "I'm constantly worried by you."

"I'm a bigger mess than you planned for, is that it? That's why you had to lie to me?"

"What did you want me to do?" His voice was softer now, almost gentle. I couldn't let him see how much I liked it. How I craved more from him. "This is what I do. What I've always done."

"You've always lied to me?"

"I've always protected you." A shadow crossed his face. "Or tried to."

I finally understood that. Hadn't that been what I'd spent my life doing? Protecting my family?

But seeing it in Hugh made it different. "It wasn't your job to protect me from all my bad decisions, and certainly not from Stavros. He was my husband, I loved him, and I will own that choice for the rest of my days." My lungs hurt as I said those words, something I don't think I had said before. After Stavros died, I had only regrets—about my notoriety, my family, my shame.

Tears flooded my eyes as I remembered good things, too. Happy, sweet, lovely memories of laughter, kisses and, yes, independence. It was all mine. It would always be mine.

Hugh reached out, as if he wanted to erase the tears from my cheek, and instead I grabbed his hand, reveling in his warm skin, his long fingers that instantly wove through mine.

God help me, I was probably making a bad decision again, but I didn't want to let him go. Not yet.

"Let's make a deal." My voice sounded scratchy and low. "No more lies. No promises we can't keep. And when this is over, it's over."

Hugh pulled me in for a hot, fierce kiss, and I guessed that answer was as good as any.

thirty-four

DIDN'T WANT TO GO. I DESPERATELY WANTED TO GO. THIS dinner was my worst nightmare. It was my biggest opportunity.

Okay. I had some mixed feelings about heading to the palace for a private dinner with the Queen and my siblings. Who could blame me?

It had been Thea's idea, obviously. She had told me, in no uncertain terms, on the drive back from the Château de Dréuvar, that the dinner was happening and I was going.

Of course, I wanted to throw it all back in her face. Her and Nick showing up at Dréuvar had ruined all my plans. Christian hadn't responded to further calls or emails, which meant he had been nearby or had someone reporting on things for him, telling him that the cavalry had ridden to my "rescue." Yes, I was still angry. If Christian wasn't caught, then all the upheaval in my life had been for nothing.

Thea had also asked if I could muster up a modicum of surprise when Gran made the big announcement at the dinner about Thea's succession to the throne.

Little did she know how good I was at keeping secrets.

I still hadn't figured out what I was going to do . . . about revealing my Cordelia Lancaster and Clémence Diederich identities, and I knew that clock was ticking. Sybil was right, it would be better coming from me and Christian could blow the whistle at any time, but I still wanted a few more days of normalcy. Maybe I could see Sophie and Henry and Felice one more time before they learned of my betrayals.

"I won't lie to Sophie and Henry about the succession," I told her, filled with guilt about all the other lies I was sort-of telling. "And Henry has leave to come?" Our brother flew planes for NATO, wearing the uniform of our military with valor and distinction. I'd always been proud—not only of his service, but that he'd found something that he loved to do, and so effortlessly, too.

Thea nodded. "He always has leave when Big Gran says he does."

That put a sour taste back in my mouth. Here we were, all of us, having to jump whenever duty called. The rebellious side of me wanted to ask Thea if she would be just as demanding when she was crowned. If she would require our presence at ribbons and trophies and unveilings and other necessary events of civilization.

Why do you care? You're not even officially a part of this family anymore, came the petty voice from inside my head. *And you definitely won't be once the truth comes out.*

So I kept my mouth shut and ignored all the complicated feelings that came with being on the fringes of the Laurent family.

But I had one more person I needed to know about.

". . . Will Hugh be there?" I asked.

"He still works for the palace," Thea reminded me. "And he's a vital part of my staff, I need him to train his replacement and, honestly, Caroline, that is a little bit more important than whatever it is you two are doing."

"His replacement?"

"He's retiring from national service in April." Thea responded carefully, but the subtext was blaring: *He didn't tell you???*

"Oh," was all I said.

"He's got fifteen years and, like most law enforcement profession-als, he'd like to retire before he's completely broken by the job. Plus, I know he has his businesses to focus on, but I think it's not unfair of me to say that I wish he'd stay longer." Thea made a regretful face. "I don't think we're too awful to work for."

"So he's just going to become a businessman?" I asked, again striving for nonchalance, but I was either terrible at it or, more likely, my sister saw right through me.

"You two haven't talked about this? About the future?"

"Why would we?"

"I guess it's not serious, then?"

"No, of course not." *Liar.*

"That's a relief."

"What?"

"You've just lost the love of your life. And Hugh is a good, solid man. I just wouldn't want him to get hurt."

Ouch. But this time, I was better at hiding my feelings. Or maybe Thea didn't care about them. "How nice to hear he has businesses," I said brightly. "What sort are they?"

Thea waved a hand. "All kinds, I think. He's very involved in investing in Koras, started years ago when he first left the army. I think he started out with renovating properties, working with local shopkeepers and offering them fair rents. I keep asking him to advise the economic development council, but he refuses. Says it would be a security risk." Thea smiled ruefully. "Although I think he just likes to stay in the background. Some men are like that, you know. They want a quiet existence with no one ever noticing how impres-sive they are."

I let that all sink in, trying to ignore the churning feeling in my stomach. "Well, that is all very nice," I said again. "Good for him."

Thankfully, Thea didn't press me or bring up any additional

pieces of information that made me feel two inches tall for the rest of the ride. I was dropped off at the Hotel Ilysium, and Thea and the rest of the vehicles zoomed off toward the palace.

Leaving me to prepare for the dinner from hell all by myself.

FOUR GOWNS WAITED FOR ME IN MY SUITE. THERE WAS A small card.

Thea said you didn't have time to go shopping with me. Next time, you're buying. Xoxo Sophie

The sweetness of the gesture unlocked a little of the reservation I had about going back to the palace. What was I nervous about, anyway? This was my family! My baby sister, my twin brother. They had my back. It would be fine.

Still, I stood and stared at the four evening gowns for longer than was necessary. Picking out what to wear had never been a traumatic experience for me. Not to brag, but I had been listed on multiple international best-dressed lists throughout the last decade. The door to the bedroom opened and Hugh came in, freshly showered and changed back into his security guard suit.

"Oh . . ." I breathed. Gone was the thermal T-shirt and wool sweater and jeans he'd been wearing while he was on "sabbatical" and chasing Christian down across Europe *with me* . . .

He came closer. I couldn't help myself and reached out to touch his face. "You shaved . . ." Gone was the piratical auburn mustache, the beard that had felt both soft and rough against my skin.

"Vacation's over," he explained as he looked me over in my thick white hotel robe. "Are you nervous?"

I managed a self-conscious laugh. "How can you tell?"

"I can tell," he said simply, and he pulled me into his arms.

Hmmm. "Magical bodyguard senses," I guessed.

"No." He nuzzled me and I felt warm. *Seen.* "When you're feeling confident, you move quickly. When you're feeling unsure or hesitant, you spend a lot of time in bathrobes."

I shook my head. I wasn't sure that was true at all. "I'd like to take this bathrobe off right now," I murmured. "But my presence is required shortly at the palace." I added those last words like someone had asked me to describe cockroach mating practices.

"Did you and your sister talk yet?" he asked, and I could tell that it was important to him. He and Thea respected each other, were even friends of a type. My sister's words floated back to me.

Hugh is a good, solid man. I just wouldn't want him to get hurt.

"Actually, we talked about you," I replied lightly. "And your upcoming retirement."

"Mmmhm," he said as he kissed me under my ear.

"I didn't know," I continued, "about how much you're looking forward to being in the private sector."

"I've never heard it called that before," he said with a slyness that made me giggle, even though I knew he was avoiding my indirect inquiries. Hugh spun me around and tucked my back into his chest so that now we could both stare listlessly at the four dresses my baby sister had thoughtfully bought for me. "Sophie did well," he said, his voice rumbling against my back.

"Don't tell me that you knew she picked out these dresses because she prefers pink or you know which boutiques she shops at on Fridays."

He laughed. "No. I saw the delivery slip earlier."

Oh. I twined my fingers with his and drew them across my body like a seatbelt. "Which one should I wear?" I asked, because I was curious about which he'd prefer.

"You'd look beautiful in all of them."

"That's a very safe answer," I replied drily. "And thank you. Now pick."

He untangled himself from me, walked to the dress rack and selected a dress. It was floor-length, like the rest of them, with long sleeves, like the others. But this one had a daring deep V-neck—more risqué than I'd ever worn in the Queen's presence before.

"Done," I said quickly. "But you have to tell me, why did you pick this one?"

"Two reasons," he said, bringing me back the dress on its padded white silk hanger. "It matches your eyes."

The color was deep forest green. Not quite my eye color, but I was, of course, flattered by the comparison. "And?" I pressed as I untied my robe and revealed the feminine black undergarments I had already put on.

His eyes darkened, his Adam's apple bobbed. "It looks good on the floor." I was in his arms before the dress floated to the carpet.

I WAS ESCORTED TO BIG GRAN'S PRIVATE GOLD DINING room (not to be confused with the formal gold dining room—you know you're rich when you have two gold dining rooms). Hugh left me in the hallway—for private family functions, the security stayed outside—with a squeeze of my fingers. And when I hesitated to walk through the wide double doors, for an instant I saw what Hugh—or other guards—must see when they watched me.

When you're feeling confident, you move quickly. When you're feeling unsure or hesitant, you spend a lot of time in bathrobes.

It was a lot to think about. Maybe I'd have to go to therapy to puzzle out whether that statement was true. Or maybe I'd just let Hugh explain me to me. He had certainly proved to be an expert in the subject.

Feeling those eyes upon me, I lifted my chin, took a steadying breath and quickly stepped over the threshold into Big Gran's dining room of doom.

I was immediately tackled from my left. "Caroline!" Sophie squealed. "Oh!" After she finished squeezing me, she stepped back and examined my dress. "You picked the green!" Her eyes lit up. "Of course you did, you're an international femme fatale with a dangerous, tragic past now."

"Sophie. Really?" my brother chided her in an exasperated tone. I turned and saw my handsome brother. Taller than the rest of us, with sharp, perfect bone structure and his blond hair cut precisely, he was dressed in a black dinner jacket and casual navy pants better suited for weekend sailing. It was like, if he wasn't in uniform, he really didn't know what to wear. Most people in the palace accepted that about him—after all, he was in the military. No one would criticize his fashion choices off-duty.

Except I knew the truth. When he bent down to kiss my cheek, I murmured, "No black pants in your closet?"

"Of course there were," he whispered back. "They came with the coat."

See, no one supplied a royal prince with one half of a suit. Henry did this on purpose. He had a private secretary at the palace and his measurements were on file with at least three tailors in the city and probably one in London and in Paris. He had access to all the proper princely clothes, had people to order a fully bespoke wardrobe. But for some reason, for years, he rejected those particular royal expectations in this small, silly way, which garnered no repercussions for him.

Now why couldn't I have followed his lead? Picked some innocuous, easily explained method of rebellion? No, instead, I had to run off and marry the first race car driver who knew how to kiss properly.

Maybe Sophie was right. Maybe I was an international femme fatale.

Just like Mother.

I gave my head a gentle shake. I couldn't get caught up in deep thoughts about matriarchal DNA tonight. I needed to stay present. On my toes. Because the show was about to start.

Sophie was still squabbling with Henry. "I said she looked beautiful—I don't know what I did wrong." She linked her arm through mine. "And there's nothing wrong with a dramatic entrance," she informed me with a very serious air. "It's something I always strive for."

"God, Sophie, you're so full of it," Henry said into the whiskey he had been gulping like he was a man in the middle of a whiskey-free desert.

"And you're such a curmudgeon," Sophie threw back. "Why are you so cranky tonight? Is it because of that American actress who's got her hooks in you?"

"Who?" Henry looked genuinely confused.

"The one at the Beyoncé concert?" I helpfully supplied.

But Henry's eyes remained blank. "Sorry. I still have no idea what she's yammering on about."

Sophie clucked. "I suppose there are so many American actresses, he can't keep them all straight. Oh, the joy of being an eligible European prince these days. Meanwhile, I have to practically throw myself at men to get them interested."

Henry sighed, as if he were in pain. "Does anyone need a refill?"

"I don't even have a drink yet," I said.

My brother widened his eyes. "Oh, no. We can't have that. You must be properly prepared for the evening. Champagne, or something stronger?"

"My usual," I said.

"Straight up vodka with a Xanax chaser—excellent choice." He turned to fetch me a drink like a thoughtful brother who wanted to escape a baby sister who insisted on saying inappropriate things.

"I don't have a drink either!" Sophie nearly shouted at his back.

"Shh . . ." I hushed her, but then started to laugh. The impulse had been an old habit, nurtured during a lifetime of being quiet and obedient on occasions such as this. Strange how it came back and resettled in my skin so quickly. "Never mind," I said to Sophie. "Make all the noise you want."

Sophie had a curious look in her eye. "You're different. I'm sorry I was so flippant earlier. About . . . your *annus horribilus*. You know I say things I don't mean, but you do have a certain air to you."

"It's the dress. It's gorgeous. Thank you," I said sincerely as I remembered the man who had helped me fasten the back of it. The way his rough hands had glided against the smooth silk.

"You're blushing," Sophie observed. "It's more than the dress, then. Good. You're too young to hide away and mourn Awful Stavros . . ." She opened her mouth and put her hand against it. "I did it again. I'm sorry."

I wasn't angry. "He wasn't awful," I said softly. "We had a good run, but I'm not sure we would have stayed together forever." I thought of the divorce attorney Stavros had contacted in Paris. How I hadn't been mad when I'd found out. I tried not to wonder if the hackers knew about that, too, and if that private bit of information would soon be plastered on every gossip site.

"I heard things . . ." Sophie let that hang out there, and it was enough. Of course she'd heard things. The circles of jetsetters were fairly small, even with all the access to private jets. And she'd hear more, if I continued to have any sort of life. People couldn't control themselves.

But then Henry came with the drinks, deftly handing a Martini to me and a glass of champagne to Sophie while juggling his whiskey.

"You do love me," Sophie sighed. "Because you could have had a footman bring these over but instead you did it yourself."

"I forgot about the footmen." Henry swore with a grimace, and I laughed because of course he hadn't forgotten. He did love us enough to bring our alcohol himself—and if that wasn't love, what was?

"Does anyone know why we're here?" Sophie asked, after a few sips of champagne. "I feel like something terrible's about to happen."

Henry frowned. "Like what?"

Sophie shrugged. "I don't know. I just have a feeling."

And right at that moment the doors opened and the stars of the evening entered. Our grandmother, the Queen, had even worn her largest tiara, with matching earrings and choker.

Sophie caught my eye. Yes, it was that serious.

Thea smiled when she saw me and made a discreet wave with her fingers, directing me to her and Gran. "You're on, sis," Henry said, hiding his mouth behind his glass.

"Don't fuck up," Sophie managed to say while keeping a wide smile on her face.

When you're feeling confident, you move quickly.

Without the slightest bit of hesitation, I went to greet my Queen.

Thea faded into the background with all the innate grace of a princess and the skill of a ninja.

And it was just me. And the woman who had thrown me out of the family.

thirty-five

ER MAJESTY QUEEN AURELIA HAD RESTING BITCH face. Which wasn't a bad thing for a Queen, if we're being perfectly honest about it. I had grown used to the fact that my grandmother had never smiled with matriarchal satisfaction when I came into a room, even when I was an adorable tow-headed child, so the face that she had on now was quite normal.

Still, the uncertainty of the situation did make me sweat a little more than was approved by royal etiquette.

She spoke first. "Caroline. How lovely that you've joined us this evening."

Translation: Thea made me invite you.

"It's my pleasure, Your Majesty."

Translation: I couldn't get out of it. See also, a passive-aggressive reminder that I was thrown out of the family nine months ago.

"Your sister tells me you've graciously volunteered to help her with some of her charitable work."

I wasn't sure what that meant. Was she talking about the meeting with Karl Sylvain von Falkenburg? Or the whole debacle with Christian?

I decided to take a shot on the most likely possibility.

"Yes. I was most fascinated by the historical site that Mr. von Falkenburg introduced me to."

Her eyebrows arched. I think that meant that I had chosen correctly.

"The Langûs battlefield and the discovery of King Fredrik's grave. Such an important development for the continued installation of our family's legacy." She paused. "Don't you agree?"

I nodded slowly. "Family is everything."

There was a cough somewhere from the direction of my siblings, who were totally pretending not to listen to my conversation with Big Gran.

My grandmother's eyes flashed with interest, and maybe my small little digs weren't going to repair my relationship with her, but I remembered that I had other family.

"Speaking of which," I continued without letting her reply, "I was able to briefly visit Astrid recently."

"The Dowager Duchess of Aronburg," she said with a hint of correction. "How is Lady Astrid?"

"She is well." I smiled blandly. "Still running her own little kingdom in the mountains."

Thea swooped in. "I believe dinner will be served shortly. Shall we take our seats?"

Gran turned without saying another word to either of us. Thea gave me a decided watch-it look and then Henry came up and whispered in my ear, "Weren't you supposed to grovel and plead for forgiveness?"

I sighed. "I think so."

"That was very poor groveling," Henry said gravely. "The worst groveling I've ever seen, in fact."

"But very entertaining," Sophie added as she swooped by us on her way to the table set for five.

Dinner started. We had always been fortunate, I suppose, that Gran insisted on delicious food in substantial quantities. I had heard some horrible stories about bland fish courses and tiny glasses of wine at some of the *other* royal palaces in the countries that bordered Drieden. They know who they are.

There was light conversation about Henry's military duties, and about Aurelia's correspondence with a beloved former American president (not the recent, disastrous one. Gran had called *him* a pompous jackass, if I recalled correctly).

Then, just after coffee was served, Thea clinked her glass with a spoon.

"A bit formal, are we?" Henry asked.

"You could have just kicked us under the table like you used to," Sophie said.

Thea lifted a brow at Sophie, who made a kissing face back.

I knew what Thea was about to say and, for one bittersweet moment, I wished she wouldn't.

I liked our family exactly as it was. The sass from our baby sister. The droll over-it attitude from our brother. Our absent but loving parents. And, I realized, I'd even made a small amount of peace with what Gran had done to me.

Yes, she'd cut me off. Taking away my title had been almost like a metaphysical amputation. Something that had always been part of me suddenly wasn't.

But. It wasn't fatal—to my self-worth, to my future, even to my relationships with my family. I'd proved that by coming back tonight in my emerald silk cut nearly to my navel, chosen by my lover, who saw me exactly as I was.

Once the imminent announcement was made, everything could change.

Maybe Sophie wouldn't make faces at her sister . . . once she was Queen.

Maybe Henry wouldn't gallantly offer to play bartender . . . for his sister the Queen.

Maybe Thea would return my titles to me.

Maybe I didn't even want them anymore.

Gran's voice interrupted my reverie. "I wanted you all here tonight so you could hear it from me. After the celebration of my Jubilee this summer, I will inform Parliament that I am stepping down from the throne."

A dramatic pause. Because she hadn't wasted the last fifty years being an idiot.

"And I intend to declare that Theodora shall succeed me."

Getting all dressed up and enduring Gran's coolness was a hundred per cent worth it to see the expressions on my siblings' faces.

Sophie's eyebrow arched dramatically.

Henry blinked two, three dozen times.

We were too well trained to swear (even though I was tempted to fully take advantage of my black-sheep status), but I was fairly certain that certain very unroyal words were flashing through my siblings' minds.

And because no one had ever informed me of the proper court etiquette for this situation, I did the only thing that felt right to me. I stood, lifted my glass of wine and said solemnly, "God save Queen Aurelia."

Henry stood, then Sophie, each following my lead. Then Thea did the same and I finally succeeded in melting my grandmother's resting bitch face into a true, humble smile.

Harald, Big Gran's personal butler, sprinted into the room. I had never seen the man move so fast before. I don't even think I had seen him turn a color besides pale ecru.

But it wasn't just Harald. Security agents appeared as if out of thin air. Two of them at every door, each of them holding their fingers to their ears, to whatever news alert or orders were being transmitted.

And then, maybe even scarier—Hugh and Nick stepped inside the room with faces deadly serious.

I had only seen these kind of acts once in my life, after a terrorist explosion in the downtown subway four years ago. It was a lockdown procedure. Henry, Sophie, and I exchanged looks. We all knew it. And then I noticed something.

Harald had bent low to whisper something in Big Gran's ear. Then she had pointed at Thea and he did the same to her.

I wasn't sure which scared me most. The fact that Big Gran had just abdicated a duty to my sister or the tears that were now spilling onto her cheeks.

"What's happened?" I asked. Hugh's eyes caught mine across the room and he gave me a small nod, making me feel like we were in this together—whatever this was.

But Her Majesty Queen Aurelia had just fully broken down, her white gloves covering her face. So Thea stood and put her hands on Big Gran's shoulders.

"What's happened!" I demanded this time. If I was part of this family, even on the outskirts, I deserved to know.

Thea looked stricken as she recounted the news. "It's Father. He's had an attack. He needs urgent surgery right away."

"Oh my God!" Sophie cried.

Henry pushed back his chair. "Where? What hospital?" he shouted at a security officer. "Sinclair! Tell the helipad to get ready."

"He's at Ceillis House or . . . he was. He's being flown into St Mary's now. The Ören wing," Thea added, but it was almost unnecessary. It was the section of the hospital that was organized and prepared for royal visits—emergency or routine.

Henry checked his watch. "Still, this time of night, we'll do better with the helicopter." He signaled to the men and held his hand out for Sophie as she got out of her chair.

Queen Aurelia's voice rose above the sounds of pushing chairs and rushing bodies. "Thea stays."

The pronouncement startled all of us until we remembered . . .

"Yes, ma'am," Henry said in his military manner. It was appropriate; he was taking an order, after all.

But Thea looked like she didn't want to obey. She even went as far as to say that one word that would have earned any of us a sharp reprimand when we were children. "But . . ."

"The Crown Prince is in mortal danger. As next in line, you must stay here." Big Gran's voice was shaky but carried all her authority. No one argued.

Henry, Sophie and I rushed from the room but, down the hall, I stopped when Henry started to turn left toward the courtyard, where the helipad was located. He said my name. "What is it?"

"I'll join you there," I promised. "I have a stop to make first."

My twin gave me a brief nod, snatched our little sister's hand and moved on. In the entire family, Henry was always the one who had always accepted my decisions without argument. Frankly, it was a relief.

I spun and went back toward the stairs, where I would find the drivers and the cars. A few minutes later, I was in the back of a palace Mercedes, speeding along the Corsicair toward the Hotel Ilysium. I told the driver to call Agent Konnor and let him know where we were going. He was back on regular duty and his place was with the rest of the security staff, but I still wanted him to know I was safe.

If the whole family had to gather at my father's bedside, then I was determined that Thea would be the only one left out.

THE HOSPITAL HAD STAFF WAITING FOR US AND THERE was a private underground entrance for the SUV to pull into, but I knew that all the precautions in the world wouldn't stop this news from getting out. That not only was Prince Albert in the hospital, but that his disowned daughter and ex-wife had rushed to his side.

I had dragged my mother out of a pre-theater private dinner party for ten that she had been enjoying in her suite, so she was dressed in her brightest peacock-blue plumage. The two of us in our evening clothes rushing out of the hotel and then into a hospital wing would automatically draw attention. It was only a matter of time. Everyone would know soon.

The memories of Stavros's death came crashing back to the present. The press, the photographers. The gruesome things they shouted as I stumbled from vehicle to building to vehicle to hotel. I hadn't even known where I was going, who was leading me, I had simply trusted people to take me where I needed to be.

It was much the same tonight. The staff led us to the fourth floor. Palace security had already stationed themselves at the entrances. Doors opened as we approached. I didn't stop and smile or thank anyone. I had one mission.

To see my father one last time.

The waiting room was probably fancier than the rest of the hospital, but I noticed none of it, seeing only the faces of Sophie and Henry and a team of white-coated doctors. "Mama!" Sophie cried, running to Felice's arms. Henry excused himself from the doctors to come and give our mother a hug as well. We were dysfunctional, perhaps, but in this fishbowl we needed each other more than ever.

"Thank you," Henry said with a kiss on my cheek. "For bringing her," he added.

"She'd never forgive herself if she wasn't here."

"And we'd never stop hearing about it," he added with a small bit of deadpan humor.

Then Henry led me back to the doctors to hear the news I had dreaded. It would be a miracle if our father survived the night.

thirty-six

I T WAS JUST AFTER DAWN THE NEXT MORNING WHEN THE doctors came into the private waiting room with the news. Father had stabilized, which was good, but they had determined that the best course of action would be heart surgery.

Among the doctors who had entered was the chief surgeon of the palace, Dr. Fabian Lao, whom I knew reasonably well. It was nice to see a familiar, trustworthy face among the white coats, who were surely very self-aware that their patient could only be the next king of Drieden if they didn't mess up.

The doctors told us what to expect, how long it would be and what the surgery would entail. "Do whatever's necessary," Henry said, as if he was gruffly giving orders to a young soldier.

Dr. Lao paused. "There is a question of consent."

"It's fine," I said. "We trust you."

"No." For the first time, Dr. Lao looked out of his element. "In this particular case, with the patient being a member of the royal family—"

"What, do you need an Act of Parliament or something?" Henry burst out. "No one is objecting to the surgery."

"The palace has an official protocol for this—"

"Goddammit, there's always a fucking rule, isn't there?"

I put my hand on Henry's arm. It had been a long night, but he could zip it while we finished this up. "Go on, Doctor," I said.

"And we must not only receive a release from the palace but also a signature from His Royal Highness's designated medical representative."

"What do we have to do?" I asked, furiously aware that yet again red tape could be stealing something precious from my life.

"We have the release from the palace. We just need a signature from the Duchess of Montaget."

Both Henry and I turned slowly and looked at our mother, still dressed in her vivid blue evening gown, curled up on a sofa soundly sleeping. "Absolutely," I told Dr. Lao as I put my hand out for the paper that would require one signature and three witnesses before anyone would dare cut into the chest cavity of the Crown Prince.

But as I watched my groggy mother sign consent for her ex-husband's surgery, I felt that silent bond of family again. When my father was better, I would try to have this conversation with him, as awkward as it would probably be. About why he still had my mother designated as his medical representative (and honestly, whether that was a practical idea, since she spent the majority of her time outside of Drieden).

Whatever his reasons—emotional, practical, or, more probably in the case of my father, accidentally negligent—this evidence of yet another way we were all connected hit me hard. When we volunteered to give blood ("Royal blood—the best kind of blood," Henry darkly joked), I thought of our DNA. The things we couldn't avoid, the things we couldn't leave behind, even when we tried our damnedest to.

Yes, so I got a little loopy after a night spent in a hospital waiting room. Who doesn't?

Thea stayed at the palace, as was required, but she sent Nick in her stead, along with the blood she'd had drawn there (she didn't want to be left out, I guessed). I caught a few minutes alone with him, telling him all the updates for him to take back to Thea and Gran. Thea didn't want to use the phones or anything digital, he said, since what happened to me had caused them to analyze all their networks again.

I hadn't thought about the hacking in nearly twelve hours. "Have you heard anything?" I asked Nick, even though my bones ached from exhaustion. "Did they catch the guy yet?"

He shook his head, his mouth a grim line. "He was gone when they got there. We're pulling surveillance, asking the neighbors and searching his belongings. We'll find him."

"Do you think it's Christian?" I asked, wondering if hope was even appropriate in this situation.

Nick shook his head. "Not unless my brother magically became some computer genius in the past year. Sybil said the security systems this guy could breach were beyond most."

"Oh." It was the most coherent response I could muster.

"Are you all right?" Nick said, his Scottish accent sharp. He took one of my hands. "You're shaking like a leaf."

"I'm fine," I said as I took my hand back.

Nick gave his eyes a slight roll. "God save me from fine women. You're coming back with me. You need a decent night's sleep."

"My mother is here," I pointed out, as if it helped my side of the argument. We both looked back at Felice, who had somehow, in the middle of a hospital, procured what looked like cashmere blankets and a satin eye mask.

"Your mother looks fine," he said, putting an emphasis on the last word. "You do not."

"What is it with you security types telling me I look like hell?"

Nick did not answer me, he just let his eyes roll down the tourist

T-shirt someone had brought in last night and which I had thrown on over my emerald silk dress.

"I'll let your brother know we're leaving, if he and Sophie want to come."

Of course, Henry wanted to stay. It was just like him, another kind of duty, another kind of post. And when Henry said he was staying, Sophie lifted her chin, yawned loudly and announced that she was, too. It was a sweet echo of how they were as children, a relationship built on hero worship and dangerous dares. Sophie, for all her flighty and feminine ways, never let a mere *boy* show her up. She did everything Henry did—with ribbons in her hair.

I kissed them each goodbye, getting closer and closer to tears with each embrace. It all seemed so terribly fragile. This family was on the brink of falling apart and any minute I could be the first one toppling the fragile pieces.

NICK HAD BEEN RIGHT. I WASN'T FINE. AND THAT WAS probably why I didn't notice when our car missed the turn toward Harvade, where the Hotel Ilysium was, and plowed firmly into the city center.

To the palace.

When we approached the gates, I opened my mouth to object. I could whine that I had no clothes at the palace or order him to take me to my suite at the Ilysium immediately. Truth be told, I really did love the view from my room there and the mattresses were divine.

But one word shot into my head and stayed there, dangling like a beautiful jewel, promising relief like an oasis in a desert.

Hugh.

Hugh would be in the palace. And that would make up for any fresh clothes, perfect mattress and soothing view of the Comtesse.

Even though the palace had been my home for most of my life, I had no current apartments assigned to me here, so I followed Nick through the halls and anterooms I knew so well. The fact that he also could navigate them so confidently was not lost on me. Once we passed the current familial crisis, and if I still had a relationship where I could enjoy such confidences, I would ask Thea to tell me what their future held.

Finally, we stopped at a door in the tower wing. I would not cry, I could not cry, I told myself, even as hot tears made it hard for me to see.

"Thea told me to bring you here," Nick said, in a half-gruff, half-soft way as he punched in a code and opened the door to my old apartments.

"Nick, I'm sorry," I said before he could leave. "For what I said at Dréuvar. I don't hold you responsible for your brother."

He shook his head. "You weren't wrong. We've all made terrible, fucked-up decisions. Some of us are just lucky we get a second chance."

He took something out of his back pocket and handed it to me. "Speaking of second chances." It was a thick clunker of a cell-phone, probably equipped to make satellite calls from a submarine or a remote island. "Your sister wanted you to have this. For emergencies."

Then he gave me a nod and closed the door. Leaving me to my demons and my fears.

My old shower still had the sticky hot-water knob (even though this was the palace, some of the plumbing had issues—that's what happened when the pipes had originally been installed two centuries ago), but I knew exactly how much force was needed to turn it past the sticky part and get all that lovely hot water sluicing over my head.

There were the same shell-pink towels with my royal monogram. How silly that swirls of gold thread could make my throat go tight.

I paused in front of the closet. If my old clothes were still folded on the shelves and hung from the rods, I would know that I was in an alternate space-time reality and I could probably also jump from the roof of the palace and fight like a black-leather-clad superhero.

But no.

This story does not go into the futuristic science-fiction genre at this point.

We were still firmly set in contemporary fantasy—as all modern royal stories should be categorized. The closet was bare except for a bathrobe and one change of pajamas. They were Thea's, I could tell from her monogram on her bathrobe, and I guessed that Lucy must have picked them out, because Lucy always preferred the men's style of pajamas and Thea enjoyed more contemporary leggings and sweatshirts.

All of these intimate details, about the lives and preferences and freaking plumbing of the place I was now in, exhausted me. I wasn't sure if I belonged here anymore, but how could I not? When I could easily walk from the closet to the bed in the pitch black because my feet had traversed the pale blue carpets so many times (and also the furniture had probably not been moved since the Second World War).

I laid in bed and gazed up at the elaborate plaster molding that resembled inverted tiers of a wedding cake. It's why I had picked these rooms out when I was eighteen. Because the palace had been built and renovated by different rulers and in varied centuries, not all the wings were alike. Thea's looked out over the city, but the rooms were smaller, boxier there. Sophie had picked a set in the tower. Amazing panoramic views, but the extra flights of stairs were a bitch. (Also, palace staff took longer to get there if one needed them. Because they were only human.)

But these rooms had high vaulted ceilings and architectural details that came out of a storybook and encouraged fanciful daydreaming about fairies and evil witches and bodyguards who were also brave, stalwart knights.

No wonder nineteen-year-old me had dreamed up the most delicious fantasies about her bodyguard. And why I still did so, even as I passed out at twenty-nine.

thirty-seven

THE SOUND OF MY BEDROOM DOOR OPENING AWAK-
ened me. There was a squeak in the hinges that palace
maintenance staff had never quite silenced, and when they'd
told me the only thing left to do was replace the beautiful, ornate brass
hinges with modern, mass-produced ones, I had politely declined.

Because sometimes beautiful things made squeaks. That's what
made them beautiful.

So it was that tell-tale squeak I knew so well that caused my
eyes to pop open. Instantly, I knew where I was. My bedroom. In
the palace.

Then I smelled the coffee and my heart nearly burst.

It was Hugh, with a bag slung over his shoulder, and then a maid
pushing a cart.

"Hello," I said groggily, with a smile. Seeing him made me feel
anchored. Rooted.

"Good morning, ma'am," the maid said. I didn't recognize her, so
I hoped she didn't mind me not greeting her by name. I thanked her
as she laid out the coffee and then left me alone with my bodyguard.

My bodyguard, who, I realized, didn't look nearly as happy as I wished he did.

My stomach dropped. "What is it?" I immediately feared the worst. "Father?" I threw back the bedclothes and my feet landed on the floor. "I knew I shouldn't have left yesterday." Wait. What time was it? Morning? I checked the Limoges clock on top of the fireplace mantel. "How did you let me sleep for so long?" I went toward the closet, where I had left my clothes the night before.

"Everything's fine," he said, catching my hand. "There's just been a lot happening this morning."

"Tell me," I demanded.

"It's only the press. Nothing I haven't dealt with before."

I saw the paper on the breakfast tray. The screaming headlines were in bold black ink across the top, middle and bottom of the first page. I made myself look. If Hugh had to deal with this, so did I, and it was awful. Terrifying. The Crown Prince on life support. Rampant rumors, specious speculation, and me and my mother making the circus complete. There was even a side column wondering, "Where is Karl Sylvain?"

Because Karl and I were engaged, apparently.

"They're camped outside the gates, the hospital. I'm not sure if you'll be able to go back."

"They're not keeping me away," I hissed.

"For your security, I'm not sure that's wise."

This was exhausting. This argument, this life. "Are Henry, Sophie and my mother still there?"

Hugh nodded.

"If they are there, then I should be as well."

"But you're different. The press is used to Sophie, they're not used to you."

"I'm going back to the hospital, and that's that."

Hugh paused for a moment, and I recognized the expression on his face. It was the same one he used when Thea gave him orders.

And I had sounded just like her. Princessy and superior and authoritative.

And . . . oh God. This was no way to have a relationship. One person constantly submitting to the other.

Well. Maybe some people got off on that. But it wasn't my thing. I tried keeping the princess out of my voice when I spoke again.

"I want to go back to the hospital, Hugh. I have to be with my family."

And when he looked back at me, I saw the man, not the bodyguard. The man who actually cared about all of the parts of me, the one who would move Heaven and Earth for me.

The one who didn't stop me as I changed into the clothes that someone had retrieved for me. The one who had a coffee poured for me to carry to the cars downstairs.

The one who held my hand, however briefly, before I ducked out and ran toward the doors of the hospital, the one who shielded my body with his own, a useless defense against the yells and camera flashes.

Henry and Sophie had spent the night keeping watch, while, due to an unexpected complication, the doctors had put Father in a medical coma in order to give him the best chance at recovery from open heart surgery.

In the Ören wing, there was a safe space for the family to gather, and I didn't see any bodyguards after Henry and Sophie left to go take their rest at the palace.

It was just me and my mother, who had woken perfectly and miraculously refreshed. The only woman in the world who could get beauty sleep on a hospital chair.

But that wasn't to say that she was bright and chipper.

No. The world loved to think of Felice as flighty and flippant, but as she waited for good news about my father's recovery, she was quite serious and subdued.

A kind nurse brought us a small breakfast and a pot of tea. Felice touched neither until I forced a buttered roll into her hand. "You must eat," I told her. "I can't worry about you both at the same time."

Felice's eyes went watery. "Darling Caroline. You were always the one keeping us all together."

"I don't know about that," I sighed, thinking of how I had been disowned, ostracized and was now only reluctantly accepted by my grandmother. "If I was so good at keeping the family together, you'd think I would keep myself in the mix," I grumbled.

Felice smiled. "Just because you take care of the rest of us doesn't mean that you don't deserve your flights of fancy."

Her choice of words rubbed me wrong. "Marriage isn't a flight of fancy."

"No, of course not," she allowed. "But eloping does indicate a certain spontaneity."

I had to give her that.

"Ma'am?" The kind nurse had returned and she addressed me with a respectful dip. If I had been less bone tired, I would have told her that I wasn't a princess, that I didn't deserve a curtsey, but it was exhausting to correct people all the time.

"This came for you." She handed me a large white envelope bearing the Hotel Ilysium logo.

"Oooh. What is it?" Felice's interest was immediately piqued because Felice loved surprises and surprise packages even more.

I broke the seal on the envelope and two notes spilled out.

The first had handwriting that I recognized still, even all these years after I used her to relay my gossip column to the editors of the national tabloids.

Caroline,

As we are under strict instructions not to call you at the hotel, I had no choice but to drop this note off. I traced the source of the medical hacking—to a company called Bionaura. They have specialized servers and only someone with access could have used these.

Will talk more soon,
Sybil

Well, that made sense. It happened all the time—an employee inside a hospital, rehab facility or government tax office looked up the files on a famous name and accidentally leaked a substance abuse problem or a previously unreleased tax return. I had been a victim of a curious and bored data clerk who was looking for some extra cash.

It was the most logical explanation. But something wasn't quite right.

I opened the next note. It was written on the personal stationery of Karl Sylvain von Falkenburg.

Dear Lady Caroline,

First, I'd like to apologize for the media attention that our outing garnered the other day. I hope the coverage has not been too distasteful to you. In spite of all that, I truly enjoyed our time together and hoped we could meet again. Perhaps you could join me for dinner this evening at my residence?

Sincerely,
KvF

PS There will be no press invited.

It was very kind and thoughtful, and when I fingered the note I realized there was another thin page stuck to the back.

PPS I was giving this to my secretary when I heard the news on television about your father. Suffice it to say, the invitation remains open if you feel that a good meal and pleasant company would serve as a helpful distraction. If it won't, then please do not hesitate to decline this invitation. There will be other dinners and warmer evenings ahead.

"Who are they from, darling?" Felice asked.

I placed Sybil's note back in the envelope. My mother had once been close to Sybil, who had served as her personal astrologer, but I wasn't sure what the current status of their friendship was. Therefore, I moved quickly on to something I knew would distract my mother. "This is from Karl Sylvain von Falkenburg."

Her eyes lit up. "Oh." She drew the word out like a schoolgirl with a crush. "He's something, isn't he? Good for you, my girl. You clearly inherited my good taste in men."

She said it cheerfully, like it would be something I should be proud of, but since we were currently in a hospital waiting room because of her ex-husband's poor health, I couldn't help but wonder about her choices. And mine. If I had inherited anything from my mother, I feared it was not good taste in partners but the ability to make bad decision after bad decision.

"Do you know why Father still had you designated as his medical representative?" I asked suddenly.

The smile slipped from her plumped lips and the tears returned to her eyes again. Instantly, I regretted asking, but I found I couldn't tell her to forget I had asked. I had to know—"Do you regret marrying him?" I asked in a low voice.

She sank into her chair, her slim shoulders rounding, as if

protecting herself from the chilly Driedish wind outside. "We were practically strangers when we agreed to marry, your father and I. It was a perfect arrangement on paper. At last, the Laurent and Sevine dynasties united." She smiled weakly. "But if he had been ugly or repulsive, I would have said no, no matter what my mother urged me to do." Her eyes closed. "Your father was not ugly or repulsive. He was what every woman would dream of. So kind, so sweet, and a prince! How could I not fall in love with him?"

And I had seen the photographs. Felice and Albert's wedding day had been picture-perfect, the ideal Driedish prince and princess. Of course my father would have loved her, so beautiful, charming and ebullient.

Felice shook her head, bringing her back to the present. "How could I regret marrying a man I loved deeply? A man who gave me my children?" She placed her palm on my cheek, a cool, light touch, and then she let her hand drop.

"And the divorce? Do you regret that?" As a child of that broken marriage, I wasn't sure which I would rather hear—that my parents could have worked things out and spared us all so much heartbreak or that all the drama was for a good reason.

Her voice grew fainter when she replied. "Perfect princesses exist only in fairy tales. Humans wear tiaras, my darling. Humans who deserve love and forgiveness, just like everyone else."

My mother inhaled sharply through her nose before continuing. "You've been married, my love, you know as well as I do what that means." She glanced away, avoiding my gaze. "You can love someone with your whole heart, but you must find someone willing to walk with you, grow with you, no matter how difficult it is. No matter the differences between you."

That familiar Felice smile returned. "Which is why someone like Karl Sylvain von Falkenburg would be so perfect for you. He's

Driedish, for one, and he's incredibly wealthy. I mean, a billionaire is the next best thing to a prince, wouldn't you say?"

"Now you're sounding like all the newspapers," I accused her. "Karl and I have met exactly once and already the press are a nightmare to deal with."

My mother laughed. "You know what Konnor used to say, when he was on my security detail?"

I ignored the sudden extra thump of my heart when I heard Konnor's name. "What?" I tried to ask, as neutrally as possible.

"He said a swarm of press was his best friend while guarding me." Felice's eyes twinkled. "Because he always knew right where to find me."

I chuckled softly along with Mother, because it sounded like Konnor and it was also, to everyone in the royal staff's great despair, eternally true. Where Felice was, paparazzi were soon to follow.

Yet another thing I inherited from my mother. Unfortunately.

thirty-eight

WHEN HENRY RETURNED FOR WAITING-ROOM duty, his driver took me back to the Hotel Ilysium. Hugh slipped in the car with me and we watched the reporters as we left the hospital and again as we arrived at the hotel.

No matter where I was, there was screaming. Hustling and jostling and scrambling.

Even if my father hadn't been in the hospital, I knew this routine. There would be no privacy. No anonymity. No peace. I stared at the crowds and the concrete and desperately wanted a view of the water. Whether it was from my hotel room or overlooking Lake Como or in a dinghy off Perpetua.

The palace did not have a view of the sea.

This was never going to work.

All of a sudden, as the limousine pulled up to the Hotel Ilysium's door, with the lines of photographers and cameras, I knew what I had to do.

No matter what fantasies a girlish Princess Caroline had dreamed up in her fairy-tale palace bedroom, my relationship with Hugh Konnor could never have a happy ending.

Not with the press wetting themselves every time I appeared in public, inventing scandalous details about non-existent relationships and making it virtually impossible for me to do normal things like visit my father in hospital or take a walk on the beach.

And especially not with Hugh.

A good, solid man.

The kind of man who risked everything to keep others safe. Who served his country, who was loyal to a fault and reinvested in his community. The kind of man who deserved another kind of life.

Like Stavros had.

Stavros had deserved to stand in his own spotlight. To pursue his career without the danger of my distractions.

Some men are like that, you know. They want a quiet existence with no one ever noticing how impressive they are.

If Hugh stayed with me, he would always be worried, always be on guard. Because this shit wasn't going away, even if I escaped to the wilds of Tasmania. Sooner or later, I'd have to re-emerge and the hurricane would be whipped up all over again.

Right before he could exit the vehicle, I placed a hand on his sleeve. I knew what was under those layers of wool and cotton: a tattoo of the coordinates of his birthplace, the roughest section of Drieden City.

His eyes met mine, waiting for my softest command.

"Stay here," I said. Oh, my heart hurt. I wanted to thread my fingers through his, drag him along with me through the crossfire.

But that way lay madness, I knew from experience.

"It's time," I said quietly. "I will formally request that I am accompanied by a different bodyguard."

The silence was suffocating.

"Just like that?" he asked, his voice gravelly.

For a brief moment, we had been a team, and I was tempted to try to explain it all to him, like a partner would.

But ever since he had found me in that dark apartment in Varenna he had steadfastly refused to leave when I asked.

So I would have to be cruel to be kind.

"As soon as Father recovers, I'm leaving Drieden," I said, in my coldest, most Laurent voice. "Don't pout. We both agreed not to make promises."

His eyes flashed gold. "Caroline—" I cut him off before he could say something sweet to make me change my mind.

"Don't worry, I'll give you an excellent performance review." It was meant to put a distance between us, perhaps be a tad patronizing.

Hugh Konnor refused to take the bait and, to be honest, it would have felt better if he had become angry or offended.

Instead, he held my gaze and for a moment the Hugh I knew so intimately, loved so briefly, was there. And then gone, replaced by the uber-cool, oh-so-professional bodyguard. "If you ever need me, my lady, all you have to do is press one button and I'll be there."

He patted my handbag and the new cellphone that Nick had given me that was safely stashed inside.

Then, before I could form any semblance of regret, I slid my large sunglasses on my face and went out to face the horde of press.

Alone.

Hotel staff escorted me to an elevator, which was convenient, because I don't know if I remembered how to walk through a hotel lobby.

The love story was over. Now I had to figure out how to keep the rest of my fairy tale from imploding into dust.

Alone.

When I reached my suite, I threw my coat and handbag on a chair, closed my eyes and thought of Lake Como. My villa with that wide, beautiful veranda where I had been alone before and there was a certain relief in not feeling anything. I was strong enough to do it again.

But did I want to?

Being back in Drieden City had changed things and—I had to admit that I didn't want to lose my family again. This left me with only one option.

Make sure that Christian Fraser-Campbell was locked up before he leaked the information about me that would result in my family disowning me for good.

My head ached at that prospect, if I was being one hundred per cent honest. My father was in the hospital, I had just told my lover that I didn't want him with me anymore, because I might ruin his life, and so I had a few emotional things to deal with before I single-handedly caught a sociopath who had nearly been my brother-in-law.

I wanted to run away. The prospect of Patagonia was still intriguing. Or a week inside of a Swedish spa. Or maybe . . . a nice dinner with an attractive and available billionaire.

Guilt immediately descended. But of course. I could not enjoy myself this evening, not unless Father was awake and well on the road to recovery. Even then, I should probably take care of Sophie and Mother, not spend time with the sexy billionaire who . . .

Oh.

OH.

OH.

I emptied the contents of my handbag, found the notes I had received earlier and re-read the one from Sybil.

The company she had named, Bionaura, was one of the organizations in Karl's billion-euro bio-technology empire. I remembered it from the file I had read on him, provided by Thea's charity advisor, and then again, when it had been listed in a helpful infographic next to all those fuzzy paparazzi photos purporting to portray me running from all my lovers' arms. (Remember, this was all very fair and balanced journalism.)

I stared at the notes. There wasn't a connection there. Was there?

Karl's company was also handling the genetic testing of the bones found at the Langŭs battlefield. And he was a distant relation—on the Sevine side. The Sevines had owned Dréuvar, and Christian had all this information about me that could only have come from hacking . . .

No, it was all a coincidence. Or, more likely, a disgruntled employee. Yes, that could be right.

Until I remembered.

What was it Hugh had said? That Christian had to be supported by people who were powerful enough to hide him? Who was more powerful than a billionaire who had met my sister at Davos, who had access to the genetic information of kings?

Coincidence . . . or conspiracy?

I rubbed my head. I was still exhausted. Worried about Father. And I had just said goodbye to a man who had broken my heart and pieced it back together.

This was the absolute worst time for me to accuse an influential Driedish businessman of supporting a stalker, being a hacker and the dark-money supporter of an ancient secret Masonic organization.

But I picked up the phone and dialed Karl's secretary's number anyway. Because if ever there was a time for bad decisions, this was it.

What did I have to lose?

KARL'S APARTMENT IN DRIEDEN CITY WAS AT THE TOP OF the Trilennia building, one of the tallest in the financial district. Less than a mile from the palace, but as I had moved back to the Hotel Ilysium, I was caught in a traffic snarl and was late.

I had changed into another one of Sophie's gowns, black crêpe with a bateau neckline and dramatic ruffles on the sleeves. It would have looked amazing with my Sophia Loren glasses and hat back at Villa Cavalletta in Varenna.

Home.

I pushed on my Dior pearl earrings and pushed all thoughts of Italy out of my head. I couldn't think of going back. Not until my family was well and whole and safe again.

The doors of the express elevator opened straight into an astonishing penthouse that was the exact opposite of the palace bedroom I had woken up in that morning.

Where my palace bedroom had been antique brass, carved marble and cherubs, von Falkenburg's penthouse was sleek leather, glass slides and black steel. It still felt regal, however, and when Karl approached me, in his cashmere jacket and open-necked white shirt, I felt that here was a man who could rule a kingdom, one that he had built and knit together with his own sweat and ingenuity and machinations.

A twenty-first-century king. And me. A princess born and bred but without a place in the world.

Okay, I saw what the journalists—and my mother—did then, when they gushed about our potential romantic future. It would be a fascinating story. And perhaps an ideal match, if I was interested.

Which I wasn't.

But was Karl? He greeted me as I exited the elevator and smiled warmly. My body reacted—what woman's wouldn't? Karl Sylvain von Falkenburg was tall, muscular and striking with bronzed skin, as if he'd just stepped off his yacht after a week in the Mediterranean. "Lady Caroline, I'm flattered that you could come."

"Please, just call me Caroline." I accepted his offered hand. It was warm and welcoming. No sign of an evil weapon or a sneaky syringe. His hand was calloused, however. Maybe from all the hacking he did?

Stop, Caroline. Don't be ridiculous.

I made appreciative comments about his apartment, and they

were sincere. The place was breathtaking at night, as if the tiny tril-lions of lights of Drieden City were shining just so for his decor.

"Thank you. I don't get to spend nearly enough time here," he said, and of course I was about to ask what other residences he spent time at, because I'm a bit of a real-estate buff, but before I could, I turned and saw that Karl had a strange expression on his face, some blend of interest and admiration.

"Is that why you invited me tonight?" I asked. "Because you wanted a nice dinner at home?"

He looked amused. "Do you want the truth?"

If only he knew.

"I received a phone call, after our outing to the battlefield."

"Only one?" I asked.

"Only one that mattered." Karl smiled. "From a Lady Astrid Decht-Sevine. Suggesting that we get to know each other better."

It wasn't what I was expecting. And clearly not what Karl had expected either.

"I've only met her once, at a horse race about a decade or so ago. But she is a legend."

I remembered what my mother had said. "That's right, you're a Sevine relation."

He reared back slightly, cocked an eyebrow. "On my mother's side," he admitted.

"So we're what . . . cousins?"

"It would seem so." He made a gesture toward the candlelit table. "Does that make this awkward?"

"For most of Driedish history, I believe they preferred that prin-cesses dated cousins."

He cocked his head.

"Date?" he asked.

I felt my cheeks warm. "Let's call it an outing. With food."

"Exactly so." With the proper manners of a courtier, he pulled out a chair and I settled in for what I hoped would be an illuminating evening.

As dinner was served, I must admit I momentarily forgot all my suspicions and reasons for accepting the invitation. Karl was a sophisticated, interesting host who was able to skillfully direct the conversation from topic to topic. He would be right at home at the table in the Queen's gold dining room—either the small or large one.

I couldn't help but think that a match between me and this billionaire might be the only thing that Felice, Astrid and Aurelia could all agree on.

It would be so easy, I thought. All my problems would be solved if I could only fall in love with a man who had the appropriate pedigree to impress my family and the right-sized bank account. Karl looked at me, again with that warm yet searching expression. "Would you care to take coffee on the veranda?"

I answered with an enthusiastic yes. My two favorite things—coffee and fresh air. Then I would artfully ask about his Bionaura company and about whether he might know how a certain almost-royal could hack into my medical records there.

Karl stood, leaving his napkin on the table. "Let me just go find out what happened to my staff. They've left us alone far too long," he added with a wink.

It was really too bad that I was damaged goods. Karl would be lovely to get to know better.

One minute ticked by.

Three minutes.

I checked my watch. Karl had not returned, obviously, and the penthouse was strangely quiet.

And I suddenly had a very, very bad feeling.

thirty-nine

WITH THE SOUND OF MY RAPIDLY INCREASING heartbeat in my ears, I checked my handbag. Swore softly. There was no cellphone in it.

Had it fallen out? Did I remove it at the hotel?

I couldn't remember.

Think, Caroline.

My eyes darted around the walls for buttons, security alarms, but Karl's systems were discreet, as became a billionaire. No doubt there was a panic room around here somewhere, but my host had not included that on his brief tour at the beginning of the night.

I bit my lip to keep from calling out. No need to alert anyone to my presence—or my distress, if it turned out that Karl and his chef and butler were simply extremely quiet at coffee preparations. And dish-washing. And . . . all of the other sounds that humans make as they live and work in a space.

A creepy slither of fear slid down my spine.

Don't overreact, Caroline.

Do something, *Caroline.*

There.

I saw a phone on a side table. As if I had no cares, fears, or worries in the world, I walked to the wall, making out that I was inspecting the . . . what was it? Oh, the Wilheim Kurad sketch. Of course. Probably an estimated two million at auction. Lovely . . . lines.

My fingers landed on the phone receiver. Casually. Paused. *Shit.*

I knew no one's numbers. Out of panic, forgetfulness, lack of use, I couldn't remember a single useful phone number.

Except one.

I hadn't called it in years, but I did so automatically now. After two rings, a very bored Driedener answered. "Newspaper tip line."

Princess Caroline is having a rendezvous at the Trilennia.

I whispered and quickly replaced the receiver and spun around, certain that I was being watched.

There was no one.

But the door to the veranda was open.

Goosebumps erupted down my arms. Had the door been open before? Had the Driedish wind raked it open?

A feminine instinct made me grab my handbag. It was hand-made, sturdy calfskin with heavy palladium hardware and a handle that fit just so in my fist.

For a weapon, I could do worse than a Birkin.

The wind on the penthouse veranda was invigorating and strong. I would have enjoyed seeing the city lights from up here, if I wasn't so terrified.

Only a few feet from the glass railing, I turned when I heard a slight scuffing sound.

"Hello, Caroline."

I sighed with a strange relief.

After all, he was a man who I had once known quite well—or so I had thought. A man who would have been my brother—of a sort. And if I had to pick a person to lurk on a dark veranda waiting for me,

I supposed I'd rather have someone I sort of knew than a perfect stranger.

"Christian," I said. "You could have called me."

He moved away from the wall, and in the dim light I could just make out his skeptical expression. "You were trying to frame me at Dréuvar."

"Would you believe that it was my sister and your brother taking control of the situation?"

"One hundred per cent," he said solemnly.

Something dark and matte was in his hand, down by his leg.

"Where is Karl?" I asked, trying to keep my voice steady even though OMG *that was a gun in Christian's hand!*

Christian cocked his head back toward the penthouse.

Okay, then.

"What was this all about, Christian? You have me here, what do you want from me?"

"At first it was about your heritage."

"What do you mean, my heritage?" I blurted out. As a quasi-journalist, I couldn't help the follow-up question.

"It was the discovery at the Langûs battlefield. We simply wanted to confirm that the tests were accurate. That it was King Fredrik who was in that grave."

"We?" I echoed. "You mean Vox Umbra?"

His eyebrows raised. "Interested parties."

My gut twisted. "And I was right. You came after me because I was the weak link. The only Driedish royal outside of naval bases and royal properties who could have her blood tested."

"Not blood. I just wanted your hairbrush." Christian smirked. "But you had an unexpected bodyguard."

"So you hacked into my medical records when you couldn't get close enough to me." It was so ridiculous. "Why didn't you just ask? I would have been happy to give DNA to test against bones found on an archeological site." Just saying the words made me realize what an absolute lie Christian had just told me. "No. You had another reason."

"What other reason is there?" He chuckled like *I* was the one spouting crazy theories.

"You wanted to know about the current heirs," I guessed. "To see if we were legitimate."

His smile faded and, finally, he lifted his shoulders. "There were questions raised. Speculation in the press during your parents' divorce. And when I was with Thea, something always felt . . . different about your siblings."

"Shut up," I snapped. "You don't get to talk about my family. Not after what you've done."

Christian paused before speaking again. "What do you know about it, Caroline? You weren't even around."

"I know what my sister and Hugh have told me. About how you traumatized them."

He stepped closer. I gripped my handbag tighter. "Don't you want to know the true story? About why I did what I did?"

His tone was so sincere, and my instinct told me that he had told the truth in those emails to me. That he did want his story told.

With a shaky voice I gave him what he wanted. "I can tell the world, Christian. Clémence Diederich for *The Times*. Front-page investigative reporting."

I had to keep him talking, after all. How long had it been since I placed that phone call to the tabloid magazine tip line? How long would it be before paparazzi were camped out in front of the Trilennia building?

How long before my improvised SOS signal was recognized?

Christian was shaking his head, though. "They'll never believe you."

"They will," I said, a little too desperately. "They know who I am. Caroline Laurent. I'll even put my own name on it."

"Don't lie to me." The silent threat was chillier than the Driedish north wind.

"I'm not," I swore. "After Stavros died, I blew up the Formula One safety procedures. If you've been wronged, people need to know. The truth must be known."

"Even if your own family is exposed?"

I shrugged, praying that my next lie would be believable. "They abandoned me, Christian. Just for marrying a man they didn't approve of. Why would I protect them?"

And perhaps that spoke to his own self-interest, because he gestured toward the low-slung chairs on the deck with his gun. Oh yes, how completely welcoming that gesture was. Please, come and sit or I'll shoot you dead and leave you to rot.

Christian nodded toward the Birkin I still clutched in my lap. I wasn't sure I could unclench my fingers around the handle if he ordered me to, at this point.

"You have something to write this down?" he asked instead.

Because sociopaths are also egomaniacs. Don't want to miss a word of this insane word vomit. "Um, of course," I mumbled, praying to the patron saint of princesses in distress that I had *something* useful inside this very expensive accessory. *If all else failed, I'll just swing it at his head before he takes a shot at me.*

There was no cellphone in the bag, as I already knew. And no, I had not thought to toss in a Hotel Ilysium pen and notepad. But then my fingers closed around a small plastic cylinder.

My heart started to race.

I couldn't be sure, here on this shadowy balcony, but it felt an awful lot like my small can of pepper spray, which Hugh had presumptuously emptied for his own protection in Italy.

Could it be?

If it was dark enough for me to not know, then I figured I had a chance.

"Oh, brilliant," I remarked brightly. "I have my recorder on me." I palmed the canister, found the button with my thumb and, feeling like a terrified idiot, spoke into it. "Interview with Christian Fraser-Campbell."

Because it was dark, because he was a narcissist, because I had my very own patron saint and security detail of guardian angels, Christian didn't look twice at my so-called recorder.

I took a deep breath. It wasn't much, but I'd take what I could get. *Five minutes? Ten? Keep him talking, Caroline.*

Until you can't anymore.

"Were you already a member of Vox Umbra before you became engaged to my sister?" I asked him, holding the mace a little in front of me.

Christian nodded approvingly. "I was. It is a birthright of my family. Thea and I, we had met casually, then one day I received a call, encouraging me to pursue her."

"Who was it?" I asked, even though I already knew.

"Your grandmother. Astrid Decht-Sevine."

"It was an arranged marriage?" I asked, my throat dry.

Keep him talking.

"No, encouraged," he said, in a tone that said he doubted my intelligence. "Beneficial for everyone involved."

"So why did you threaten the Driedish monarchy?"

He lifted a shoulder. "There was a better offer." And then, as he realized how that would sound in a newspaper interview: "But really, it was because the people needed to know that the Driedish royal family was stealing from the people."

Whatever. I didn't care. This was all fake and any second now he was going to figure out that I was bluffing with a pretend voice recorder. I had to catch him by surprise if I was to have any advantage at all, so I readied myself to hurl my Birkin at Christian's smug face because I was tired of hearing him talk—

Crack.

I screamed.

I sprayed.

Another scream. Christian's.

Crack.

Gunshot.

Shove.

I fell to the cement. Tasted blood, grit, pepper, salt.

Heard my name. "Caroline!" In the same instant, I was clutched more tightly than I had been in my life. Surrounded by heat, male, darkness.

An embrace I would know anywhere. In heaven or in hell.

"Hugh."

His hands went to my cheeks, my chin was lifted to meet his face. "Are you all right?" A desperate demand.

I nodded. Then his mouth took mine. An altogether different demand.

Mine. Yours.

I broke away. I couldn't help it. Still in survival mode. Adrenaline off the charts. "What about—"

We looked down at Christian twisting and wailing on the ground several feet away from us. He had been shot in the face with pepper spray (mine) and shot in the arm with a bullet (Hugh's).

Teamwork.

Hugh was grim. "It's time to finish this."

I watched his first punch. And then the second.

I turned my head on the third, the fourth and the fifth. And then things went still. And Hugh returned to take me into his arms.

forty

WE FOUND KARL UNCONSCIOUS IN THE KITCHEN, along with two of his staff members. I said a silent prayer of thanks to that patron saint of mine and promised to never work her that hard again.

Hugh called Nick at the palace, and I heard obscenities through the phone. When Hugh ended the call, he looked at me with a grim expression. "You're going to have to explain what happened here."

I opened my mouth, and then closed it when I realized that Christian was still alive—barely. When he was turned over to palace security, he would start talking and, boy, did he have secrets to spill.

Finally, I shook my head. "They're not going to like what they hear."

Hugh walked over and kneeled in front of my chair. "We only have a few minutes—what do you want me to do?" I realized that Hugh was offering to do the unthinkable. Darkly, I thought it would be so much simpler if Hugh had pointed his gun a little closer to the chest cavity region when he'd taken a shot at Christian. But there was only so much I would ask of this man.

So all I said was, "You found me," because it was enough.

And he replied, "All I had to do was follow the cameras."

In the next moment, the emergency responders spilled out of the elevator, followed closely by more palace security officers, who bundled me up and swept me away without another word.

IN THE BASEMENTS OF THE PALACE, THERE WERE ADMINistrative offices, the maintenance offices and the security offices. This is where I was led, with a guard on either side of me, one at the back and one in the front with one hand on a radio.

They brought me to some kind of a conference room, where Thea and Nick were waiting, along with several other people who I recognized from my brief stay on Perpetua.

"Caroline!" Thea breathed a sigh of relief when she saw me, but it was me who should have been worried, because she looked ragged. The fluorescent lights did our fair skin no favors, but even then she looked exhausted, like she hadn't slept in days.

"I thought you said you were going to take care of her," I said to Nick, whose lowered lids said he was in no mood for my sass. So I moved on to more important things. "Has Christian arrived yet?" I needed to know what he had said.

"What happened, Caroline?" Thea was so angry she looked like she was about to spit nails—golden ones, of course. "Did he kidnap you?"

"Kidnap me? Why on earth would he do that?"

Almost as one, every set of eyes in the room rolled toward the palatial chambers above our heads.

"I'm not a princess," I objected.

"Don't be stupid," a scratchy voice said from behind me. "You're that and more."

Hugh Konnor. Oh, how you slay me.

I closed my eyes tightly and let it all sink in. And when I opened them, I knew what I needed to do.

To protect my family. "Karl von Falkenburg simply invited me to dinner." When Thea's brow lifted in surprise, I said, "You can confirm with him if he's talking again. I'm not really sure why Christian showed up. Maybe he wanted to kidnap Karl. He's certainly worth more."

I continued with the lies. "Anyway, he cornered me on the balcony, and I'm very lucky I had my pepper spray on me." I wished I could see Hugh's face, thank him somehow for ensuring that I was always protected. "Christian's been a sick bastard who gets off with toying with this family and I, for one, am glad it's come to a mostly peaceable end." I sent an apologetic look to Nick. "Sorry about the bastard bit. I'm sure your mother was a lady."

"She had me, didn't she?" The ends of Nick's lips flicked up and I had the distinct impression that he could see right through me.

But that was impossible. No one had all the pieces to the puzzle except me. And therefore, I was the only one who could find the solution.

"Has Christian said anything? Did he indicate that anyone else was responsible?" I let my eyes fall on Sybil. "For the medical records?"

She shook her head.

Thea cleared her throat and said, "No. He's being treated by the physicians, but he's acting like he took a vow of silence. He hasn't said a word." Her face was drawn, and I realized how difficult this must be for her, dealing with the man who she thought she'd have children with and then had traumatized her in so many ways.

I wouldn't let my sister get hurt again.

"Well, then. I'm sure you all have very important things to finish up with law enforcement." I turned to Sybil. "Can I steal a moment of your time? I have a recent astrology question that I need answered and we haven't had a consultation in so long."

Sybil kept her face disinterested and nodded like she couldn't care less.

"Thea? Is this all right?" I asked, and my sister nodded wearily. "Please get some sleep soon." I kissed her cheek and gave her shoulder a squeeze. "We need you healthy."

Then I marched from the room with Sybil right behind me. I'm sure it looked very purposeful but, as soon as I left, I realized that I didn't know where we could go next.

Sybil must have noticed my hesitation because she pointed down the hall to a door that led to a boiler room.

"Really?" I asked after the door closed behind us. I gestured at the steam pipes and tanks and valves. "Here?"

"It's probably the safest room in the whole complex," she noted wryly. "Too much noise and interference for anyone to hear anything."

Interesting. I'd file that away for the next time I arranged a covert conversation. "I need a new secure email," I said, going straight into the business portion of our meeting. "Preferably something that can't be hacked into. Do you have any recommendations?"

She immediately named a provider. "It's the best. Even government officials with access to top-secret channels use them." Her lips twitched. "Unofficially."

"Great. When I get my new address, I'll need you to send me everything the hackers have got on me." When I saw the approval in her eyes, I knew I was on the right track. "And then, I'm going to give you the password."

Which earned me an immediate frown. "Whatever for?"

"There will be a draft email saved. If something ever happens to me or a member of my family, I need you to send it."

Sybil's sophisticated, calm air dropped. "What are you getting into, Caroline?"

"I'm taking care of my family," I said simply.

forty-one

AS SOON AS WE STEPPED OUT OF THE BOILER ROOM I felt it. Something had happened.

It felt like lightning had struck, like the walls would burn you if you touched them.

Sobs echoed from an office down the corridor.

I started running toward them.

Then a man shot out of a door. Unlike all the other times he'd sneaked up on me, this time something deep down in my bones had told me he'd be there.

Waiting for me.

"What . . . ?" Before I could finish the question—whatever I was going to ask; I wasn't even sure myself—he answered me.

Because he knew.

"His Highness."

"Oh." My head spun, my knees went soft. But before I could fall, Hugh's strong arm was wrapped around my waist.

"Thea?" I asked.

"On her way."

I shook my head. "She's not supposed to leave. Gran said . . ."

"Thea said."

Oh. Of course. What Thea said—whatever she said now—would be obeyed. Now that she was truly the heir to the throne. The next Queen of Drieden. Who would argue with her?

"What do you want—"

I cut him off. "Upstairs."

It wasn't what he had expected, I could tell. But his arm slipped from my waist. His fingers twined in mine and we walked up the winding maze of corridors and stairs toward the Queen's residence. Together.

I WALKED IN WITHOUT KNOCKING, SOMETHING I HAD never done before. The parlor was already full of Big Gran's closest staff. Her ladies-in-waiting, her butler, her secretaries. They parted like the Red Sea for me and the path to her inner sanctum was clear. Harald was by the door, stalwart and ferocious. "Is anyone in there?" I asked him softly.

"No, Your Highness."

I didn't correct him on my title. Protocol didn't matter today— but it never had.

"What did she say to you?"

Harald flinched slightly. "Leave."

Well. That was a positive sign.

I reached for the door and turned the old, worn handle. I swore I heard multiple gasps in the room behind me. Such things weren't done. But what was Aurelia going to do to me? Throw me out of the castle?

I took a deep breath and headed into the dragon's lair.

Her Majesty Queen Aurelia sat on a chair next to the window, looking out on the great courtyard below. Soon enough, there would be a crowd gathered at the gates, there would be a wall ten feet high of flowers and offerings. Wreaths would be laid, photos of Prince Albert would be affixed to the black iron fence. And none of the mourners would really know that their Queen sat here, watching all of them, silently grieving with them.

I could tell that she had heard the door open because her shoulders drew back. She wouldn't want just anyone to see her sad. It simply wasn't in her DNA.

"It's me, Gran," I said, so she might feel like she could relax. She did not.

I pulled up a chair to the window anyway, and sat. Until she told me to leave, I would stay.

We stayed like that for however long it took for the news channels to report the death of His Royal Highness Prince Albert of Drieden. It could have been minutes or hours. Time was sticky and slow there in my grandmother's private rooms, catching each of us in our own web of memories and regrets.

Finally, the first news truck showed up. Then the second, right as a group of Driedish women collected, their arms wrapped around each other.

My father had not been the most charismatic of princes. The most exciting thing he'd ever done was marry my mother, which surely led to him swearing off excitement for the rest of his life. He never liked fast horses or speeding cars, but he enjoyed fishing, reading, a good game of chess and an exceptional glass of whiskey. And he was a dutiful, if absent-minded, father.

"It's all changed," Gran said suddenly. "The family has changed, just like that."

"No, it hasn't." I was surprised at how confident I sounded, given all the upheaval the House of Laurent had experienced in the past year. "Not unless we let it change."

*

THAT WAS ALL THAT WAS SAID FOR THE HOUR THAT I stayed by my grandmother's side as she silently processed the death of her eldest son.

An hour later, just as the bells chimed, there was a knock on the door. Harald entered, followed by Dr. Lao. Harald cleared his throat. "Your Majesty, the palace surgeon has arrived."

Dr. Lao waited with his head lowered until Gran stood and acknowledged him. In very official language he formally informed his sovereign of the death of her son. There would be certificates and seals and letters to Parliament and back again, all to certify that the next king was dead.

Long live the Queen.

Briefly, I wondered if Father's death changed any of Gran's plans for abdication after her Jubilee, but they probably didn't. Gran wasn't the type of Queen to change course. At least there wouldn't be any awkward explanations about why my father had been skipped over.

He was dead. What my father wanted didn't matter anymore.

After the formalities were over, Gran nodded at me. "Please see Dr. Lao out."

And that was that. Whether my grandmother and I would ever have a close, healthy relationship, I didn't know. Maybe this would open the door to family Christmas at her estate in Kasselta. Maybe I'd never be allowed in the palace again.

So I needed to make the most of this opportunity. "Dr. Lao," I said, "could I speak with you for just a few moments? In private?"

I directed him to a nearby sitting room, which he seemed to recognize. The thought gave me pause. How many times had he come upstairs to speak with Gran on medical issues?

But that wasn't what I asked him. No, I had an altogether different question. "Would it be possible?" I finished.

Dr. Lao nodded slowly. "Yes."

"Good. Let me know when it's done."

THE NEXT FEW DAYS WERE A HAZE OF TEARS AND FAMILY and details. So many details went into a royal funeral.

So. Many. Details.

If there was ever a time that I was tempted to beg off my responsibilities because of the whole—I was disowned from the family—uncomfortable truth, this was it. At the same time, however, it was my father's funeral.

Thankfully, there was a whole palace staff that stood ready for such occasions, and I learned that the palace made funeral plans for each royal family member whenever they turned twenty-five, so that was a warm, fuzzy feeling. /sarcasm font/

Henry briefly returned to his base, which was probably exactly what he needed. He seemed to be dealing with our father's death in a different way than the rest of us.

Felice withdrew to the château at Dréuvar, which seemed to be the practical choice for all concerned. While our parents' divorce had been explosive and dramatic, I knew they had loved each other, in their own way, from afar all these years. Maybe knowing the other was out there, living their life exactly as they wished, was all they ever wanted.

In the breaks between consultations and cuddling sessions with Thea and Sophie, I thought of my own lost love. Hugh Konnor had, predictably, slipped out of sight . . . as long as I stayed within the palace walls. I noticed his presence whenever I ventured out of doors, to the shops or back to the hotel where I was keeping a room, for my own sanity.

Maybe Hugh and I would live the rest of our lives like my

parents. Happy enough to know that the other was safe and sound and alive.

The idea left me hollow and fidgety.

Go.

The word had been whispering at me again, flicking around my ears like a pesky mosquito. I wasn't sure if it was the specter of another public funeral or the weight of the choices that I still had to make, or both, but I knew my temporary reprieve was fast running out.

As soon as Father was interred at St Julian's Cathedral, I had to be ready. To go. To stay. Or to fight.

forty-two

THE FUNERAL WAS BEAUTIFUL. THE BOYS' CHOIR was angelic, the flowers divine, the homily heavenly.

It was fit for a would-be king, but nothing like Albert Laurent, the man, who probably would have preferred a quiet service by his favorite trout stream with a small but satisfying luncheon of roast chicken and potatoes.

Technically, I shouldn't have been included, but as this was the twenty-first century and no one was cruel enough to exclude me from my father's funeral, I sat with Sophie and Henry and Felice on the third row of the cathedral while Thea and Gran sat at the front of the church.

I never said that protocol was completely ignored.

There was a short procession (he was only a prince, not the monarch, after all) and then a reception for politicians and VIPs in the state hall. Henry had liberally shared his flask in the limousine back to the palace so the event passed by in a blur. Of course, all of us behaved ourselves. We were professional royals and we could shake hands and murmur politely no matter how much whiskey had been consumed.

The word had been passed around . . . to meet in the library after the event. Okay, it was me passing the word around. I knew Henry wanted to return to his unit as soon as possible, and Sophie had said some things about the invitations that were coming her way. Her friends wanted her in Courchevel. Or St Bart's.

And then there was Thea. I was still worried about her. She had been a workhorse over the last week, but I suspected that some time with Nick on an island somewhere would do her good.

No, I needed to get us all together one last time, before we all scattered and everything changed.

Because change was inevitable.

Instability was not, however.

It was nearly evening when the four of us convened in the palace library. It was a true library, rivaling many universities in its collection of rare books and encyclopedias on Driedish history, economics and politics. It was generally a deserted spot in the palace, which is why I had picked it for this occasion.

Sophie entered the room with a groan and promptly lay flat on a library table. "*What now?*" she asked dramatically.

"Good God, please make this quick," Henry said, pulling his flask out of his jacket pocket. I had noticed earlier that he had taken care to make sure his suit matched, a sign of his distraction.

Thea was the one who still seemed to be holding it together, albeit with thread that was quickly unraveling. "What's going on, Caroline?"

I pulled four envelopes from under my arm and laid them on a table. "I asked Dr. Lao to pull these for each of us."

Henry cracked open one of his eyes. "What is it?"

"They're your blood tests. From when we all gave blood when Father was in the hospital."

"Isn't this illegal?" Thea asked shrewdly.

I shifted uncomfortably. "Under the policy between the hospital and the royal family, the blood we give is retained for family use only.

It would be destroyed once Father died, but it was the property of the palace while he was alive."

Thea raised her eyebrows at me. "So you presumed to have each of us tested? For what?"

"To make sure we're not bastards," I said. It was a joke that only Henry got. Sophie looked intrigued. Thea's eyes went cold. "No, that's not why," I said hastily. "I mean, none of us really knows . . . but that wasn't why." Here was where I started telling partial truths, but it was necessary.

"They're testing the bones found at the Langûs battlefield, to confirm that they're the remains of King Fredrik, our ancestor. And after what happened to my medical records, I realized that, in this century, the royal family needs to protect its own genetic information, now more than ever."

"This is crazy," Sophie declared. "Do you think someone would try to say we're not legitimate heirs, based on what some old bones look like?"

"That's exactly it," Thea said, rubbing her forehead.

"So these are for each of you," I said. "Certified genetic tests, overseen in a hospital, from samples that were kept separate from any other donations."

"And what do you want me to do with this?" Sophie asked, holding her envelope by the corner as if it contained something creepy and crawly.

"Take it immediately to your vault and lock it away," I explained patiently, reminding her of the large vault in the safe room attached to her apartment in the tower above us.

"I've forgotten how to open it," she whined.

"I'll show you," Henry said, almost as if he was bored. But he had been staring at his envelope intently since I'd said what was in it.

"Can we go now?" Sophie asked, and I replied that she could. We all needed rest, space and time away from the palace, I added.

"Especially you," I said to Thea after Henry and Sophie had nearly run into each other on their way out of the library, leaving just me and my older sister.

"I don't understand what has happened," she said. "But I know there's more to it than you're telling me."

"Just like there's more to what you've told me about what happened after Christian disappeared."

Thea gave her head a little shake. "That's different. You, my sister dearest, keep secrets."

"We all do," I said. "Look at Father."

My sister frowned. "What did he keep from us?"

"All these years after the divorce, Mother was still his designated person to give medical consent."

"But Father wasn't exactly good with those kinds of details." Her face was drawn, thinking of the man we had buried so recently in St Julian's Cathedral.

I left it alone because I didn't want to cause her more stress or grief, but I knew there was no way that Father had simply forgotten to update a form for the last decade. No, the palace had secretaries and administrators and couriers all double-checking and triple-checking such things, planning ahead for all sorts of unlikely events. Mother's name had been left on his paperwork for a painful reason.

Love.

"Take care of yourself," I told my sister. She really did look ill.

"You're leaving. And not to the hotel."

I nodded. I didn't want to keep it a secret. "I need to go and take care of a few things."

"You'll be back for the Jubilee, though." It was more of an order than a question. "And I'll want you by my side when Gran abdicates. I want us all to present a united front."

"I would like nothing better," I said honestly.

"And then it will be that much easier for me to slip you back into all the paperwork," Thea said, making a little check signal as if she were signing a document. "I'm righting Gran's wrongs," she said in a very earnest tone. *"All of them."*

I left it at that. Whether I was named a princess again, whether I was given back my HRH, seemed inconsequential at the moment.

Not when I still had a firewall to erect around my life—and that of my family.

MY GRANDMAMA WAS WAITING FOR ME, WHICH WASN'T A surprise. I'd had to announce my name at the gate, after all: Caroline of Sevine.

I knew it would get her attention.

Astrid was standing at her bookshelves and took off her reading glasses as I entered her study.

"I suppose we need to talk," she said.

"Only one of us is talking," I told her.

Because she was a smart woman, she kept her lips together.

"Your actions have been unacceptable. Arranging marriages, manipulating your own granddaughters, sending Christian after me to gather my DNA . . ."

Her eyebrows raised. "I don't know anything about that."

"Don't you dare," I scoffed. "There are exactly two people in the world who would care enough about the DNA in those bones at Langůs. Two people who would really care if I was a descendant of that Fredrik. And they are both my grandmothers."

Several expressions flitted across Grandmama's face—surprise, calculation, then . . . humor? "Really. I wouldn't have done anything with it, even if the test showed that one of the Laurent bastards had illegitimately taken the throne at some point. It would have been worth it just to see Aurelia's face when I told her that her precious legacy wasn't quite as untarnished as she believes."

"And what about Thea's face?" I demanded. "Your own granddaughter? What would she look like when she learned that you were the puppet master behind her biggest humiliation and betrayals?"

Astrid looked shamefaced, which was somewhat satisfying. "I never encouraged Christian to leave Thea. That was a mess he got into all on his own."

"But you continued to harbor him, enable him, use him to do your bidding when you wanted information after the bones at Langûs were discovered."

"He went rogue," Astrid stubbornly insisted. "And anything he tells you is a lie."

It didn't matter now. At the end of the day, I had only come to Switzerland to tell my grandmother one thing.

"There is something I want to make perfectly clear," I said. "If you or Vox Umbra ever releases any of the information it is keeping on me or anyone I love, or does anything to hurt my people, there will be consequences."

Grandmama looked intrigued. "What should I expect? Some retribution from that Konnor fellow you dragged in here?"

A dull stab of pain blossomed in my gut at the thought of Hugh. "No. My answer will be published in the biggest newspapers around the globe. All of your dirty secrets—Vox Umbra, the spying, the lies. I have a document that will be sent to major news outlets around the globe in the event that you or your fellow colleagues attempt to manipulate the royal family of Drieden again."

"Under your pen name? Will it be Clémence Diederich or Cordelia Lancaster or a yet to be assumed nom de plume?"

"No. My revenge will be under the name of Caroline Laurent."

Finally, I had done my grandmother proud. She beamed at me and said, "And that is how it should be."

I spun on my heel, intending to march out of the convent, having said all that I had come to say, but stopped as my grandmother's voice rang out.

"Is that it?" I closed my eyes at the hint of pain in her strong voice. "Am I the next to be disowned?"

Go.

Being an outcast hurts; no one knew that more than me. And Astrid deserved my rejection and more for all the trauma she had caused.

What would a Sevine woman do?

My fists closed tightly at my sides. A savvy Sevine woman wouldn't turn her back on another Sevine woman.

"That depends," I said finally.

"On what, exactly?"

"On how well you make this up to us."

With a slow, meaningful nod, Astrid signaled her acceptance of my terms and I left to return to my home.

forty-three

ONE MONTH LATER . . .

THE VIEW FROM THE TOP OF THE DILAPIDATED CAN-
nery was not quite as picturesque as the view from my Varenna
veranda, but it was exciting in its own way. I stood on the
roof of the old building, looking out at the old docks and industrial
buildings of Koras. Of course, there were boarded-up buildings and
crumbling brick but, like flowers blooming from the cracks of a
sidewalk, there were also brightly painted doors, fresh signs, the
indications of busy tradesmen and motivated youngsters.

The air smelled of diesel and saltwater but also of falafel and fresh
bread. Sounds of buzz saws filled the air, trucks honked, a group of
schoolchildren played a game of football.

Koras was alive, and when I heard footsteps behind me on the tar
paper and metal roof, I was, too.

I turned and tried to keep a cool, sexy demeanor even as my heart
tried to jackhammer itself out of my chest when I saw Hugh Konnor.

God, retirement had never looked so good on a man.

While I was wrapped up in a cashmere cape, due to the fact that it
was still cool and crisp in Drieden in April, Hugh was only in a white

shirt, his sleeves pushed up to show the black ink on each muscled forearm. He hadn't grown his beard, but his hair was longer than it had usually been while in service to the palace. The thick auburn waves ruffled with the wind and my fingers twitched with the need to touch him.

"Hello, Hugh."

"Caroline." My only clue to his feelings was that I noticed his knuckles turned white on the hand that clenched a yellow safety hat.

"This is quite a coincidence," I managed to say.

"It's not," he admitted. "There's a crowd of photographers who are covering the main entrance to this shitty cannery. It was like a neon sign directing me to you."

"Shitty? Watch how you describe my newest real-estate investment."

"You outbid me," he growled.

I couldn't help the feminine pleasure that swept through me. "I heard you're starting a private security business." I knew everything about him, actually, and the empire he had built when he thought no one was watching. My real-estate advisor had pulled up his invest-ments, his corporation holdings. He had the largest real-estate portfolios in this quarter of the city and was creating jobs and safe apartments and raising the security of every person in this district.

But right now, he was more than all of that.

So much more.

Hugh took a step forward. Then another one.

"You heard about my company, hmm?"

I nodded quickly. Maybe that had revealed too much. Shown my cards. "I was looking for some advice—from a professional security expert like yourself."

That got his interest, as I knew it would. "What's going on?"

"Where should I go next?"

"What do you mean?"

"I've been trying for a while now to figure out the next phase in my life. After Stavros died, I escaped to Varenna. And now I need to find a new residence. So tell me, where in the world will I not be found? I've narrowed it down to a charming bungalow close to Goa, a small village in Bolivia, or North Dakota." I checked them off my fingers and, when I was done, I looked back at him. He had moved closer. I could almost touch him now. Smell his lavender soap.

He looked displeased with me.

"Do you know somewhere else I should go?" I asked, still going for that wide-eyed insouciance that came so naturally to Felice—or Sophie, for that matter.

"The edge."

"Where is that?"

His jaw clenched. "The edge of the roof. You're very close to the edge. Could you please move away from it?"

"Yes, I see." I looked down. "But it's only a four- or five-story drop. I don't think I'd die. I'd probably only break my legs."

"I'm serious, Caroline."

"Of course you are. When are you not serious?" I asked fondly because . . . I was fond of him. Rather desperately, in fact.

Hugh held out the yellow safety helmet. "Put this on, then."

"But right there—that's when I'm not sure," I mused. "Was that serious or not serious? Because that yellow plastic does not go with this fabulous cape." Of course, I was teasing him. Because I decided I needed to see him smile or some other expression which demonstrated that his current feelings were something more than mildly irritated professional curiosity.

"What are you doing here?" he finally sighed, and there—right there—I thought I saw . . . something. Something vaguely vulnerable or hopelessly hopeful. A mirror of how I was feeling.

"Don't you want to know? Where I've decided? I've done a lot of

thinking in the past month, and I thought, as a private-security person, you'd want to know——"

He looked pained. "I don't——"

"Here. Right here," I said in a panicked rush. I didn't want
to hear that he didn't want to listen to me. He absolutely had to
hear this.

"On top of a cannery in Koras?" Not surprisingly, he was confused. "Be serious."

"I was serious when I bought the building."

"Caroline——"

"It's a good investment. We can develop it together. You do have
a construction company, right?"

"For the last fucking time, step away from the edge of the roof!"

I stepped away from the edge of the roof, into his personal space.
Which was more dangerous—the five-story fall or being within
arm's reach of Hugh—I wasn't sure.

The words came tumbling out. I hadn't planned this, and certainly not on top of a cannery but, if this was my opportunity, I had
to grab it. "After Stavros died, I thought there were only two options
for me: be like Mother—or Father. Notorious or cloistered. But I've
come to the conclusion that everyone is wrong about me—including
you, by the way. I won't be limited by just those two paths. I have my
own path——"

"Which one is that?" he grumbled.

That was good. He was listening.

"The one where I go after everything I want," I explained. "Privacy, love, adventure, career." I laughed into the wind, the excitement
of the unknown making me feel a little dizzy. "I don't know what
that's going to look like yet, but I know that as much as I don't want
to be like Mother, I also don't want to be like Father."

Hugh frowned. "You mean buried in St Julian's?"

I shook my head. "My father never stopped loving my mother.

And he let everything fall apart, he let her slip through his fingers. Because he wasn't brave enough to try to walk with her."

I reached out, brushing my fingers against the line of buttons on his shirt. He didn't step back. Instead, his warm rough hand closed around mine.

"Even though I'm no prince, I like to think I'm as brave as one." His hazel eyes were warm on me, like an early spring sun, which encouraged me.

I closed my other hand around his. "If you're not a prince, I don't know who is. And you're absolutely the bravest man I know."

Our bodies leaned into each other. This was natural. Unavoidable. Irrevocable. The as-good-as prince and the not-so-much princess. The fearless bodyguard who had made it safe for me to feel again. We needed and deserved each other.

Hugh's head lowered. I met him halfway with a kiss that was pure and powerful, without pretense, full of promise. His right arm wrapped around my waist, and I imagined those Koras coordinates tattooed on his skin as an anchor, holding me in the one place where I belonged.

Right in the middle of my own city.

The kiss broke; we needed air. He laid his forehead on mine and I worried what he might say. This was typically the moment he said something heartbreakingly beautiful and something just plain heartbreaking.

"You want to protect me, I know, but please don't protect me from this," I said, in the narrow space between us. It was a plea from my heart. "Please just stop trying to protect me from bad decisions."

He chuckled. "You're calling me a bad decision? When you're the one who just bought this building that might crumble beneath our feet at any second?"

"You're right. Then how could you let me go? There are so many other bad decisions I could make. At any time, actually. Who knows what I could do next? I probably need a permanent bodyguard at all times."

His brows drew together. "You raise a good point."

"I always do," I assured him.

"I think there's only one thing left to do." For some reason, he looked at the edge of the roof, grabbed my hands, then took one giant step closer to the edge. His eyes were twinkling, but I could also tell they held a secret.

Huh. It seems I knew him as well as he knew me.

He took a deep breath. "You'll just have to marry me."

I weaved a little. Hugh slapped the safety hat on my head. "What?" I managed to say.

"After I get your sister's permission, of course."

"You . . . want . . . me?" Yes, I am a very witty woman of the world, you know.

His face softened. "I've wanted you since I first set eyes on you."

It was like someone had taken one of Grandmama's swords, stuck it in my gut and swirled all my insides around. It was a beautiful, dizzying kind of heartbreak.

"And?" he prompted.

"What?" I asked, still dazed and dizzy from his proposition.

"What's your answer, so that we can get off this deathtrap of a roof?"

There was no way to express so much *yes* into a single word. So I wrapped my arms around him and kissed him again as hard and as well as I could until we were both breathless.

"You were meant to be mine, Caroline Laurent." He said it with that steady, cocksure confidence I knew so well. "Now I'm taking you to solid ground." He interlaced my fingers with his and we started walking toward the stairs.

My legs shook as we descended, knowing that the next step was terrifying, world-changing, death-defying.

Irreversible.

He placed his hand on the steel door and gave me one last look. "Are you sure about this?"

I laughed—a crazy sound. "Me? What about you?"

His mouth slid to the side and his arm wrapped around my waist. "This part's easy."

"You're a brave man, Konnor."

"That?" He nodded at the scrum of hustling paparazzi that were sure to be on the other side of the door. "That's nothing we can't handle."

And with that, he pushed open the door and we walked into the glare of a hundred flashbulbs.

Together.

forty-four

WE WERE IN ONE OF MY HIDEY-HOLES.

You didn't think I had just the one spare house in Varenna, did you?

This one I bought years ago, a sun-bleached stone cottage on an olive-tree-lined hill in Aix-en-Provence. Lush lavender bushes encircled the garden and, on clear days, one could see the Mediterranean from the bedroom window.

The window in front of the bed where Hugh and I had slept for the past three weeks after our small wedding in Scotland, on Nick's estate. We had wanted a private ceremony, so anywhere in Drieden was out of the question, unfortunately. I still wasn't sure I had reached the point where people would ignore my second wedding to a millionaire ex-bodyguard and I did not want any negative press to shadow either Gran's Jubilee celebrations or the announcements about Thea thereafter.

It also felt like a fitting conclusion to the whole Christian Fraser-Campbell drama. Good defeats evil, love wins, every time, and then your foes get married in your family chapel. There was something vaguely medieval about the idea that Hugh especially enjoyed.

And then, while we were all in Scotland, there was one last medieval twist. In a cell that was electronically monitored 24/7 on an island in the middle of the North Sea, Christian died of a heart attack.

Thea ordered an immediate investigation, Nick hit the whiskey hard for a day or so, but I felt it was safe to say that the instigating cause of Christian's death was likely lost to history, never to be discovered.

I thought I'd been so quiet, but when I tiptoed back to the bedroom still wearing nothing but his shirt, which I had tossed on, he asked, "Who was that?" Hugh's voice was drowsy, but I knew he'd been yanked out of sleep as soon as the phone rang. Once a bodyguard on alert, always on alert.

I hesitated with my answer, which made his next words sharper. "Caroline? Who was on the phone?"

It wasn't that I didn't want to tell him. It was that I wasn't sure I *should*.

Hugh and I had promised each other, no more secrets. I had told him all of mine after we became engaged. Hugh agreed with Sybil's security assessment—I, along with Cordelia and Clémence, was a blackmail risk. But I decided to wait until after Thea's ascension to the throne to tell her the truth about my forays into journalism. It would be the biggest moment in her life and I didn't want my previous mistakes to distract from that.

If, after that, she couldn't forgive me, then I was ready to accept it. If I had inherited anything from our mother, it was—finally—a peace about the mistakes I had made and the person I was growing to be.

Finally, I decided to just spit it out. "It was Dr. Lao, from the palace. I'm fine," I added, with a reassuring smile when his frown instantly deepened with my answer.

"What did he want?"

I lifted my hands. "Apparently, there's some antiquated rule of the office of palace physician. He's not quite sure how to handle it at the moment."

"And he thought you could help?"

"I think he might be trying to narrow the suspects."

Hugh's hazel gaze sharpened. Again, I should have really picked my words more carefully. Note to self: Don't refer to oneself as a suspect. It makes one's husband suspicious of your activities. "Explain, please."

"The blood tests I arranged for Thea, Sophie, Henry and me. Remember, the ones I told you about?"

He nodded.

"They were analyzed blind by an independent lab. Dr. Lao's nurse assigned each of the samples random code names and only she had the key, which was destroyed by a different clerk once they were returned."

"Was there something wrong with one of the tests?"

I bit my lip. "I don't know if I can say that. But Dr. Lao says there's this very old royal decree that requires the court surgeon to tell the monarch whenever he gets evidence that an heir is expecting a child."

Hugh threw back the bedclothes and was crossing over to me in one blindingly fast movement. "Caro—"

I stopped him. I knew what he'd assume. "It's not me," I insisted. "The blood test was two months ago. I'd know it by now."

His shoulders relaxed, but he still seemed concerned, going by the way his eyes were searching over me, as if trying to detect evidence of injury or pregnancy.

"Besides, it's . . . you know . . . too soon," I stammered, suddenly wondering if it *was* too soon for . . . *that* . . . *with us*. But when Hugh closed a hand around my waist and pulled me to his naked, muscular body my hormones snapped to attention. Yeah, maybe not too soon.

And the way Hugh's body reacted to me seemed to indicate that he also agreed with that conclusion.

"So what is Dr. Lao going to do?" Hugh asked. "If he's got to report this? Call each of you and . . . inquire about your . . . ah . . . months?"

I helped him out. "No, I volunteered to do it." Hugh gave me a you-didn't look and I tried for levity. "The good news is, Henry says he's definitely not pregnant."

"That's a relief," Hugh said.

"And then I called the sister I thought most likely to get knocked up . . ."

Hugh knew who I was talking about. "And?"

I shook my head. "It's not her."

author note

Dear Reader,

As in *The Royal Runaway*, in this novel I borrowed and stole from real-life historical places and events that have long intrigued me.

As far as I know, Vox Umbra is a complete and total figment of my imagination, however, I did draw inspiration from the long-held beliefs and myths surrounding the Knights Templar and Freemasonry that go back to the Crusades. The Chinon Parchment is an actual document, discovered in the 21st century in Vatican archives. It amazes me that there are documents and relics that are yet to be discovered stored beneath the Vatican — *Indiana Jones and the Dusty Trove of Lost Books*, anyone?

When I was searching for a name for Astrid Decht-Sevine's Swiss fort/convent, on a hunch, I decided to google "Perpetua," which was the name for the abandoned island/convent in *The Royal Runaway* and this novel. I soon discovered that there are two Catholic saints, Perpetua and Felicitas, who were martyred in Carthage in the first century, CE. When I originally created the island of Perpetua, I pulled the name from Mozart's Requiem and Latin-Catholic liturgy.

But after discovering the two female saints whose names have been joined together for two thousand years, I felt it was meant to be; Perpetua and Felicitas, two fictional convents influenced by two powerful matriarchal lineages.

And if you didn't already know, yes, there was a real-life king buried in a car park. It was not, however, King Fredrik II of Drieden. In 2012, the remains of King Richard III were found under a car park in Leicester. Maybe it's because I'm American, but I've long been mildly obsessed with this bit of history and all of the story possibilities that it could inspire (who killed the king, who tried to hide the evidence, what if someone switched the genetic testing?), however, I restrained myself while writing *The Royal Bodyguard* and didn't let myself go too crazy. Although, I will say, it was an excellent idea for the Driedish royal heirs to get DNA testing done. Just saying.

Keep Reading,

Lindsay

acknowledgments

A million and one thank you's . . .

To my agent, Louise Fury, and the team at The Bent Agency for helping me tell my stories.

To my editor, Kate Byrne, and the team at Headline, including Sarah Day and Lucy Bennett. As always, thanks for making this book a reality and helping me make it 100 times better.

To my HBICs, Mary Chris Escobar, Laura von Holt, Alexis Anne, Alexandra Haughton and Julia Kelly, who inspire me to keep digging deeper and reaching higher. (And a shout out to Laura and Alexandra who celebrated a royal wedding with me and then listened to me figure out how the first draft of this book was absolute rubbish.)

To my readers, you have excellent and refined tastes. I think about you every time I sit down to write and I pray that this story brightened your day and lightened your heart, even in uncertain times.

As always, to my husband J and my children, E & M. I love you to Drieden and back.

Filled with intrigue, romance and mystery,
Lindsay Emory's
THE ROYAL RUNAWAY
will whisk you away on a romantic,
glamorous and royal adventure!

Turn the page for a preview...

HEADLINE
ETERNAL

one

I T WAS MY WEDDING DAY. I IMAGINED OTHER BRIDES HAD
similar days. They, too, softly smoothed their white skirts, brushed a
piece of lace with their fingertips, and clutched a handkerchief into a
crumple.

Other women felt like princesses on their wedding day. Me? I really
was a princess. I had the tiara, the palace, the framed certificate, and
everything.

They delayed telling me about my missing groom as long as
they could, until it became apparent that the schedule would have
to change, that we wouldn't leave for the cathedral in the flotilla of
white carriages drawn by horses in matching ostrich-feather head-
dresses.

Because I, Princess Theodora Isabella Victoria, second in line to the
crown of the Kingdom of Drieden, had been stood up.

Left at the altar.

People spoke in hushed tones around me, trading whispers I couldn't
make out and didn't really want to hear.

Before I found out the truth, I knew we were behind schedule. I
should've been loaded into the carriage by now, waving and smiling at

the adoring public lining the streets. I shouldn't still have been sitting here, waiting.

My mother was called out of the room, which should have alerted me that something was up. The palace staff usually did everything they could to avoid talking directly to my mother—she had a way of making their lives difficult.

Then Caroline was called out. Caroline was my emotionally stable middle sibling. My maid of honor. Not because she was older than Sophie, the youngest, but because Caroline could be counted on to think through any unexpected problem that arose—the train, the bouquet, the . . . missing groom.

Caroline returned, her mouth in a sharp line. She knelt at my feet, took my hands, and laid out the problem.

My fiancé was nowhere to be found.

I simply stared at her. An avid amateur historian, I racked my brain for any similar situation in the Driedish history books. What was the proper protocol for a canceled royal wedding? What does a jilted princess do next?

Then the whispers stopped. The atmosphere froze. My grandmother had entered the room. Tall and straight, she held her head as if there were always a crown balanced upon it—the big one with the Jaipur sapphire. She came to me and held out a box of tissues.

Something about that gesture undid me. I could be as regal and disciplined as the next royal princess, but my gran handing me a tissue made it real somehow. I had been humiliated in front of my country, in front of the world.

Five minutes passed and my grandmother lifted my face and blotted my wet cheeks. "There will be no more tears shed for him. His name will never be spoken in this house again."

It was an order from my queen.

My eyes immediately went dry.

two

I T WASN'T A SURPRISE THAT I'D BEEN SENT AWAY. IT WAS easier for people to manage the fallout if there wasn't a lightning rod continuing to draw the electric attention of the world.

All of the Queen's advisors agreed that the best place for a jilted princess was a cold island in the middle of the North Sea, a Driedish territory called Perpetua. Why they couldn't have agreed that jilted princesses should spend four months in the Maldives, I would never understand.

I'd returned to the palace three days ago, and since then my nights had rapidly deteriorated into an endless cycle of nightmares, herbal teas, and television reruns. It was really so boring. I was over Christian Fraser-Campbell. Completely. The man had left me at the altar. Why I kept having the same dreams about him, I had no idea.

He would be in a dark tunnel, running away from me. Then I would run after him (which would never happen in real life—I have my pride). I'd call his name, praying that he would stop running, that he would shout something back in his charming Scottish brogue. But he'd always stay silent; he'd always keep running. And I'd keep chasing. Until the headlights of an oncoming train would overtake us both.

It was clichéd and predictable.

I disliked being both.

The palace doctor had left the sleeping pill prescription wordlessly on my desk the day of the wedding, after being among the group of ten Big Gran had ushered into my suite to deliver the bad news.

I hadn't taken a single pill yet, and now I was wondering if I should. I had an interview scheduled tomorrow—"PRINCESS THEODORA'S FIRST POST-JILT INTERVIEW"—with Chantal Louis of *The Driedener*. Another lost night of sleep would mean that the dark circles under my eyes could not be concealed by the usual layer of makeup. My makeup artist, Roberto, would have to bust out the hard stuff, which he would moan about, and then I'd apologize for it and there would be a whole uncomfortable balance of power over heavy-duty concealer. #Princesslife #thestruggleisreal

I was over my ex. Really, I was. Which is why I was heading toward my bathroom to fill a glass of water and take a pill. To forget about the bastard. And to prevent under-eye circles.

But instead, something drew me back to the large window that over-looked the city below. The palace stood above the city on a bluff that probably had been quite daunting in the Middle Ages. In the twenty-first century, the city had climbed up to meet the palace, many of the buildings standing at or above the height of the tallest tower of the ancient home of the rulers of Drieden.

I pulled the thick brocade curtains back and stared at the lights of the city, still beaming bright even after midnight.

Sharing the name with the country, Drieden City was a beautiful mix of modern and historical, quaint and contemporary. It had started to crumble into redundancy in the early twentieth century with the decline of the traditional shipping industry that had sustained it for centuries. But then oil was discovered. First, crude oil bubbled out of the marshlands, then it oozed out into the triangle of the dark, cold North Sea that Drieden controlled, and a nation was given its second life.

Growing up royal, every minute detail of Driedish history had been drilled into my head. As the second in line to the throne—after my father, the Crown Prince Albert, God help us all—I took its study seriously and applied myself dutifully to the stories of my homeland. Often I would close my eyes and imagine what the kingdom looked like in 1350, when Olaf the Conqueror first claimed the fertile lowlands. Or in 1650, when King Henry III refused to send colonists to the New World, condemning colonization as a foolish, wasteful enterprise.

I loved those stories. I loved this view and the city lights that seemed to throb inside my veins.

Later, I would look back on this moment and wonder why I hadn't simply popped the sleeping pill and crawled back into my gilded four-poster bed, the same one that my grandmother and great-grandmother had slept in before their ascendancies to the throne.

I'll never know what made me change into street clothes, pull my hair into a bun, and slip on running shoes. But that's exactly what I did.

I knew the covert ways out of the palace like the back of my hand. Part of it was due to a natural gift for observation and investigation; part of it was thanks to my formal education. It had been impressed on me by my tutors, secretaries, and Big Gran herself that a good princess should learn everything about her country.

That included secret ways out of the palace.

This wasn't the first time I'd slipped out undetected. That had been when I was a teenager, a university student. There were things I'd wanted to do, places I'd wanted to go, people I'd wanted to see without my official security detail getting involved. For years, it hadn't been a problem. Drieden is a small country and the monarchy can still be informal if it wishes. My uncle John, the Duke of Falender, works as a banker in the financial district. My brother serves in the armed forces. Until my engagement, I produced documentary films. With a discreet and small security presence, my family has been able to keep up the pretense that we're normal folk who just happen to live in that big old house on the hill.

With my recent notoriety, though, and my resulting cloistering in the palace and assorted hideaways, I hadn't been outside royal boundaries in over three months.

And sometimes a girl just needed a change of scenery.

My feet flew over the carpet, down the southwest stairwell, across the landing, into the upper gallery through a service entrance, then down another set of stairs that led into the herb garden, which was next to the kitchens with their loading dock and abandoned at this time of night.

Just like that, I was outside in a small courtyard. There was a guardhouse at the bottom of the cobblestone drive, but I pulled up the hood of my jacket and hopped into a nearby white Fiat with plates that matched the keys I had snagged from the loading dock bay.

The gates opened swiftly (as they should for an official palace vehicle) and I drove two hundred meters and . . .

I had no idea where I was going.

To the lights?

Why?

Because the lights were pretty?

Was I insane?

Probably. Now I was talking to myself. Just like Prince Karl the Holy when he believed a trout told him to invade France.

My foot pressed the gas pedal, indicating that I was, in fact, insane. Sleep deprivation had sucked all the common sense out of my head.

But I kept driving. Instinct and a memory pulled me forward.

There had been a night, two years ago, right after I had started dating Christian. I had gotten a call from him; he had flown to Drieden to surprise me. "Come see me," he had urged. He had given me the name of a bar where I was to meet him in an hour. And like tonight, I had managed to slip out of the palace completely undetected.

Romantic, right?

Without being aware of my destination, I now suddenly found myself parked outside that same bar. It seemed just as I remembered it. A cocktail lounge in the theater district, its raucous crowd was decidedly different from the posh, upper-crust circle Christian usually ran with. As soon as I walked into the disorienting mix of shadow and neon, I remembered that I hadn't brought any money or identification. Another sign of my deteriorating mental state. Still, I took a seat at a table covered with chipped red paint. After all, the point of this excursion wasn't to drink. If I'd wanted to get drunk, the palace had vast cellars full of very expensive spirits at my disposal. If I'd wanted to lose myself, I would have just taken the damn sleeping pill.

The point of this trip was . . .

I had no idea.

Now I closed my eyes.

I saw Christian, as he was the night I met him here. His longish blond hair curled around his collar. His skin still tan from the ski season. Was this what I wanted? To see Christian again? Was that why I came here?

"Excuse me. Is this seat taken?"

A deep voice. A Scottish accent. *Christian?*

"No," I answered, wondering if I was dreaming. A new part of my nightmare, perhaps? I peeked through my eyelids.

My new tablemate settling into the chair opposite me was not Christian Fraser-Campbell, ninth Duke of Steading. This stranger was the complete opposite of Christian, dark and rough, but not altogether objectionable.

"Hello," I said, automatically being polite and proper even though I desperately wanted him to leave me alone.

"Hallo there. What brings a beauty like you out on a night like tonight?"

At the word *beauty*, the rest of my defenses rose. I was in a dim bar with eyeglasses I'd borrowed from my secretary and a hood still pulled over a messy bun. Any man who thought I was a beauty at the moment was either delirious, drunk, or dead.

I said the first thing that popped into my head. "I'm meeting someone."

"A boyfriend someone?"

I noted that he did not offer to get up. Instead, he leaned back in his seat and crossed his arms, all ears for whatever my answer was.

Rude, I thought.

"No," I informed the ill-mannered Scottish stranger. "A coworker." It was the blandest answer I could imagine. Maybe boredom would make the man go away.

His eyebrows rose. "At this hour? Here? What kind of a job are you working?" His eyes draped over me in a perfect expression of sarcasm and speculation. "You're not . . . picking *up* anyone?"

It took me a moment. "Are you insinuating that I'm a prostitute?"

"Well, if you are, you're a badly dressed one."

"What, are you an expert?"

His mouth slid up on one side, clearly amused. "Not regarding fashion, no."

Ugh. How could I get him to go away?

I imagined the most boring profession ever. "I'm actually a historian." It wasn't too far off from my former job producing documentaries.

"Are you now? How fascinating."

Damn. Now I'd really have to turn on the boring. "I specialize in Driedish rural agrarian history." I made a tenting motion with both hands. "Specifically the congruence between animal husbandry, agricultural economics, and women's health."

There. Dull-level ten. That should do it.

Instead of running away from the madwoman ready to discuss the most obscure, driest subject ever, though, the stranger leaned forward, as if he were eager to hear more.

"Ah." He brightened. "Farming. A noble profession, indeed, although given to long days, uncertain futures, and way too much drink." He waved a hand and caught the attention of a nearby waitress. "Two whiskeys, please."

"I couldn't—"

He interrupted with sparkling eyes. "But my lady, you already have."

HEADLINE ETERNAL

FIND YOUR HEART'S DESIRE...

VISIT OUR WEBSITE: www.headlineeternal.com
FIND US ON FACEBOOK: facebook.com/eternalromance
CONNECT WITH US ON TWITTER: @eternal_books
FOLLOW US ON INSTAGRAM: @headlineeternal
EMAIL US: eternalromance@headline.co.uk